RANDOM
HOUSE
LARGE
PRINT

IN THE COMPANY OF KILLERS

IN THE COMPANY OF KILLERS

—

BRYAN CHRISTY

RANDOM HOUSE
LARGE PRINT

Published in the United States of America by Random House Large Print in association with G. P. Putnam's Sons, an imprint of Penguin Random House LLC.

Cover design: David Litman
Cover images: (city skyline) Wenjie Dong / Getty Images; (Capitol Building) Dominic Labbe / Moment / Getty Images; (giraffes) Verónica Paradinas Duro / Moment / Getty Images; (trees) Danm / Moment / Getty Images; (bird) Thomas Winz / The Image Bank / Getty Images

The Library of Congress has established a Cataloging-in-Publication record for this title.

ISBN: 978-0-593-39580-6

www.penguinrandomhouse.com/large-print-format-books

FIRST LARGE PRINT EDITION

Printed in the United States of America

10 9 8 7 6 5 4 3 2 1

This Large Print edition published in accord with the standards of the N.A.V.H.

For my wife, Jennifer

Let not any one pacify his conscience by the delusion that he can do no harm if he takes no part, and forms no opinion.

—John Stuart Mill

Whoever fights monsters should see to it that in the process he does not become a monster.

—Friedrich Nietzsche

IN THE
COMPANY
OF
KILLERS

FALLEN GUARDIAN

Samburu County, Kenya

Captain Bernard Lolosoli looked down at the American journalist. "You were right."

Tom Klay, sitting with his back against the tire of a Land Rover, looked up from his notebook. Klay wore a faded safari shirt, brown field pants, and hiking boots. A droplet of sweat rolled off his chin and struck the page at the exact spot where he'd just finished a line, destroying the word and his thought along with it. "It happens," he replied.

"Are you ready?" Bernard asked.

Klay closed his notebook and dropped it into his shirt pocket. "All packed."

"Good." The ranger extended his hand. Klay took it and got to his feet. "Three men entered our east gate two days ago. We located their vehicle this morning. Their plates are stolen, and there is no exit record. Their passports were fakes."

"Passports," Klay said. "Not locals then."

"Ugandans. On holiday, they said."

Klay caught a flicker of movement out of the corner of his eye. A small male dog emerged from behind the Green Guardians' field station, carrying a feathered chicken wing in its mouth. The dog was scarred head to tail, with that compact build common to developing-world canines. "You get many of those?" he asked.

Bernard followed Klay's gaze. "Dogs? Or chickens?"

"Ugandans."

"We do. It was rail workers. Now it's tourists." Bernard smiled. "Thanks to your article, everyone wants to see our famous elephant."

Klay watched the dog. Every few steps it glanced over its shoulder toward the guardhouse, checking to see if anything was following it. The dog set the chicken wing down in the dirt. It looked back again, expectant. There wasn't much to see. The concrete field station and next to it the Guardians' makeshift field armory, a steel shipping container under a thatched roof. Between the two structures, the dirt was stained black with motor oil.

The little dog yipped, and Klay heard agitated

scrabbling on hard ground as a large dog emerged at speed from behind the building and rocketed toward the mutt. The bigger dog was a Belgian Malinois, a shepherd breed with relentless drive, making it a favorite among law enforcement. As the Malinois bore down, the smaller dog snatched up its chicken wing and sprinted across the clearing. It hopped onto an overturned bucket and into the crotch of a large acacia tree.

The Malinois didn't need the bucket. It leapt straight into the tree and chased the smaller dog up a thick branch into the tree's umbrella. The little dog barked as it climbed. Suddenly a third dog—a female as small and scarred as the first, but heavy from nursing—emerged from behind the field station, carrying a whole chicken, minus a wing. The female crossed the open space, dragging the dead bird between her forelegs, and disappeared into the bush. A moment later her mate leapt from the acacia tree onto the field station roof. The Malinois tried to follow, but it was too heavy and crashed to the ground instead. The big dog was about to climb the tree again when Bernard whistled. The dog froze. "Pfui!" Bernard said, and pointed. "Platz." The Malinois slunk obediently to the outpost's front door and lay down.

Klay looked up at the dog on the roof. The skinny male lay with its back legs spread on either side of the roof peak, looking down at Klay, chewing its wing.

"What do you think?" Klay asked. "You think it's lost tourists—or something else?"

Bernard sighed. "We paid one hundred thousand dollars for that animal," he said, looking at the shepherd. "Our donors insisted we have military dogs. I flew to Berlin to buy him. I had to learn German to speak to him. He has a better education than most of my family, and he still falls for that old dog-and-chicken routine." Bernard nodded at two vehicles speeding in their direction. "It doesn't bloody matter what I think, Tom."

Klay squinted. Two black SUVs were racing toward them from the south, kicking up clouds of dust. "I'm going to say it again. If Botha is running this operation, you do not want a political ride-along anywhere near it."

"I know it and you know it. He knows to stay in the truck," Bernard said.

"So, why's he coming?"

"Someone might have told him you want his photograph for your famous magazine."

Klay groaned. "I should have brought a camera then."

"That would have been nice."

Two of Bernard's rangers waited nearby. The Green Guardians were a privately funded counter-poaching force made up of Samburu warriors. Bernard's men looked the part. In addition to their desert fatigues and tan boots, they wore their hair in long, ocher-dyed braids pulled back severely from their scalps, adorned with feathers and narrow, brightly beaded headbands. Beneath their uniforms, the men's lean ribs were tattooed with chains of coffee-bean-sized scars representing bravery. Like their Maasai relatives, the Samburu were nomadic pastoralists. When not on duty, Bernard's men—Goodson Ltumbesi and Moses Lelesar—tended their animals, lived on milk and blood drained from the necks of their cattle, and warred over livestock with neighboring tribes. With their hair tied back, their dark eyes, and their cheekbones as sharp as cracked shale, they resembled a pair of young eagles swiveling for prey, with well-oiled and well-used HK G3 battle rifles for talons.

Bernard was a contrast. The Samburu warrior had gone to boarding school in England. He wore his hair short, sported a closely trimmed goatee, and carried a baby's arm of fat around his middle. When Klay had first met him, years ago, Bernard was working as a fixer, taking journalists to difficult locations throughout East Africa. He emerged shirtless from his hut wearing an orange-and-black-checked shuka over one shoulder, multicolored bead necklaces that wrapped his neck from chin to chest, tire-rubber sandals, and a gold belt adorned with tiny dime-shaped metal circles dangling on gold chains. A thin chain stretched from one ear, under his lower lip, and over the other ear. He jingled when he walked, like a child's toy.

"You always dress up like this?" Klay had asked.

"Like what?" Bernard had replied.

Bernard took Klay up in a rented Cessna 172 to look for elephants. It was the first time Klay saw Kenya's largest living elephant, a local tourist attraction named Voi. The super-tusker was standing among a group of five males on the west side of a low hill. All six were big elephants, but Voi was mammoth, with tusks so long they rubbed the ground. Bernard pointed him out, then banked the plane to take a second look. "Watch!" As the plane came around, the five male elephants looked up, then quickly encircled Voi. Brandishing their tusks, they shook their heads violently, while Voi turned his back to the plane and lowered his head.

Klay was astonished. "Like they know," he said. Bernard tapped the earcup of his headset to indicate he couldn't hear. Klay bent the mic closer to his lips and shouted again. "Like they know," he repeated, "it's because of his tusks . . ."

"Of course they know!" Bernard had replied. "We say, 'An elephant is born carrying two gravestones: One for himself. One for his species.'" Klay had included the line in his article. "The Last Great Tusker," he'd called it.

Klay's cover story had come at a cost. The big elephant was now world famous. Voi's enormous tusks, revered by Kenyans, were now priceless to Asian ivory collectors. To protect him from poachers, Kenya's president had declared the animal a national treasure, and had deputized the Green Guardians to protect him.

Only a few criminals had the connections and the wherewithal to kill the well-protected Voi and smuggle his tusks to China whole. Klay's information was that Ras Botha, a man known all too well to Klay, was about to try.

Klay watched the politician's vehicles approach. "Long haul from Nairobi."

"We flew him in," Bernard said. "Same as you. He's trouble for us, Tom. Ras Botha may be our immediate threat, but if we're not careful, Simon Lekorere will become our long-term problem. The Chinese completed the Uganda rail line since you were last here. They have built another line from Addis to their military base in Djibouti."

"The Ultimate Silk Road Project," Klay said. "I know."

"Do you know they want to connect them?"

Klay whistled. He imagined a gigantic Roman numeral **I** burned into the side of East Africa. The Kenya-to-Uganda rail line would be the numeral's base; Addis, Ethiopia, to the port of Djibouti would be its cap. China had built the southern line for economic reasons. The northern line was strategic: Djibouti was a gatekeeper to the Suez Canal.

Klay looked up at the small dog still crunching its chicken wing. "Oil," he said.

Bernard nodded in the direction of the politician's incoming vehicle. "He extorts payment from us to keep his voters from poaching our elephants. That's nothing new. Our donors pay him off. But he will get more money than we can afford by selling our land to the Chinese. Connect those two rail lines and everything we have here will vanish."

Klay looked out over Kenya's idyllic landscape. Bernard was right. Whatever China's ultimate plan, if a third rail line was built through here, everything he was seeing would be lost. "No protests?"

Bernard laughed. "The Chinese hired Perseus Group."

Klay cocked his head toward the other American in their group, a lanky blond software engineer wearing a pale blue Perseus Group polo shirt. The engineer leaned against the Guardians' outpost, rapidly typing something into his iPhone. "I thought **you** hired Perseus Group?"

Before Bernard could respond, the two SUVs braked to a hard stop, covering Klay and Bernard in their dust. Klay ran his tongue over his teeth and spat. Two bulky Kenyans wearing sunglasses and business suits emerged from the lead vehicle. They hurried across the clearing, inspected the Guardians' Land Rover, gave a nod, and a third bodyguard opened the main car's back door. Inside sat Simon Lekorere talking on a mobile phone. The heavyset politician wore a dark brown cowboy hat, gold-framed Gucci sunglasses, and an orange kitenge shirt.

"Jesus," Klay muttered.

"He's Samburu," Bernard said.

The politician sipped a bottle of beer.

"Deep down," Bernard added.

Bernard whistled, and his rangers swung themselves into the open Land Rover. The Perseus Group engineer did not move.

"Let's go," Klay yelled to him.

The engineer glanced momentarily in Klay's direction, then returned to his phone. He spent a few more moments typing before finally crossing the clearing to join them.

"I sent my report to Tysons Corner," he said to Bernard.

"That's your prerogative, Greg," Bernard replied.

"Our contract is very clear with respect to all anti-poaching operations."

"So you said. We'll be leaving in a moment. You'll have the second row to yourself."

The engineer climbed into the truck.

"Welcome to Kenya, Mr. **Sovereign**," Simon Lekorere boomed, extending his hand. The politician's hand was small in Klay's, but surprisingly calloused. The portly man laughed, as if he knew what Klay was thinking.

"Come," he said, climbing into the Rover's passenger seat. "Let us see if we can save some of our elephants today."

A bodyguard placed a small cooler between Lekorere's feet. Bernard walked Klay to the back of the vehicle.

"What's your play to hold him?" Klay asked quietly.

"Pride," Bernard said.

"Pride?"

"Samburu understand the importance of land. We have to remind him that he is Samburu first and a greedy politician second. He's wily. He's been playing the Chinese for us, getting us a new school and a clinic." Bernard reached into the back of the vehicle and withdrew a rifle. "Take this."

"No, thanks," Klay said.

"You said it yourself," Bernard said. "If this is a Botha operation, we should be ready." He nodded toward the politician. "Let's give him the idea we've got something worth protecting, shall we?"

Klay accepted the rifle, a battle-scarred, bolt-action Mauser, no doubt confiscated from a poacher. He shouldered it. Checked the action.

"Make a better club," he said, working the ragged bolt.

"Good." Bernard smiled. "We are out of those." He handed Klay a five-round stripper clip. Klay pressed the cartridges into the magazine, pushed the bolt forward, and let the clip fall to the ground.

Bernard bent down and picked it up. "We recycle these."

"Sorry," Klay said.

Bernard tapped him on the shoulder with the piece of metal and nodded toward the politician. "We need him. So try not to shoot him."

"That only happened once," Klay said. "And it was an accident."

Bernard was still chuckling as he started the vehicle.

Bernard drove fast, the Land Rover shuddering over a dry and broken landscape. In the truck were the three rangers, the politician, the software engineer, a monitor from the Kenya Wildlife Service, and Klay. Their route traced the Ewaso Nyiro River. The river's seasonal ebb and flow had lately been accelerated by the earth's rapidly changing climate, floods in dry season, droughts in wet. It was late November, time for the short rains, but none had come. They crisscrossed the river's desiccated bed, plunging down and then up its steep banks, dodging fallen trees, spinning in deep sand, crashing through thornbush.

Standing behind Klay, Bernard's rangers scanned the landscape for threats, barely touching the truck's roll bar despite the vehicle's bucking. Klay did not ride as easily. At each jolt his thick knees punched the back of the politician's canvas seat.

Klay didn't fit well into the truck's second row. He didn't fit well into most places. He was a large, broad-shouldered man. With his amber eyes and graying brown hair, he was still handsome enough, but etched now, salt overtaking pepper. The same applied to his personality. More than one grade school teacher had described young Tom Klay as troubled. Now, in middle age, he was a hardened brooder. He ground his molars. He spoke sparingly, in a voice so low it often sounded as if he were talking to himself. He carried himself in a way that suggested any number of past careers, not one of them journalist. If you were a boxer, you might recognize the forward roll in his shoulders and the slight tuck of his chin. If you had law enforcement experience, you might notice his tendency to stand with one hip forward, the other canted away. He was best appreciated in geologic terms, a cairn of irregular boulders stacked above a very active fault line.

"Tuskah!" the politician shouted over his

shoulder, too fat to turn. He held a bottle of beer above his head. "You like it, right?" he called to Klay. "Tuskah?"

Klay ignored Lekorere and looked out over the savannah, two fingers balancing the Mauser's barrel against his thigh. A male lion dozed beneath a tree in the late-afternoon sun.

He wasn't here for the animals, or for the conversation.

"Doesn't it get to you?" readers asked him from time to time. "The killing . . . all those poor animals?"

The question surprised him the first time. "It's not easy," he replied, "but I grew up in a funeral home, so I guess I was born for this job."

Years later he was still giving the same awkward response, only the truth behind his answer had changed. The truth was the killing had used to bother him a great deal, and he wished it still did. The transformation had happened surprisingly quickly, he realized looking back. One trip he had returned home and discovered that he hadn't noticed any baboons, though they had surely surrounded his camp. On another, he found himself irritated by a tower of giraffes blocking the road. Eventually, even the elephants became invisible.

Nature had become his murder book. From **A** to **Z**—from the spiral-horned addax to Grevy's zebra—he exposed crimes against endangered species in the pages of **The Sovereign,** and then, like a television detective with a season to fill, moved dutifully on to the next victim. One didn't linger over the dead, in fiction or in life. One moved on.

Klay was a criminal investigator. He was selective in the stories he took on. Winnable cases only. He was no Don Quixote. He didn't investigate crashing insect populations or stranded polar bears. He didn't report on the global warming crisis for the same reason he didn't investigate Russian money laundering, Mexican drug trafficking, or Wall Street's financial crimes. Those stories weren't winnable. He identified traffickers, designed investigations, reported his stories, and hoped the system did the rest. Enough of the time it did. But not always.

For years Ras Botha had run a continent-wide syndicate that defied categorization: Diamonds from Sierra Leone. Arms to Charles Taylor. Counterfeit pesticides to Kenyan farmers. Fake HIV meds to Nigeria's poor. Botha controlled crystal meth labs. He trafficked Thai, Czech, and Russian prostitutes through his nightclubs in Cape Town, Johannesburg, Pretoria, and Musina. Elephant ivory and rhino horn were sidelines for the South African, holdovers from a trophy-hunting business he ran with his brother.

Klay had tangled with Botha once before. Prosecutors cited facts from Klay's story in their indictment, but corruption runs thick in South Africa's courts, and days later Botha's case was dismissed.

That was South Africa. This was Kenya. Kenyans would love to lock up a foreigner trying to kill their most beloved elephant, especially if that foreigner was the notorious Ras Botha.

And so, by broad agreement, if the Green Guardians captured Botha's poachers tonight, Klay would be in the room for their interrogation. He would ask a few questions of his own, and then he would follow the trail back to take another bite of Ras Botha.

"Tuskah!" Lekorere managed to turn in his seat. The politician was looking at Klay, offering him a beer.

Klay forced a smile and accepted the bottle. When the politician turned forward again, Klay poured the beer out of the door and shoved the empty into the seat seam.

Bernard pulled to a stop at the edge of a deep ravine and his rangers jumped out. "We'll go in here," he said. "Tom, drive the truck up to Mitchener's Point and we'll meet you there." He checked his watch. "Give us three hours."

Four hours later, standing on Mitchener's Point, Klay studied the terrain below through binoculars.

"You're wasting your time." The Perseus Group engineer held up his iPhone. "I can see exactly where the elephant is."

Klay continued to glass the valley, moving his binoculars in a grid, trying to pick out the Green Guardians among the thick cover.

"See?" said the engineer.

"Maybe," Klay said, without looking. "Maybe you're giving away his exact location."

"The signal's encrypted. It's Perseus Group encryption, used by the Israeli military."

"Glad to hear it."

"He should have let our Askari drones handle this. It's in our contract."

"Why don't you go sit in the truck with the politician," Klay said.

"I have a right to be here," the engineer protested.

Klay lowered his binoculars and faced him. "You don't have a right. None of us does."

The engineer shook his head as he walked away. He waved his phone over his head. "This technology might actually save your elephant, you know."

On the far edge of the clearing, leaning against a tree, the Kenya Wildlife Service ranger smiled. He was a lean older man, his dark face lined from years in the bush. Klay felt bad for him— this was a babysitting assignment. The Green Guardians were permitted to carry automatic weapons as long as KWS had a ranger present. If he stayed out of the way, the seasoned ranger would receive a little cash at the end of the night to salve his pride. The ranger reached two fingers into his shirt pocket, withdrew a loose cigarette, and offered it to Klay.

"I quit," Klay said, putting the Sportsman cigarette in his mouth. He leaned forward and the ranger lit it with a match.

Klay inhaled deeply and blew the smoke out slowly. "**Jesus,** that's bad."

The ranger nodded in agreement. He drew another cigarette from his pocket, and Klay lit it for him with the tip of his. The two men smoked together in silence.

Klay heard a clicking sound to his right. He turned as Bernard and his rangers materialized from the bush. There was no other way to describe it. One moment there had been trees and bushes; the next they were there. Bernard first, followed by Goodson and Moses. Bernard looked straight at Klay as he approached, the heads of his subordinates swiveling.

"I thought you quit," Bernard said. He took the cigarette from Klay's fingers and put it to his own lips. "No elephant," he added, returning Klay's smoke.

"No Botha," Klay replied. His eyes strayed to the darkening ravine. He hadn't expected the man himself, of course, but his intelligence had been solid: a Botha poaching team was in the area.

Bernard smiled. "You'd have heard a bit of gunfire." He patted Klay's shoulder. "Looks like you were wrong after all."

"It happens," Klay said.

"Not often. Someday you'll have to tell me how you come by all that brilliant intelligence sitting at a desk in Washington, DC."

Klay drew on his cigarette, then dropped it and stepped on it with his boot. Bernard began walking toward their vehicle. Klay followed. "I hear you're part of their drone program," Klay said.

Bernard checked to see that the engineer was out of earshot, and nodded. "They made us an offer we couldn't refuse."

Klay grunted. "I thought it was just collars."

"It was. In the beginning."

"Right. Well, makes sense for you."

"Are you saying you wouldn't?"

"I'm just talking," Klay said.

Bernard halted. He turned and faced Klay. "But you are saying something."

Klay looked into his friend's eyes. He forgot sometimes how dedicated Bernard was. "Yeah, all right. Would I take Perseus Group money? Terry Krieger money? If I had your problem? Sure."

"No, if you had **your** problem."

"What's **my** problem?"

Bernard smiled. "Imagine you had something you actually cared about."

Klay allowed himself a rare laugh. He knew somebody in just about every country on earth, but he needed only half the fingers on one hand to count his true friends, people he respected and trusted no matter what. Bernard was a true friend. If Bernard said he would do something, it was guaranteed. Klay had bet his life on it more than once. He didn't just trust Bernard; he admired him. Bernard Lolosoli knew as much as Klay did about the world's complexities, but he maintained a generations-deep connection to his family and to the earth. He possessed a joy for life that managed to flourish in spite of all that was happening around him—the poverty, the corruption, the killing. Despite it all, Bernard kept his center. After a few days in Bernard's company, Klay always felt a little less angry, and a little more human. For a while, he felt peace.

"Okay," Klay said. "Yeah, I'd take his money. I'd take his elephant collars. But Askari drones? Those are people trackers."

"I know. They wanted facial-recognition cameras at our gate. They're building a database by tribe, tying it into a cross-agency police cloud. I drew the line at their face harvesting. They weren't happy. I won't be able to hold them off forever. We are a Perseus Group laboratory now."

He nodded in the engineer's direction. "That one is our minder."

"Do your donors know?"

"Our donors care about our animals, Tom. He came out here, you know. Terry Krieger. Very knowledgeable in the bush. Said he's always loved elephants. Wants to give something back. They all do it. Come to Africa. Wanting to cleanse themselves of something . . ."

Klay's jaw muscles knotted.

"Perseus's drones have knocked the hell out of our poachers. Herd stress has declined. Birth rates are rising. Mothers are producing again." Bernard kicked a rock with his boot.

Klay waited.

"After our latest annual report came out, Nairobi said to us: 'Right. Done and dusted. Wildlife sorted. Let's approve the north-south rail line.'"

"That's the play?"

"Krieger supports us. Anything we need, he says. But I hear otherwise from Nairobi. His interest is the Chinese and they want the railroad." Bernard turned to him. "A north-south rail line would run straight through our land, Tom. Destroy our way of life. My family would have to leave here. My mother . . ." Bernard paused. "Why don't you write about that?"

Klay looked away. A troop of baboons had emerged from the trees and was crossing a field of dry grass, led by a very large male. A baby sat on the big male's head, its tiny hind foot causing the adult to squint and swat it away.

"A story on Perseus Group?" Klay shook his head. "That's outside of scope. I'm here for Botha."

"You do remember Congo, right?"

Klay ground his back teeth, still looking in the direction of the baboons. "I remember," he said.

"All that great intelligence you're able to pick up in Washington. I thought maybe . . ."

"Maybe what?"

"Maybe you could get someone important to listen."

Klay turned and studied Bernard, wondering what his friend knew. "Look," he said, finally. "I'm just a hack. I'd have to spend, what? Three years to get into Perseus Group? Two at a minimum. Even then. Even if they gave me the pages, even if I didn't mind spending the rest of my life buried in lawsuits—because they'd definitely sue me—even then, there's no one to act. Who would prosecute Perseus Group—world's biggest private military company? No one. Not here. Not in Congo. Not in the US. Nowhere. And that's just the corporation. There's no way I could get close to Terry Krieger. Even if I wanted to."

"Even if you wanted to?"

"I take on fights I can win. I'm not—" Klay struggled to find a word to convey his meaning.

He looked down. An ant crawled across his boot. "I am not a fucking safari ant."

Bernard smiled.

"What?" Klay demanded.

Bernard nodded toward Klay's foot. "The ant never works alone, Tom. Didn't you know that?"

Klay looked down again. Ants were swarming his boot. Several had their jaws locked into the leather. Klay knocked them loose with the toe of his other boot and stepped away. "Scale matters," he said. "Look, take his money. Set some boundaries for him, **like you have,**" he added, quickly.

"If you say so." Bernard increased his pace, opening the distance between the two men.

Klay had to jog to catch up. "Botha is our meat," he said. "If we get him, maybe I can do a little good for you here."

"Sure, Tom."

After a moment, Bernard paused and turned to him. " 'Hack.' "

Klay shrugged.

"No. You said 'hack.' What if Botha hacked Voi's collar?"

"It's encrypted." Klay saw intensity in Bernard's eyes. "You don't mean the transmission. You mean the access?"

Bernard nodded.

Klay considered the possibility. Voi's collar was part of the TIPP program. TIPP was the

Total Information Project for Pachyderms software designed by Perseus Group. It recorded the movements of all collared elephants across the conservancy. Someone with access to the TIPP app might be able to manipulate Voi's given location.

Klay thought of an even simpler explanation. Technically, they weren't tracking an elephant; they were tracking an elephant's collar. "Move the collar, move the elephant," Klay said.

"Move a dot on his app and you move them both," Bernard agreed.

Klay puffed his cheeks, squinting in thought as he blew out the air. "Who has access?"

"To the software? Just Greg and whoever he works with at Perseus. Maybe some of the biologists. To the physical collar? Anyone, really."

Either option was a hack of the Green Guardians' system.

"If Voi is not here, but his signal says he is, maybe it's because Botha wants us—"

"—where the elephant isn't."

They strode quickly through the trees to the Land Rover. Standing beside the vehicle, the Perseus Group engineer was typing on his phone again. Lekorere, the politician, wearing headphones, was also reading his phone. Lekorere smiled and raised a bottle of Tusker to salute their return. Bernard shook his head.

"Did you find Voi?" the engineer asked.

"No," Bernard said.

"I told you we should have used the Askari drones."

"He's not here," Klay said.

The engineer tapped his phone and opened Voi's tracking app. "Look at his TIPP." He handed Klay his phone. A small green dot in the shape of an elephant blinked on the program's map. "Red means stopped. Yellow is streaking. Green moving normally. He's right there." The engineer pointed at Bernard. "**You** missed him."

Klay backhanded the engineer with a withering look. He had seen Bernard glance—**glance**—at a clean stretch of granite and then describe in detail the poacher who had crossed the rock hours earlier, including his age, weight, how fast he was moving, and what he was carrying. Then, calculating how much of the poacher's load was likely water, and where the area's water sources lay, Bernard had driven ahead of his quarry, set up camp, and was having tea when the poacher arrived. "I'll be having those," Bernard had said, taking a sack of bloody tusks from the surprised man. "Good tracking follows a trail," Klay wrote of the incident. "Great tracking leads it."

"Voi's not here, **Greg**," Klay repeated.

Looking at Bernard, the software engineer scoffed, "I'm not talking dowsing sticks."

The blinking-green elephant on the engineer's

phone suddenly jumped. Klay pushed the phone hard into the engineer's chest. "What's that?"

The engineer looked down. "Oh," he said.

"Oh, **what**?"

"Must be the satellite." Greg tapped at his phone. "There may be a lag. It happens sometimes." He turned and pointed west to a single mountain that rose above the plain. "It says he's up there."

The KWS ranger shook his head and dropped his cigarette.

I don't like it," Bernard said after they had parked and surveyed a portion of the mountain's base. "No spoor."

Klay, too, had seen no tracks—neither human nor elephant—and it was getting late. "Okay," he said. "But if my intel's right, and Greg is right, and we don't follow?"

"Then we've said goodbye to a national treasure."

Bernard spoke to the KWS ranger and returned to Klay. "There's a plateau just before the top. Our cattle end up there sometimes. That's where he'll be. Follow the trail. We'll clear the area and meet you at the plateau."

"What about those two?" Klay asked.

"The MP stays in the car."

When Bernard didn't continue, Klay shook his head. "No."

"Babysit him, would you?"

Klay looked at Greg again and sighed. "Beer's on you."

"Fair enough."

Bernard gave a few hand signals, and then he and his rangers vanished up the steep slope, dancing over rocks and among trees, like ghosts.

The climb was steeper than Klay had expected. After an hour he was using vines and roots to pull himself upwards. After two hours, he was struggling to silence his breathing. It came out of him in deep, cave-emptying gasps. His thighs burned. At each step he ordered his foot to clear the next rock, then watched as his boot kicked the rock loose and sent it tumbling down the mountain. Behind him, Greg climbed easily.

Klay wiped a damp forearm over his muddy face. Sweat burned his eyes. It was a poacher's moon, nearly as full and bright as daylight. Tracking is easiest at dawn and dusk, when angled sunlight casts a shadow in each footprint, enabling even an average tracker like Klay to read the ground. In the moon's bright light animals and men stood out, but the earth for Klay was illegible.

Finally, he reached the edge of the plateau where the elephant was supposed to be. He wiped his eyes with a dry corner of his shirttail and raised his binoculars. The clearing was empty. Klay grabbed the engineer's phone from him.

According to the TIPP app, the biggest elephant in Africa was standing right in front of them.

Bernard appeared at Klay's side. He put a finger to his lips. "No elephant," he mouthed, gesturing to indicate a trunk. He scissored his fingers to indicate a man walking, and pointed. Klay understood: someone was on the plateau with them.

Klay heard the crack of a rifle shot. Bernard's eyelids fluttered. The Samburu ranger seemed surprised, as if someone familiar had called out his name. Klay dove forward, tackling Bernard to the ground. He didn't hear the second shot. Klay's senses inverted. Sound turned to light. Light became touch. He tasted the bullet's impact, he would later recall. And then he was falling.

HOMECOMING

Dulles, Virginia, and Washington, DC

Klay awoke as the plane dipped toward Dulles International Airport and the green fields of northern Virginia came into view. It was late morning. He adjusted his arm uncomfortably. The bullet had passed through his right shoulder below the clavicle. He'd suffered bruised ribs and a brain-numbing concussion in the long fall. The doctors in Nairobi said he would be fine.

Bernard was dead.

The politician was dead, too, and the elephant had been nowhere near their location.

"Are you finished, sir?" a flight attendant asked, and he realized she'd already asked him once.

He looked down at the tiny Chivas bottles littering his tray. "I'm finished," he replied.

An anti-poaching operation gone bad, Kenya's **Daily Nation** had speculated. Land dispute, ran a competing theory.

Klay knew differently. He had the Botha file. Ras Leopold Botha, age forty-nine. He was born in Musina, South Africa. Father a local police officer, mother a housewife. Botha himself had been a cop once, supplementing his policeman's salary running stolen cars across the border, shipping them on to Mozambique. Working the syndicate with his brother, Dirk. The two men buying up property, opening a professional hunting company, Botha Brothers Safaris. Ras was the dominant brother, the imaginative one.

They had met once before. Klay was investigating elephant poaching in South Africa, and Ras Botha was a necessary stop for any journalist making that trip. Most reported Botha's name without speaking to him. Botha was not an easy man to track down, and he didn't talk to the press. Klay got lucky. Botha had been on trial in Pretoria, charged with murdering one of his Russian dancers. Klay attended the trial. On the last day, Botha had testified on his own behalf. The Afrikaner's defense was simple. "You don't **vermoorden** ass like that," he told the judge. "You fuck it."

Afterwards, Klay sat in a visitors' room,

looking at the man through scratched Plexiglas. Someone had ripped the phone off the wall on Klay's side of the window, so they yelled at each other through holes drilled in the Plexiglas.

"**I** run the ivory trade in Africa," Botha shouted. He was short and stocky, with a square head, protruding ears, and black crew cut hair. Two prisoners flanked him, a cell phone in each of their hands, all of them Botha's. The Octopus, they called him.

Klay laughed at the bold confession. Botha saying it matter-of-fact, like he was a businessman.

"You mean the **poaching,** Botha," Klay had replied. "You run the **poaching** in Africa."

Botha slammed a fist into the Plexiglas. "I'm not a fucking poacher. I'm a **hunter.** I use the resource. Those elephants are South Africa's elephants. It's our decision what to do with them. Not some bleeding-heart Yanks on holiday or some fucking Pommies with an orphanage. Those elephants are **property.** We own them. And **we** decide to sell their ivory . . ."

Klay pushed himself up from his airline seat, sending shock waves of pain into his brain. The plane had arrived at its gate. He retrieved his backpack from the overhead bin using his left hand. He looked down to see that his right hand was trembling. He opened and closed it, trying to steady his nerves. Without succeeding, he filed off the plane.

. . .

Erin Dougherty was waiting for him as he exited the secure area. He wasn't expecting anyone, and he might have walked past her, but he couldn't miss Erin's big mess of curly red hair. She stood on her toes, avoiding his slinged arm, and kissed him in a way that drew attention, including his.

"You didn't have to," he said, looking down at her.

"Don't be silly," she said, picking up his duffel bag.

Klay followed her up the ramp and outside to the parking lot, noting the men turning to stare openly at her as she passed. Erin walked quickly. Her wild hair and pale skin, her athletic body in clothes that didn't hide it, made her a constant target of male attention. He'd tried to get used to that during their time as a couple, but never had. He would glare into their wolfen faces, or pretend they didn't exist. It never made any difference. He drove a shoulder through more than a few. That never made a difference, either. She'd laughed at him. "You think walking down a street full of leering strangers is hard? Try fighting off your parents' friends, the college professor you looked up to," she said. "Just about every male editor at every place I've worked, including **The Sovereign**." He tried to imagine it, but he had nothing in his own life that offered a reference, so he went back to glaring and knocking into people.

But that had been years ago.

Erin oversaw what most people would call photo captions, but staff at **The Sovereign** referred to as legends. "God forbid a **Sovereign** photographer should touch a keyboard. And God help the journalist who thinks she can summarize a picture taken by a **Sovereign** priest," she said. Her legends department wrote tiny stories, no more than forty-nine words long, about people, places, and animals they often knew little about. "I was Twitter before Twitter was cool," she liked to say.

As they walked to her car, Erin's perfume floated back to him, carrying memories of Sunday mornings in their house on Capitol Hill, drinking coffee while Aretha played on the stereo, reading the **Washington Post,** then wandering over to Eastern Market for fresh vegetables. An afternoon workout at the gym. An evening workout in their bed.

But Sundays had seldom actually been Sundays, he reminded himself. And certainly weren't once a week. His travel schedule meant "Sunday" came at best every few weeks, and sometimes not for months. Odds were that first day back wasn't peaceful, either. They almost always fought on his return. The redbrick townhouse was in his name, but they'd picked it out together, intending to make it their home. Six months into their first home improvement project, the place had looked worse than when they'd started. Wallpaper on the open stairwell too high for either of them to reach was left half stripped for months, exposing a wall of cracked plaster to be patched. Painting he'd promised to do remained nothing but unopened buckets and rollers stacked in the coat closet. A small roof leak he said he'd fixed had quietly returned, weakening a bathroom ceiling until it had collapsed on her while she was in the tub. She paid all of their bills not because he didn't have the money, but because he didn't do it, and she couldn't bear the late fees. Duffel bags full of his clothes lined their bedroom, it being easier for him to pick one up and leave again than to refold his clothes and put them in the dresser.

It was **his** house, **his** terms, she said—Was it ever going to be **theirs**? He had thought so. He bought the damn house intending to fix it up for them to share. Chores weren't the real issue, of course. Nor were bills. It came down to baggage, but baggage of a different kind, baggage he couldn't unpack.

Even before Erin, he found the transition back to daily life in Washington difficult. He spent his first days home from the field lying on the couch, remote in hand, staring at the television to turn his mind off. Depression was always there, like a grizzly bear wandering around a campsite, alarming but not dangerous most of the time. When the bear became aggressive, he took steps to protect himself. He drank less, went to the gym more. He wrote. He searched the internet for his next story. If his depression became overwhelming, he removed the clip from the Glock he kept in his nightstand and hid it from himself.

Erin changed things for the better, but then came Jakarta, and that one terrible night no one could repair. He'd been sitting in a bar, an Indonesian cover band was playing "Hotel California." An American woman slid up beside him. She was beautiful, with wavy black hair and green eyes, drinking Arak Attacks, pineapple juice and coconut palm liquor. She offered him a sip from her straw: "They make you go blind." She smiled. He ordered one. But how many more? The next morning he sat alone in his hotel room, his head pounding. Something terrible had happened. He couldn't recall what it was. He reached up and felt a lump on his forehead. He remembered the bar, the woman. He remembered getting behind the wheel of her rental car, saying something about all of the more difficult places he'd driven around the world. There had been a problem with the car's lights or with its windshield wipers. He remembered squinting against the darkness and the rain. She asked him something, and he turned to her, he remembered that. And then she screamed. The sound of her scream in his mind brought it all back. He turned his attention back to the road just in time to see a boy on a bicycle. He jerked the wheel. He felt the **thud** of the impact in his chest.

The events of that night changed everything. He had killed a boy, Adri had been his name, and there was nothing he could do to fix it. He drank less in public after that. More when he was alone. He told Erin about the accident, leaving out the American woman and the extent of his drunkenness. The omission cursed their relationship, of course.

He tried to be present for her, to overcome what he'd done and who he was because of it. He saw well how he did in her eyes. She had been eager to help him in the beginning, but grew increasingly frustrated. "It's one thing not to hear from you when you're gone," she told him, "but you're standing right here!" His protective instincts ran too deep, she said. "You protect yourself first and foremost. You know that, right?"

And so, after a few drinks to dull the impact he would forever feel in his chest, he would get up from the couch and do what happy couples do— go out for dinner, meet up with their friends, tour that new art exhibit.

. . .

She drove a red Audi. He lowered himself into the passenger seat and she closed his door for him. As he pulled the seat belt across his chest, he noticed a bill from the Congressional Country Club wedged beside the passenger seat and his head cleared. "How's Grant?" he asked, buckling in.

She turned to back the car out of its space. "He's good. He's in Chicago."

Was that an invitation he heard? It had been a decade since their breakup. It had been almost that long since they'd slept together.

Grant was head of Nike's government affairs office. Fit, of course. A competitive marathon runner. Intellectual. They'd met while Klay was away. He couldn't remember the assignment, or even the continent. He remembered all too well the day he returned home. He'd dropped onto the sofa with a beer, switched on the television, and noticed two copies of **Runner's World** poking out from underneath the sofa. That was it. No muddy shoe prints exiting the back door. No foreign underwear in their bed. Just two copies of **Runner's World** that weren't current. Erin wasn't a runner.

"He's a good man," Klay said.

"Yes, he is," she said, and smiled expectantly.

He caught sight of the ring on her left hand and shook his head. "You're engaged. Wow. Congratulations!" He smiled, pleased to discover he was genuinely happy for her.

"Yeah, we decided it was about time."

He cracked his window and felt a warm late-morning breeze blow across his face. She steered onto the Dulles Access Road, and the Audi gathered speed. Adele was playing on the radio. She turned down the volume. "Do you want to talk about it, Tom?"

"Not especially."

She took her eyes off the road and looked at him. "It's not your fault."

He didn't respond.

"Look, it's not my business, but don't go to that place. Okay? Bad things happen around you because you put yourself in places where bad people are. The Jakarta boy was a terrible accident. Bernard was not your fault."

Reductions. **The Jakarta boy. Bernard.**

"Do you have any Advil?" he asked.

"Look in the glove box."

He found a bottle and took several.

"How's it feel?" she asked.

"Comes and goes."

"You're not going to like this," she said as they crossed Arlington Memorial Bridge into Washington, DC. "Porfle has arranged a small party for you."

"I'd like to go home."

"I know," she said uncomfortably. "I gave him the spare house key from your office."

He sighed. He'd forgotten that he still had a key taped to the back of his top desk drawer.

"Sorry," she said. "You don't have to act surprised."

She pulled to the curb in front of his townhouse and parked. She went first up the wrought iron steps, opened the front door with his key, and ushered him in.

"Surprise!"

Sovereign staff filled his narrow home. Snaps Kennedy. Mitchell Fox. His research assistant, David Tenchant, and Tenchant's pregnant wife, Maggie. Tom Burkey and Karen Forsythe, photographers he worked with when Snaps wasn't available. Two senior editors who were having an affair they thought no one knew about. Staff called them Tweedledee and Tweedledum behind their backs. Other faces. A handful of hipsters dressed like summer lumberjacks he assumed were from television. More strangers sipping mimosas filled his hallway, all the way back to his kitchen.

A familiar voice rose above the din. "Dr. Livingstone, I presume!" Klay's editor, Alexander Porfle, made his way forward from the dining room. Porfle was lean, a few years older than Klay, and British. He had narrow-set blue eyes, sparse hair he parted on the side, and that stiff-legged, terrified posture they appreciate at the

Westminster dog show. He wore a navy-blue blazer over an open-collared white dress shirt and penny loafers, no socks.

Porfle thrust out his hand to shake Klay's, saw the sling, and awkwardly patted Klay's chest instead. He turned to the room. "We're all sorry for your loss, Tom. But it is a reminder, a **lethal** reminder to us all, that it is a dangerous world out there our Mr. Klay inhabits. He is—and I have long said this, so I don't feel it inappropriate to repeat myself now—a sniper, a man who trains his rifle on unsavory human beings few of us can even countenance, let alone confront."

"Oh, honestly, Alex." Hadley Porfle pushed her husband aside and kissed Klay lightly. "We won't stay," she whispered into his ear. "I am sorry for your loss."

"That's what he is," Porfle continued, for everyone to hear. "And you all should know it. Mr. Klay, our Good Christian Soldier, identifies targets with me on the scope, and he takes them down. This was a small setback," he said, turning to Klay. "We'll get that bastard, my boy. Your pen and my pencil. The old **Sov** is behind you." Porfle raised his glass. "To Tom Klay, master of the upright pronoun!"

"Hear! Hear!"

Klay thanked Porfle, drank his champagne, greeted colleagues clustered in his front room, and then made his way deliberately down the crowded narrow hallway to the kitchen. He didn't recognize a single person nibbling catered Greek food, sipping white wine, talking across his granite island, leaning against the stainless refrigerator.

Klay didn't cook, but shopping for this house he'd liked the **idea** of himself as a cook, with a wife like Erin who liked to cook, too. She'd had the same idea. And though the house needed plenty of work elsewhere, they'd walked in, seen the farmhouse sink, the gas-fueled Viking stove, and the Sub-Zero refrigerator, and they felt sure this would be their home.

They talked about throwing dinner parties, their many interesting friends laughing together in the living room, pouring really nice, full-bodied cabernet using those big-bowled glasses actually designed for drinking cabernet, while he and Erin, wearing amusing, insider-joke aprons they'd bought for each other, served dishes discovered in **Bon Appétit.** Although none of that had remotely come to pass—not Erin, not learning to cook, not matching wineglasses, not a single dinner party—it had been that idea, and this kitchen, that had sold him on the house.

"Going to get some air," he muttered, squeezing past his guests. He slid open the kitchen's glass door and stepped onto the small deck. He was closing the kitchen door when Erin stepped onto the deck with him and slid the door closed.

"Hey," she said. "I'm sorry about the party."

"It's fine," he said.

"Everybody was worried about you, you know. Even Porfle, no matter what he was talking about in there."

"I get it."

She waited a moment, then sighed. "You're already closed down, aren't you?"

It was what he did. No distractions. He wanted Botha.

"Look," she said, finally, "I'm going back to your party." She looked at the deck's back gate. "Wherever you're off to, don't blame yourself, okay?"

He unlatched the gate, walked down an alley to the street, and hailed a cab.

"**The Sovereign,** please," he said. He didn't need to say more—every cabbie in the city knew the famous magazine's headquarters. The driver took East Capitol, turned right past the Supreme Court, and headed up Constitution. It was about as impressive a commute as one could ask for, Klay guessed. He leaned back in his seat and closed his eyes.

He'd had only one good relationship in the years since Erin.

Hungry Khoza was brilliant and funny and stunningly beautiful. They'd met at an Interpol conference in Lyon, France, where she was leading a panel on balancing the power between a state and its citizens. As a South African, she spoke with captivating authority. He raised his hand and asked what difference rules made when the state in question was corrupt. "American, right?" she responded. It was the beginning of a conversation that seemed destined to last forever.

But Hungry lived in Pretoria. "Geographically challenged" was how they explained their eventual breakup to friends and family. Anyone who knew them could have offered a hundred other reasons why they hadn't worked out: Hungry was too dedicated to her career as a prosecutor; Klay was too dedicated to his as a journalist. One was steady; the other transient. One black; the other white. One outgoing; the other quiet. One upbeat; the other, well, Tom Klay.

The truth was their many differences had made Klay love Hungry even more. And he was pretty certain the same had been true for her. When Hungry discovered the walls he had built inside of himself, walls Erin, despite valiant efforts, had been unable to break down, Hungry had not given up. She had picked up a hammer and chiseled away at those barriers, working patiently. And she had been successful in ways no woman ever had.

He told her about the Jakarta car accident—all of it—and how it made him feel. He told her about his childhood, his parents, and the loss that had laced his adulthood with despair. He told her about his fear that no matter how hard he tried, the world would simply absorb his efforts and get worse. He told her he wasn't a good person; he was a bad person who did good things to hide the truth. He was afraid, deep down, that he liked to hurt people. Feelings he didn't know he had. Fears he had never shared.

But then, on the verge of what felt like true intimacy, he would pick up his duffel bag and leave. Erin thought he was repeating his same sins. She encouraged him to try again. "This woman is good for you, Tom," she said. "Go back."

Hungry **was** good for him. She knew how to love and be loved. She was willing to go more than halfway in their relationship. She understood him, and loved him anyway. "Don't you see?" Hungry said to him. "You never take a case you won't win. I am that case, Thomas. Your unwinnable case. You have to **commit** to love, and risk losing it, to find happiness."

Commitment wasn't the issue—he wanted a relationship with Hungry—but he had made another commitment years ago, and that commitment left no space for her. And so he would disappear again, and months would pass before his heart drove him back to South Africa. And when he returned their cycle would begin again: she chiseling away, he pretending he was an honest man struggling to make a happy life together.

But he was not an honest man.

. . .

The DC lunch crowd was heading back to their offices when Klay stepped out of his taxi in front of **The Sovereign**'s headquarters. Klay looked up at the wedge-shaped brick building and felt a twinge of pride. **The Sovereign** was about to celebrate its 150th anniversary. In a world of media bankruptcies, buyouts, mergers, and takeovers, **The Sovereign** had endured, protected against time by a gift from a railroad baron named Hiram Prendergast, and his cousin, a botany-loving inventor named Thomas Edison, who together had endowed the nonprofit institution in perpetuity. For the next 141 years, including the moment Klay stepped onto the sidewalk, a Prendergast had controlled **The Sovereign.**

Meanwhile the Sovereign Society had evolved from a producer of survey maps and expedition journals into the most widely recognized science-and-exploration media platform in the world—producer of four glossy magazines, two television channels, an Oscar-winning documentary film studio, a research institution, a website, travel services, licensed adventure products, and the planet's most viewed social media. All of it collectively known as **The Sovereign,** voted the world's most trusted media brand.

Klay climbed the marble steps. He walked rapidly, with his head down, shoulders stiff and rolled forward, as if he were wading into a brawl. He winced as he pushed the building's heavy revolving door.

"Hi, Tonya," he said to the guard behind her desk.

"Good afternoon, Tom. I'm glad you're home safe," she said, looking at his sling. "Mr. Eady?"

"Yes, please."

Klay entered a small, oak-paneled elevator set slightly apart from the building's four main lifts and pressed its only button. After a slow, rumbling ascent, Klay stepped off the elevator into a modern gallery of photographic images and exhibits arranged in a labyrinth. The photographs were eight feet tall and suspended from the ceiling on black wires. Several had been taken by Eady himself back when he was a staff photographer. Ahead Howard Carter stepped forward into Tutankhamen's funerary chamber. A left turn and Dian Fossey bottle-fed a baby mountain gorilla at Karisoke. A right turn introduced Tsavo's red elephants. In the labyrinth's center squatted an original bathysphere, that one-eyed Volkswagen-on-a-rope that Beebe and Barton rode deeper into the ocean than any human had gone before.

Officially, the maze was designed to force visitors to reflect on their place in history and the potential each of us has to be an explorer. But

Klay knew better. The top floor of **The Sovereign** was Vance Eady's aerie. The labyrinth existed to remind people just who they were about to meet.

Eady stood in his secretary's doorway, hands on hips, dressed as always—dark wool slacks, V-neck sweater over a white shirt, shined John Lobb shoes—like an Anglican minister relaxing between sermons on a perpetually autumn day. "Well," the Society's president and magazine's editor in chief said as Klay approached. "That's fine. Very fine, indeed. Welcome home." He patted Klay's shoulder gently and ushered him toward his office.

"Hello, Sally," Klay said, nodding to Eady's secretary as they passed.

The Sovereign's beloved caretaker shook her gray head. "You boys," she scolded. "Welcome home, Tom."

"Hold my calls please, Sally," Eady said. He led Klay into his office and closed the door. "I'm paying for a party at your place, aren't I?" Eady said, and without waiting for Klay's reply, asked, "Drink?"

Klay nodded. He tossed a Mongolian eagle hunter's cap out of his way and took a seat on Eady's worn leather sofa.

Eady crossed to a large standing globe beside his Resolute desk, split the globe in half, and withdrew two crystal whiskey glasses and a bottle of scotch, while Klay absently read for the hundredth time the lines from Kipling framed on the end table beside him.

> **NOW this is the Law of the Jungle—as old and as true as the sky,**
> **And the Wolf that shall keep it may prosper, but the Wolf that shall break it must die.**
> **As the creeper that girdles the tree-trunk the Law runneth forward and back;**
> **For the strength of the Pack is the Wolf, and the strength of the Wolf is the Pack . . .**

Eady was indeed leader of a pack of journalists, photographers, and explorers who circled the world and brought their discoveries home. Every wall and flat surface in Eady's office held some exotic treasure of **Sovereign** men and women returned: A blue-green dinosaur egg fossil, five curare-tipped poison darts in a jaguar-skin quiver. Unidentified teeth, disconnected bones, pieces of gnarled fur. A stuffed zebra head hung opposite Klay with its **Well, what's your excuse?** expression. Next to the Kipling, a gold-ringed Kayan necklace had been turned into a table lamp. On one corner of Eady's desk, an inverted hawksbill sea turtle shell held Eady's car keys.

Klay's gift to Eady hung on the wall behind the old man's desk, a wooden loom strung with Indonesian double ikat cloth, purchased for Eady the day before Klay struck the boy. On receiving it, Eady quoted Henry Ward Beecher. "'. . . the pattern which was weaving when the sun went down is weaving when it comes up tomorrow . . .'"

It took Klay a few years to find his place at **The Sovereign.** He had thick wrists and fingers too broad for the Macs the staff used, so they bought him a PC and somebody dug up an old IBM keyboard from the basement as a joke, but the older design turned out to be easier for him to use, and the joke was on his colleagues. The keyboard clacked so loudly anyone on the east end of the third floor knew when he had an idea. He ignored the company dress code. Maybe it was the suits he'd worn as a boy, or the images of the bodies he'd dressed, but he couldn't bring himself to wear khakis or a dress shirt. He dressed the way he did in the field.

No one asked him about his past directly. They scattered hints. "Did you see the piece **60** did on the Russian mafia last night?" Porfle might ask. Klay said no, whether he had or not.

He didn't share his personal story with anyone. They knew his name, where he'd grown up. They had Google.

"So where'd you study journalism?"

"I didn't."

"So where'd you learn to write?"

"My mother," he answered, which was the truth.

Much of who he was came from her. She read to him every night as a boy. Whitman and Frost and guileless Mary Oliver. "Tell me," Oliver asked years after his mother was gone, "what is it you plan to do with your one wild and precious life?" When he first read the line it was his mother's voice he heard asking the question. His first writing was poems he composed for her. He had a gift, she said, smiling at the images he created with his pencil. "Words don't have to flow in order," she encouraged. "Your life doesn't, either." If he didn't want to follow in the family business, he was free to leave it. His father agreed, she said.

He wasn't about to share any of that with his colleagues any more than he would reveal that he still wrote a poem a week in the Moleskine notebook he carried in his shirt pocket, something she taught him to do. His silent prayer to her.

With little to go on, his coworkers crafted their own narrative to explain Tom Klay. Some called him Eady's pet. They wove a story together from his muttering, his clothes, his family's business, his interest in crime. An incident in Mexico City provided his weavers a prominent thread. Klay had turned a corner and discovered his photographer pushed up against a wall by a police officer who wanted to impose a tax on the American with the big camera. Klay had walked toward the cop, his hands held in front of his chest with the palms facing out, patting the air, gently saying, "We are on an assignment for your president." The officer pulled his Glock .45 and pointed it at Klay's head. In a single motion, Klay snatched the pistol, ejected the clip, jacked the slide, depressed the slide lock, and with a twist of his wrist reduced the weapon to a pipe, a spring, and a piece of black plastic. "He's with me," Klay said, and handed the cop his deconstructed gun.

The photographer had ended his tale on that "He's with me" line, cementing Klay's reputation throughout the building, turning half of the staff into open admirers, but more than a few the other way.

Eady could have corrected the rumors, could have ensured that Klay's reputation stayed within certain boundaries. But he hadn't, and that told Klay a good deal about who Vance Eady was, too.

Eady handed him his scotch and took a seat in a wingback chair, crossing one leg over his other knee. Eady reminded Klay of his grandfather. He had the same full white head of hair parted straight as a rifle barrel, same blue eyes and strong jaw. Even the same leathery neck skin with crosshatching that, in Klay's grandfather, had fascinated Klay as a child. Physically, the main difference between the two men was in their smile. When he was amused, his grandfather had broken into a broad, chipped-tooth grin. Eady's smile was always controlled. Even when he was pleased, Eady's mouth barely opened.

"You look like death itself, Tom," Eady said.

"I've been better." Klay shifted his position, trying to get comfortable.

Eady shook his head. "It's good to have you home." He raised his glass. "To Ellsworth."

Ellsworth, Klay thought.

Porfle had his sniper-spotter fantasy, and Eady had his Ellsworth. Every year, during a cocktail reception for incoming journalists, Eady stood on the roof of **The Sovereign** and gave a toast to Elmer Ellsworth, the young Union colonel who crossed the Potomac to Alexandria, Virginia, cut down a confederate flag for the president, and was promptly shot dead with the rebel banner in his arms—making him the first casualty of the Civil War. "Remember Ellsworth!" became a Union rallying cry.

"For a scrap of cloth," Eady liked to say, lifting his glass, "that wasn't." The implication as subtle as a cannon ball: **Bring me back stories. Survive if you can. I am your Lincoln.**

"To Bernard," Klay countered quietly, and drained his glass.

"Any more on the shooter, or shooters?"

Klay studied Eady, surprised. "I was hoping you might help with that."

Eady nodded, sipped his drink. "Botha's gone quiet?"

"Why would he do the politician?" Klay said.

Eady gestured for Klay to repeat his question.

"Why kill Lekorere?" Klay asked. "He wasn't a threat."

Eady shrugged. "Wrong place, wrong time. Shooters took your vehicle to get away. For some reason Lekorere was in it. That was a mistake." Eady repeated his question. "Have you heard more on Botha?"

Klay's mind was elsewhere. He was thinking about Bernard on his hands and knees outside his mother's hut searching for his rungu. Klay teasing him for losing his club again. "You should put a string on it." Bernard smiling his joy-filled smile, leading Klay on a hike, his gold belt jingling. "This blue flower tells us rain is coming. This is the candelabra tree. The sap will blind you. The only cure is to wash your eye out with blood." Klay, bandaged, standing beside Bernard's mother as she poured milk on her son's grave.

"Tom?"

"I don't know, Vance," Klay said. "He texted me while I was in the hospital."

"**Texted** you?"

Klay nodded. " 'Hope your food's worse than mine,' it said. 'Get well soon. Hahaha.' "

" 'Hahaha,' " Eady echoed, looking quizzically at Klay. "How do you know it was Botha?"

"I don't **know** it. But he signed it. 'Ras Botha.' "

Eady shook his head. "The Octopus, you called him, right? He's a murderer, Tom. We knew that before, but now you know it firsthand. That changes things, I'd say."

"There was something else on that plateau," Klay said. "Something just before the shot . . ."

"I know. Bernard. Pity. But you're a hero, Tom. Your actions saved the rest of—"

"No, something else. It's on the edge of my memory. I can't quite get it."

"Something else?" Eady looked at Klay thoughtfully for a moment. He seemed to decide something, then got to his feet and began to pace. "Good. Keep at it. Though it might not be a memory at all. Had a gorilla subadult hit me on the head once. Just a punch right on top here—" He poked a finger into his white hair. "Woke up thinking the old man had popped me for playing hooky from Exeter. Saw the whole thing down to the shine on his wingtips. Called for my mother, only mother wintered in Palm Beach and I wasn't sixteen anymore. You never know. Memory is a tricky thing." He turned to Klay. "If you think of anything, any clue at all, let me know. We want to get the bastard. By that I don't just mean me. The public has an interest."

The public has an interest.

Klay looked at Eady. It had been a while since Eady had used that particular phrase. Klay felt a sharp pain run down his injured arm.

ASSIGNMENT

Washington, DC

Klay was sitting on his usual stool at the end of the Gray Pigeon's dimly lit bar with a laptop open in front of him, thinking. Eady had gone quiet. He'd seen the old man three, maybe four times since Kenya, and each time Eady had somewhere else to be, something more important on his mind. Klay sipped his drink. Maybe he was making too much of things, over-thinking it. It's why he was here, wasn't it, watching Billy Thurman stack glasses behind a bar on a Saturday morning with a bourbon in front of him? For the thinking.

"You mind if I switch to the game?" Billy asked.

Klay didn't have to ask the bar's owner which game he was referring to. Any other day Billy wore a black T-shirt and jeans, his smoker-veined arms and faded tattoos exposed. But today he had on a blue sweatshirt, sleeves pushed to the elbow, and the word "Navy" emblazoned across his chest in gold. It was eleven o'clock. Except for Phil the Economist, perched on his regular stool, the Pigeon was empty.

Empty. Like his list of ideas on how to take down Ras Botha. That's what he should have been focused on. Klay raised two fingers off his glass signaling Billy to do as he pleased. Billy looked up at the television, a box the size of a small refrigerator bolted to the ceiling, and flipped channels with a remote.

The Gray Pigeon was what used to be called a reporter's bar, a Pennsylvania Avenue watering hole where veteran journalists and their powerful subjects could mingle after work and off the record. Photos in black metal frames memorialized the Pigeon's glory days: David Halberstam at his word processor. Sy Hersh on the telephone. Molly Ivins sporting John Tower's Stetson. Helen Thomas wagging a finger at Marlin Fitzwater. Even **Washington Star** columnist Mary "Fawn not upon the great" McGrory had allowed her photo to be taken at the Pigeon, albeit walking out of the place. Klay avoided sitting across from a framed note, typed on FBI stationery, which hung behind the bar. The note read, "Jack Anderson: Lower than the regurgitated filth of vultures.—J. Edgar Hoover." Both Hoover and Anderson had autographed the yellowing note in ink that was now faded.

The Gray Pigeon had faded, too. The internet, Craigslist, and—Billy's pet theory—Jim Fixx's **Complete Book of Running**—had each taken a turn knocking the wind out of smoke-filled evenings downing dry martinis and pickled eggs. In a corner sat Billy's one effort to keep up with the times: a piña colada machine that looped a warm mint-green liquid.

"It's just the march on yet," Billy said, backing away from the television set. "Then they got the tailgate. Kickoff's at three." He set the remote down next to the cash register and refilled Klay's ice water. "What's next on your agenda?"

"Wait and see," Klay said.

Billy eyed Klay for a moment. "Emphasis on 'wait'?"

"You got it." Klay glanced at his phone again.

He was ready for a new assignment. He'd told Porfle, but Porfle said he didn't have anything for him. He could have been wrong, but Porfle sounded like he didn't **want** to have anything for him. The only good news from all this delay was that physically he was much improved. His sling was gone. His range of motion had returned. Nerves in his right hand tingled from time to time, but his doctor said that would resolve.

Klay picked up his phone and texted Eady.

"Anything?" He held the phone in his palm for a moment, willing a response to appear, then set it down on the bar, facedown.

He nodded at Billy's sweatshirt. "How's your grandson doing?"

"Good," Billy said. "Carl's doing real good. They got him on the **Shiloh.**"

"Sounds exciting," Klay said.

"Sure," Billy said. "It all sounds exciting."

Klay didn't respond. Instead, he did what a good reporter does when he's having a conversation: he kept his mouth shut.

"Ah, you know," Billy continued. "His old man left my daughter. Kid had to be a man straight out of the cradle. Said he wanted to do something with his life. Not just a job, an adventure kind of thing. I told him there's lots of adventures don't mean getting your head blown off, but what does an old man like me know, right? I'm so smart what am I doing pouring rail booze to has-beens? Present company excluded," he apologized. "Anyway, kid says he wants to be like his granddad. I told him I was drafted. He thinks I was a war hero."

"From what I hear you were."

"What's that get you?"

"You feel responsible," Klay said.

Billy shrugged.

"Go Army!" Phil the Economist blurted.

Both men looked down the bar. Billy pointed

his finger. "I'll give you that one," he said. "No more."

Phil's eyebrows shot up. He wasn't used to being addressed directly. He was large and soft with a few sprigs of hair left on a pale head. He wore a gray sweatshirt over gray sweatpants and black sneakers, giving him the appearance of a manatee with a Jack and Coke between his flippers. He sipped his drink and watched the game.

"Carl did real well in school," Billy said to Klay. "Loved engineering. Had plenty of offers in the private sector. Turned them all down. Says there's nobody doing what the military does. But I do worry about him."

"I'm sure he's in good hands. Seventh Fleet, right?"

"That's right. Lucky Seventh," Billy said, bitterly. "MacArthur's Navy. Twenty thousand sailors now. All circling the South China Sea." Billy looked at a tattoo on his forearm too old and faded for Klay to read. "Seems like we can't ever get away from that place."

"Well, it's a different world now," Klay said.

On the television, the midshipmen were marching onto the field, lining up by company.

"Doesn't look different," Billy said. "They've got the **Shiloh** on stand-down. You've seen the news, right?"

Klay had not paid much attention to the news

since his return from Kenya. Everything on it seemed like a version of Bernard's killing.

"No, Bill. What'd I miss?"

"Carl says it's nothing. Seventh Fleet's been having accidents. The **Fitzgerald** got rammed by a Japanese cargo ship. Dead of night, sent her into a full 360 spin, full red over red. Seven dead. Then **McCain** turns into the path of a thirty-thousand-ton Liberian oil tanker—ten more boys gone. Maybe it was girls. I don't know. **Champlain** ran over a fishing boat—that's an Aegis cruiser like the **Shiloh.** All South China Sea. Modern Navy. How modern is that?"

"Not very," Klay said. He glanced at his lifeless cell phone.

"I asked him, 'How can a destroyer sail into an oil tanker?' 'All explainable, Pops,' he tells me." Billy reached under the bar and brought out a dented Famous Amos cookie tin. He pried off the lid. Inside were carefully folded letters. "I don't go in for email," he said, digging through the papers. He took out a letter. "He says it was the OOD plotting radar track for the wrong goddamn ship. SCS screwup, the CO shifting thrust control to the lee helmsman without telling him. Sloppy anchoring. Radar malfunction." Billy looked up. "How does that happen?"

"I don't know, Bill," Klay said. He hadn't understood a word Billy had said. On the television, CBS was showing drone shots of the

Naval Academy brigade lined up by company. "You gotta be proud of him, though."

Billy smiled. "Yeah. He said all that time on those video games of his would pay off, and I guess it did." The older man tapped the bar in front of Klay. "Kid says the computers they're using onboard are twenty years old. He's praying the next systems upgrade goes to somebody like Microsoft or Perseus Group."

Klay nodded. He almost said, "Makes sense for them," but caught himself. He sipped his drink and concentrated on the television. West Point's cadets were marching onto the field now, dressed in somber gray and black.

"Sink Navy!" Phil shouted, raising a fist.

"That's it." Billy came out from behind the bar with a nightstick in his hand. "Up," Billy said.

Phil hunkered his head into his shoulders and stared straight ahead. Billy took hold of Phil's collar with his left hand, inserted the tip of his nightstick under Phil's right armpit, and pressed. The big man sprang from his stool—arms and legs out—like a wooden toy, and Billy marched him from his stool. To Klay's surprise he didn't lead Phil to the door. Instead, he moved him three seats down and released him. Then he slid Phil's half-empty Jack and Coke down to him. Phil gulped the rest of his drink, visibly shaken. He reached into his sweatpants, slapped his money on the bar, and waited for Billy to pour him a fresh one. Billy set a fresh Jack and Coke in front of Phil. "You can have your seat back when the game starts, Phil. But you keep your opinions to yourself."

Phil sipped his drink, staring straight ahead, a quiet smile on his lips.

"Remind me not to mess with you," Klay said.

"Little shore patrol move. I learned it the hard way." Billy folded his grandson's letter and put it back in the cookie tin. He returned the tin to its place under the bar. "Anyway, I'm hoping no more accidents."

Klay's cell phone buzzed. It was a text from Eady.

On Monday morning Klay looked up to see Eady standing in his doorway. He checked his watch. "I was on my way up in ten."

Eady shut Klay's door. He navigated the stacks of unfiled documents littering Klay's floor and placed a thin red folder on Klay's desk.

Klay opened the folder and scanned the top document, a two-page file summary printed on pale blue paper. A priest. The Philippines. Unholy.

"You said it was going to be Botha."

"He's Botha's Asia connection," Eady explained. "Ivory on its way to China. We may have to slay this Hydra one head at a time."

Klay shook his head as he turned the file's pages. "This priest's a pedophile, Vance."

"A chance to do some extra good," Eady said.

Klay closed the file. "I don't know what your source is on this, but I've studied Botha. He wouldn't partner with a pedophile."

"You know this for a fact?"

"My gut says," Klay said.

"Fortunately, your gut doesn't work for me."

Klay pushed back from his desk. Eady rarely visited the third floor. His colleagues would be at the edges of their cubbyhole offices straining to hear their discussion. Fox's office was next door. If Klay struck the wall with his fist, he was sure he'd hear Fox yelp.

"Look, Vance. Botha had . . . Botha has a younger brother, Dirk. They say when he was a boy, Dirk showed extraordinary promise as a swimmer. He was so good that his swim coach, the local priest, would drive out to the Botha farm and pick Dirk up to make sure he didn't miss practice. The priest took the boy for drives sometimes, because if he was going to be a world champion, he needed to see the world. Then one day Dirk told his brother what happened on those drives. They found the priest with his throat cut, hanging from a tree. His car was parked nearby. Ras had written 'I did it' on the windshield with a bar of soap, and signed his name and address. He was thirteen."

Eady cleared his throat. "Not a perfect fit. I'll grant you. That's fine. No criminal network is consistent all the way through. I am a bit surprised, though. I assumed you'd take every opportunity to go after Botha."

Klay punched the wall. There was a commotion from Fox's office. It sounded like a chair falling over.

"You know I would," Klay said. "I'm on it."

"Good," Eady said, and tapped the file with his fingertip. " 'There's always a who,' isn't that what you like to say? Well, this is one of them." He turned as he was opening the door. "And just so we're clear, Tom. This is an assignment. It's not a democracy. The public—"

"—has an interest," Klay said. "Yeah. I know. I have an interest, too."

ON THE HUNT

Manila and Cebu Island, Philippines

Klay arrived at the Open Orchid, a shabby hotel in Manila's old red-light district not far from the American embassy. He set his duffel bag on the floor beside the front desk. "Reservation for Flanagan," he said, and handed over a passport. "Three nights," he added, and paid in advance, though he would only stay for one. Klay leaned an elbow on the counter while the thin Filipino clerk jotted his details with a ballpoint pen. "This hotel was recommended by Monsignor Martelino." The clerk's pen paused, then continued scribbling.

Across the lobby, a big man who looked to be in his fifties waited for an elevator beside a Filipino boy, maybe nine or ten years old. The man had a football lineman's size, but there was something not American in his carriage. Hawaiian shirt. Too-short shorts. Sandals with the socks pulled up. German or Australian, Klay guessed.

Klay cleared his throat to get the man's attention. He wanted to see his face. The big man tilted his head and spoke to the boy. Klay heard bits of German. The man kept his back to Klay until he and the boy were inside the elevator. Then he turned and stared at Klay without expression, his hand on the boy's scrawny shoulder as the elevator doors closed. Ownership.

Klay felt revulsion turn in his gut, but he had his assignment, and it didn't start here. He accepted his fake passport back from the clerk and shouldered his bag. Next to the front desk was the doorway to the hotel's bar-restaurant, the bar a five-stool setup serving bottom-shelf liquor under brown palm fronds. An elderly woman sat behind the bar turning pages in a magazine, smoking a cigarette. Beyond the bar was the restaurant. Klay smelled overheated food. "Pork sisig," a chalkboard said. He ordered his dinner with the bartender and went up to his room.

A waiter arrived with his food, laid a tray on the foot of his bed, and asked if there would be anything else.

"No," Klay said, handing him a tip.

"Are you certain?" the young man said. "Boy or girl, doesn't matter."

There was a shrewdness in the teenager's eyes. A certainty in his smile.

"I'm tired," Klay said and pointed a finger toward the door.

He ate his dinner of a roasted half chicken and French fries, drank the beer. He checked his phone. He carried his dinner tray to the hallway and left it outside his door, then returned to his room and looked at the bed. It was just after seven in the evening local time. For him it was three a.m. He wouldn't sleep. He popped a ceiling tile in the back of his closet and hid his laptop there. The safe was anything but. He put on his boots, took the elevator down, and walked the neighborhood. He could move his arm without real pain as long as he didn't try to do anything too sudden. His ribs hurt just enough to remind him he needed to exercise.

It was early evening, but late enough in this part of town. Prostitutes dotted Ermita's sewage-damp sidewalks. Thin men rose up like grass eels, calling out, "Cialis!" "Viagra!" A block from his hotel, he passed a man walking a dwarf on a leash. The little person wore a leather harness around his body with a handle along his spine. His T-shirt said, "Toss Me!"

"Mister, mister!" A woman tugged his shirt. She held by the hand a young girl, perhaps eight, wearing a pink dress. The little girl turned her palm up. Klay felt street eyes on him, watching to see what he would do.

"Mister," the girl's mother pleaded.

He bought a cup of coffee from a street cart, and left ten times the coffee's cost in change on the counter. He looked at the mother and kept walking. She snatched his money and rejoined him. "Mister. You like my daughter? You want to marry her? Take her to America? Marry her for one hour?"

Two blocks later she was gone, and so was his interest in exploring the neighborhood. He returned to his hotel, got a few hours' sleep, then took a cab to the airport, and boarded a flight for Cebu Island.

Klay's target wore black-framed eyeglasses and long white robes emblazoned with the head of a Christ child in gold thread. The fat priest stood at the front of his altar and raised an ivory Christ child above his head for his parishioners to admire. This was the beginning of the annual ceremony called the Hubo, a Cebuano word meaning "to undress." The Santo Niño de Cebu icon in his hands was the size of a house cat, dressed as a boy king.

Martelino removed the icon's tiny crown, slipped off its little black boots, unfastened its scarlet cape and gold belt, and removed its tunic. Then he produced a curved knife from the sleeve of his tunic and sliced the back of the doll's white underwear, which fell to a golden bowl held by an altar boy. Hundreds of sweating parishioners sang out, **"Christe exaudi nos."**

He carried the naked doll to a large barrel of water and began to bathe it, before handing it to his assistants, who quickly redressed it in simpler clothes. Afterwards, Martelino used the bath-water to bless his followers.

I enjoyed your service, Father," Klay said, and accepted a mango slice from a dish an altar boy held out to him. The priest sat behind a heavy Spanish desk across from Klay, in his modest office at the back of the church. Outside, the church's recessional bells chimed. Sunlight filtered into the priest's office through a capiz-shell screen.

Martelino leaned forward and plucked a date from the dish. "You were easy to recognize," he replied, chewing his date. "Few kneel before God anymore." He glanced at the altar boy, whose dark eyes dropped to the floor and stayed there.

"That's Sister Marie," Klay said. "No one eats that flesh without first adoring it. It was on the tongue or off to hell." He rubbed his knuckles. "She was a tough one."

Martelino sighed. "Paul the Sixth." He spread his hands. "So, what can I do for you, Tomas. Is it Tomas?"

"Tomas, yes," Klay said. "Thomas O'Shea. O'Shea Funeral Home Corporation." Klay placed a business card on Martelino's desk.

"Ah, a mortician. So, you understand the importance of rituals."

"Without them we are out of business."

"Which did you enjoy most?" Martelino asked, chewing.

"The Hubo—"

"No, of course. What else have you seen?"

"Well," Klay said. "The fluvial procession was something. It was overwhelming for me, as an American Catholic."

Klay was tired. He had decided to approach the priest during the country's Santo Niño festival, when millions of Catholics flock to Cebu. Klay had risen at three a.m. to walk, carrying a small white candle with tens of thousands of believers, talking quietly with them about faith. It was hard not to be moved by the conviction of the people he encountered, especially the many poor, sick, and frail. Most of these ceremonies involved a passing of the hat, taking whatever these faithful could spare. Theater was everywhere. At its most extreme, he watched a Santo Niño icon declared the navy's supreme captain general and granted command of a navy patrol ship, which it then captained across Mactan Channel, escorted by four patrol ships, two coast guard cutters, a pair of helicopters dropping flowers, and a maritime parade of devotees in hundreds of small boats.

"Oh, I know you Americans find our traditions absurd."

"Oh no, Father."

"Please," Martelino said. "I myself find it all ridiculous. But the people want these things. They insist. And it doesn't weaken their belief to see the Santo Niño sailing a battleship. It strengthens it. I myself have no doubt of our Lord. I've seen too much of Satan's work not to believe." He waved his hands. "The circus acts. The magic shows. The baby clothes. We need them. I even make things up and the people follow," the priest said. "We had a vigil last night. The camareras sat in a room all night waiting for the Santo Niño to come alive." He laughed.

An air conditioner was doing its best, but the room was hot and Martelino was already growing rancid beneath his heavy robes. Klay could smell him.

"You seem to know exactly what the people need, Father," Klay said.

The priest waved an arm dismissively. "I told them I had a bad stomach. I went home to bed. Let them stay up all night. Now, what would you like to talk about?"

"I am a mortician. A family tradition. When my great-grandfather started the business, death was a solemn occasion. A time for religious reflection. Families went to church. Now my nephews play video games on Sundays. My brother's wife can't be bothered to take them to church."

"Women are weak," the priest said. "You are not married?"

Klay gave a short laugh and shook his head.

"But you are not young. Forty-five?"

"More or less. I'm wondering, Father . . . I saw the ivory Santo Niño you used in your ceremony, the carvings here in your office." He pointed. "They say you have the best collection of carvings in the Philippines. You know master carvers. I am thinking if people in the US could see these images, it might strengthen their faith."

"Possibly."

"We have a chain of funeral homes across the United States."

"Is that so?"

"Do you visit the US much, Father?"

"Not for a long time. My home is here."

Klay paused, annoyed at himself. He hadn't needed to ask that question. He knew the answer already, and he didn't need the priest's lie. According to Eady's dossier, Martelino coordinated a network of child exploiters. He traveled to the US an average of four times a year, entering by car through Mexico or Canada. Klay had copies of the priest's Mastercard charges, Facebook posts, WhatsApp texts, and logs of his cell phone calls. Many of the calls were to a convent-orphanage on the other side of the island, which Klay suspected was supply for customers who preferred young girls.

Klay looked at this overfed, satisfied man smiling back at him through his folds of skin. He took in the ivory crucifixes hanging on the priest's wall, the ivory child sculptures lying on his bookshelves—the living trophies who were everywhere. All of it a single tentacle leading back to Ras Botha.

Control yourself, he told himself.

"My brother is in the meatball business," he continued, wondering where the hell that lie had come from and what he was going to do with it now that he'd said it. "He left our family funeral home to work for his wife's father, making meatballs . . ."

"He left your family."

"He told my father, 'People die only once, but they need to eat every day.' It broke my father's heart, but my brother was right, you know? Funerals and faith are a dying business . . ."

The priest nodded.

"So, Father, I'm in charge of marketing."

He reached into his backpack and brought out a brochure for O'Shea Funeral Home. On the brochure's cover was an old black-and-white photograph of a little boy with his arm around a puppy, the pair sitting together on the front seat of a horse-drawn hearse. Klay Funeral Home was no longer in business but the photo was real. Beneath the photograph of Klay's grandfather, the brochure read, "O'Shea Funeral Home. Serving the community since 1898."

He'd designed the brochure on his laptop and printed it in the business office of Cebu's Radisson hotel, where he was staying. Working up the brochure, seeing his grandfather as a little boy, brought back happy memories. Klay and his brother playing pirates in the chapel, riding casket carts and swinging gladiola sabers. The time he forgot to close the hearse door. His father's humor.

"My stretch limousine, eh, champ?" his father had joked, sliding into the Cadillac's front seat that last day, with a shoebox in one hand and a cigarette in the other. Klay started the car. When they arrived at Lewisburg prison, Jack Klay opened his shoebox. It was empty. He took off his Hamilton watch and his diamond pinkie ring and dropped them into the box. He leaned back in his seat, reached into his front pocket, and took out his Tiffany money clip. He took out his wallet and put them both in the shoebox, too. Then he closed the lid, set the box on the seat between them, and looked into his son's eyes. "So, this is where I'm supposed to give you life advice. Okay, remember this: There's always a who. If he's done you a service, you thank him. If he's done you a disservice, you never forget it. Use your head, hit before you get hit, look after Sean, and visit your mother." He winked. "You'll be all right. Sal has an envelope for you."

His father got out of the car, tossed his cigarette, and walked away. Klay had walked away, too. He had not done enough for his brother. He had not visited his mother. Or his father. "Memories," Klay said now, looking at the priest. "That's the funeral business. What cemeteries are about. And gravestones. But Americans no longer live near their families, Father. They move all over. They don't visit family graveyards. So, I thought, why don't we make gravestones people can take with them? Carvings they can keep on a shelf to remind them of their loved ones, of their faith. Gravestones for their bookshelves . . ."

The priest smiled. "Bookstones!"

"Yes! Like that." Klay crossed to a bookshelf. "May I?"

On the shelf lay a sleeping Christ child, naked and anatomically correct, with the thumb of one hand touching its lower lip. The child lay incongruously next to a plastic gumball machine filled with candy. Klay hefted the ivory, feeling the weight in his hands. It was the size of a human infant but much heavier, carved from a single tusk. The elephant had been enormous, as big as

Voi. Klay ran a hand along the infant's pale arm. It had the same cold feel as a dead man's skin.

"Extraordinary craftsmanship, Father. Ivory is elephants, right? This must have been a big one."

"I think so," the priest said. Martelino signaled the altar boy to help him to his feet. The priest circled his desk and joined Klay. He wore purple Crocs, Klay noticed.

"See," Klay continued, "we could put the name and date of birth and death on its back here, just like on a gravestone. How much would something like this go for?"

"Depends. This one is Delarosa. I designed it myself." Martelino touched a fleshy index finger to his upper lip in the same way as the finger of the infant touched its lips. "Delarosa brought it to—"

"Here you go, Father."

Klay handed the sculpture to the priest, but Martelino wasn't prepared for the icon's sudden weight. He pitched forward, and would have dropped the sculpture if not for the altar boy, who darted to the priest's aid. The boy steadied Martelino, but in his rush he knocked the gumball machine off its shelf. The plastic toy hit the floor and shattered. Blue candies skittered across the tile floor.

"Idiot, Sixto!" the priest shouted. "You pick up every goodie!"

Klay bent down to help the boy. The candies

weren't candies. They were quaaludes. The fat fuck was drugging the altar boys.

The young boy looked terrified. "Sixto," Klay said to him quietly, smiling. "I'm six two, too."

Sixto looked back at Klay with uncomprehending eyes. Klay helped him scoop the quaaludes up with a piece of paper and pour them into a tissue box. Sixto retrieved a dustpan and swept up the broken dispenser and dropped the pieces into Martelino's wastebasket. Watching the boy, Klay felt the weight of powerlessness in the face of evil. He got to his feet. "You know, I don't think we could do ivory, Father. It would be better, certainly, but it could be a problem. There are laws about ivory, aren't there? Let's think about wood, okay?"

The priest dropped heavily onto a sofa. "Batikulin is the best wood," he said without interest. "Santol is cheaper."

"I would only want to do this for our wealthy clients. Price is no object. They only want the best."

"Then ivory! Ivory is what we want, Tomas!"

We.

Klay looked at the ivory sculpture. "It is beautiful."

"Of course. Ivories will be the perfect memorial for your dead ones."

"How would I get these to the United States?"

"There are ways. For the Vatican, I wrapped a

dormido in dirty underwear, covered the underwear in chicken blood and human shit, like a dirty diaper. No one opened it. When the cardinal asked about it, I told him his Niño was so real he even smelled like a baby."

Klay laughed.

"Could we get the Vatican to bless it?"

"The Holy Father, no. The papal nuncio, no. But I have many contacts in the Holy See. They know my relics. First, we will discuss with my carvers. Get me my phone, Sixto."

When the boy had left, Klay continued, "We would need a supplier in Africa. Do you know someone?"

Martelino slapped Klay's knee. "That's the easy part!"

The priest leapt from his sofa with surprising speed, crossed the room, and took a book from a shelf above his desk. It was a Koran. He opened it, and a handful of photographs spilled from the book onto his desk. "The Muslims bring it from Africa."

"The Muslims?"

"On Mindanao! Look at this." The priest handed Klay a photograph of a commercial pier, and a pair of large ships rigged with purse seine nets in the background. In the foreground rows of plastic tubs the size of refrigerators appeared to be filled with small fish in crushed ice. Klay did a quick count of the tubs, multiplying the number he could see on each axis; there were hundreds of them. Standing among the tubs were four men holding automatic weapons.

"That's a lot of fish."

"Zamboanga is the sardine capital of the Philippines."

Martelino handed Klay more photographs featuring the same pier. A steel nozzle sucked sardines out of the large plastic tubs and dumped them onto a conveyor belt rolling into a building Klay assumed was a cannery.

"I tell my supplier his ivories stink like fish. It gets me a discount!"

Klay studied another photograph and suddenly realized elephant tusks were poking up among the sardines. It was not only a sardine cannery. It was an elephant graveyard on ice.

"Oh, that's clever, Father. How much can your people get for us?"

The priest shrugged.

Klay felt a growing urgency. His digital recorder had been running all morning. He needed a connection to Botha. The public had an interest. He had an interest. "Which countries would it come from?"

The priest's eyes sharpened. "Why do you care?"

"We'll need a reliable supplier. Not from a country at war . . ."

"Yes. Well, I don't know that side. They talk about Zanzibar because of the Muslims. But

I don't know. I don't need to know. It's not a problem."

"I used to hunt with a South African who might be able to help us," Klay said. "Ras Botha. He's a professional hunter, works all over southern Africa."

The priest shook his head.

"He does a lot of international business," Klay said.

"I don't know him."

Klay studied the dilation in the priest's pupils, the moisture along his upper lip, the flush in the capillaries in the man's cheeks. Martelino was telling the truth. He picked up a photograph and pointed to a pair of men on the pier holding assault rifles. "Is it dangerous, Father?"

"Oh, it is some crazy people down there. Very, very bad," Martelino said. "Abu Sayyaf. The communists. But not all . . ."

"That's right. Mindanao. It's a Muslim state, isn't it, Father?"

"It deserves to be. Full of very proud people, Mindanao. Never conquered. You Americans promised them independence during your war with Spain, so they stayed out of that fighting. Then you put us, the Catholics, in charge of them. Now they have what you call 'trust issues.'"

"I don't understand, Father. Islamic State is there, isn't it? A Catholic priest trades with Muslim terrorists?"

"My mother is Moro. I have cousins on Mindanao. It is family I see when I look at these people, not terrorists. It is why I was selected by the president to facilitate the peace negotiations. We have created a new region for them called Bangsamoro Autonomous Region. It is here." A map of the Philippines hung on the wall beside the desk. Martelino pointed to Mindanao Island, and put his finger on a thin sliver of the large island that was colored red.

"Not much," Klay said.

"Not much," he agreed. "But a start. Contiguous territories will be permitted to opt in over time. We are a poor country, and these are our country's poorest people, Tomas. Over half cannot read or write. They work the Zamboanga docks, but they need more to have a future. We talk so that we do not fight."

Klay had encountered ironies all over the world, but nothing beat this: the pedophile ivory trafficker was a peace negotiator.

Martelino sifted through his photos. "I have something." He opened a desk drawer and shuffled through papers. "Their troops have agreed to turn over their weapons. It is wonderful. We will have peace after so many years. Yes, this is what I mean." He withdrew a color photograph from a manila envelope and handed it to Klay.

In the photo, six men and a woman stood in a line behind a long table covered in food.

"This is a boodle fight. Do you know boodle fight?"

"I am not a fighter, Father."

"Oh, ha ha. You could be. A boodle fight is not a fight. It is a feast. Like your Thanksgiving. It's how the cadets used to eat at the Philippine Military Academy, you know . . ." He shoveled at his face with his hands.

Klay was looking at the figures, memorizing their faces.

"We cover a long table with banana leaves. Then lay down a wide road of rice. Let's see. It is shrimp, mussels, crabs, bangus—milkfish, which is our national fish. Ampalaya, which I don't like, too slimy. Adobo. Tilapias. Pork. Chicken. Duck. Anything." Martelino licked his lips. "You must repeat the ingredients over and over so that everyone can get some of everything. You eat it with your hands. Oh, not pork." Martelino tapped the photograph. "I remember. We did only seafood and chicken for this because pork is haram. You see, I wanted to honor my uncle. They eat boodle-fight-style because they need to move quickly and cannot have glassware breaking. And also, you eat standing up, shoulder to shoulder, for the team building."

"Who are these people, Father?"

Martelino leaned forward and lifted his glasses. "Of course that is me." He pointed a chubby finger to himself at one end. "I am the president's peace negotiator. There is the leader of the Abu Sayyaf. That one is MILF, who is my uncle. There is the one for the communists. Here is Mr. Wei from the Chinese embassy."

"China?"

"Ah, so close to the South China Sea. The president said we must involve them. I told him it is a mistake—the Moros will not do business with China. But he has other concerns . . ."

Klay studied the photograph. At the photo's edge was a tall woman with closely shaved hair and skin the color of milk tea. She seemed uncomfortable, leaning at the edge of the photo as if to evade it. "This one?"

"Ah, that one is called Mapes, or something. The Moros would not accept an American government observer, so then we got her. She is a businesswoman." He shrugged. "She works for the Perseus Group companies."

A SURPRISE ENCOUNTER

Ninoy Aquino International Airport
Manila, Philippines

He was wading through Manila's crowded airport, on his way home, when he saw him. It was only for an instant, but Klay was certain. Crew cut, protruding ears, dark eyes. Botha's head had appeared in a gap among Filipinos. Then he was gone. Klay hurried forward. He spotted Botha again walking toward a fast food restaurant.

"Botha!"

The South African turned. He scanned the gallery and seemed not to recognize Klay. Then, suddenly, he smiled. Klay pushed through the crowd. He felt his heart pumping, his adrenaline rising. Ras Botha waited, still smiling. Klay broke from the crowd, and paused. A young boy stood beside Botha.

Botha seemed pleased at Klay's hesitation, as if he had achieved something. "Merlin," he said, "this is an old friend of mine, a very famous journalist from **The Sovereign.** Tom Klay. This is my son, Merlin."

Botha and his son wore matching red-and-yellow rugby shirts. The boy was the spitting image of his father.

"Hello, Mr. Klay," Merlin said with none of his father's harsh Afrikaner accent.

"Hello," Klay said awkwardly and shook the boy's outstretched hand.

For a moment no one spoke.

"Are you here for the rugby, Mr. Klay?"

Botha smiled even broader, his eyes awaiting Klay's response.

"No, Merlin. I'm here on a project." He looked at Botha.

"Merl, pick us out a table inside and I'll get the food."

"Okay, Papa."

Botha nodded toward the Jollibee counter. "Walk with me," he said. "You look upset, my bru." Botha stepped to the counter. "Ya, hon, I'll have us two Yumburgers. Two chocolate milkshakes. And a halo-halo for my boy." He turned to Klay. "And something for my big friend here. What'll you have? How about the Aloha Yumburger? That's a good one. And a Coke for him, too."

She brought the drinks. Botha handed Klay the Coke. "You here for the girls? I know you'll stay away from little boys. But the women, if that's what you want, it's worth your trip. I got even better ones, though. You come see me. Czechs. Russians. Thais. I don't go in for the fish heads, myself. Like getting sucked off by a bull-frog, you know? But Russians. They got noses and real tongues."

"I heard you like Russians," Klay said quietly. Inches from the man who had murdered Bernard, Klay could barely contain his fury.

"What's got your broekies in a knot?"

"You murdered my friend," Klay hissed. "You shot me."

"I shot you?" He sounded genuinely surprised. "Hang on." Botha accepted a tray loaded with food from the girl at the counter. "You was in the wrong place wrong time what I heard. You know, miss. Could I have his Aloha burger packed up separate to go? Thank you." He turned to Klay. "Wasn't me. But that oke was going to cut you was a real meat butcher. I got you the best doctor I could."

"Say again?"

"I did what I could," Botha said.

Klay stepped toward Botha. "Those were your people in Kenya. I know it."

"Know? You know it? Knowledge is a very interesting thing. Thank you, sweet. Like I said, I did the best I could." Botha handed Klay his sandwich.

Klay set the bag on the counter. Botha's eyes lingered a moment on the bag; then he plucked napkins from a dispenser and grabbed a handful of ketchup packets.

"I see they put you up for a big award on that story," he said. "You'll look good in a tux. I got five tuxes. One I wore to Pablo Escobar's wedding. You let me know when you're ready to spend some time. We'll share a cognac, two or three girls. Have ourselves a braai. We can do a little elephant hun—"

Klay grabbed Botha's shirt front, driving him backwards along the counter, crushing the milkshakes into his chest. One dropped to the floor and splattered. People gasped. Merlin looked up. Klay saw the boy's wide eyes and released Botha.

Botha laughed. "You a crazy motherfucker, Klay!"

A security guard was moving in their direction.

"You'll find out," Klay snarled. "I'll see you again."

Botha was still laughing, wiping milkshake off his shirt as Klay left the restaurant.

"Ya, okay," Botha called after him. "You want me in prison. Okay. But remember, my bru, the cage you're in is not always the cage you're in."

That night, on the long flight home, Klay closed his eyes and replayed the events following Bernard's murder. There was a ball of sound, Bernard's head pitched forward. Next he was lying in the back of a Land Rover on his way to Nanyuki army base, Moses the Green Guardian beside him, Goodson shouting into his phone, "From **The Sovereign**! A man from **The Sovereign**!" Then a helicopter ride. A room with pale green paint peeling off the wall and a sputtering fluorescent light. The smell of rubbing alcohol. A fat black man with jaundiced eyes and a small mustache leaning over him, sweat in the creases of his neck. The doctor rushing, barely examining him. More yelling. Bernard's voice. No. Bernard was dead. Maybe his own voice. Then a boy on his bicycle. Crunching metal, screeching brakes. A thud in his chest. The red lights of an ambulance . . .

Klay wrenched himself upright in his seat. Cold sweat covered his forehead. His memories and dreams were becoming one nightmare, the accident in Jakarta weaving itself into his experience in Kenya.

He forced himself to focus on the details he knew to be real. After the fat doctor, he had awoken in a different room. This one was clean, brightly lit, cool. A padded strap held his arm to his side. His wound had been dressed and bandaged. A tall woman stood beside his bed listening to his heart with a stethoscope. She gave him a bright smile, and ticked off his vitals to a nurse. "You are very, very lucky, Mr. Klay," she said. "You will be fine. Able to fight for our elephants again . . ." The strap was for his wound, she told him. He had been dreaming. "Throwing your arms every which way."

On his return home, Klay had gone to Georgetown University Hospital for a follow-up. The doctor who examined him said there was nothing more he could do for his injuries. "Your Kenyan surgeon was excellent," he said.

Had all of that been courtesy of Ras Botha?

And what cage?

THE PUBLIC HAS AN INTEREST

Washington, DC, and Shepherdstown, West Virginia

It was Saturday at the Pigeon. Klay was typing up his notes on the priest, sketching a story. Phil the Economist was reading a newspaper. A couple of French tourists were sitting at a table behind Klay. He could see them in the bar's back mirror. The French newspaper **Le Figaro** had recently done a feature on the decline of American journalism, and had included a mention of the Gray Pigeon. The story had inspired a few tourists to visit over the past month. Billy asked one for a translation. "You are like Popeye," the tourist explained, and made a muscle. Billy smiled, but the tourist continued, "Like Popeye with no ship to sail."

Next to Klay's laptop was a tuna fish sandwich and a bag of chips he'd bought at the bodega next door. He was drinking cranberry and seltzer in a pint glass. "You want an umbrella with that?" Billy had asked.

His cell phone rang. It was Porfle.

"You did it again, I see."

Klay ate a potato chip and typed in another search. "What's that?"

"Went over my head for your assignment."

"I assumed Vance cleared it with you."

"Nope. Didn't."

Klay plucked a corner of the plastic wrap around his sandwich and tried to shake it free. "Okay, sorry," he said.

He wished he'd been able to steal the priest's photo of the peace negotiations dinner, but Martelino had scooped all of the photos up and returned them to his desk drawer.

"What are you working on?" Porfle asked. "Botha again?"

"I'll tell you when I get back to the office."

"The thrill is gone from this relationship, Mr. Klay," Porfle said.

"What do you want from me, Alex?" It was a mistake to engage the passive-aggressive Porfle, but Klay was tired, and the smell of the priest and his sadistic crimes still lingered in his nostrils.

"I want you to follow procedure," Porfle said. "I want you to discuss story ideas with me in advance! I want you to write up the formal proposals we've agreed on and submit them for consideration at our pitch meetings—with projected word counts and budgets included. I want you to get your expense reports in."

Klay pictured his editor sitting pencil-straight in a home-office desk chair, eyes watering, hand trembling as he gripped the phone. "Our essential Brit," Eady would say, followed by a caution: "We need him in place, Tom." Klay understood Eady's desire to have a malleable and obedient deputy, but it didn't make working for Porfle any easier.

"When you get back, I want your expenses turned in promptly," Porfle continued, his voice rising. "The next day."

Klay didn't have the heart to tell Porfle he was already home. Eady had been clear: "You are to endure Porfle. It took me years to find him . . ."

Klay gritted his teeth. "Of course. I apologize, Alex. It came up suddenly. I'll get them to Accounting right away."

"You're not the only wildlife crime investigator in this city, you know."

"Tell that to Vance," Klay said, and instantly regretted it.

"Uncle Vance won't be around here to protect you forever. You should keep that in mind."

"You know something I don't?"

"Humph," Porfle said, and hung up.

"Everything okay?" Billy asked, wiping down the bar.

Klay shook his head. "Just the usual, Bill." He munched another chip, unwrapped his sandwich, and thought about his peculiar double life.

He had been with the magazine five years when one bright February afternoon Sally had phoned from upstairs to say that Vance and Ruth Eady had an extra ticket to the Kennedy Center. Schubert's **Trout** Quintet. Would he like to join them? A dinner party invitation followed a week later at the couple's Watergate apartment. "Bring a date if you like." Klay was with Erin at the time, against office policy, so he went alone. A few weeks after the Eadys' dinner party, Vance appeared in his doorway. "Do you flyfish, Tom?"

The Eadys owned a big old house in Virginia horse country about sixty miles west of DC. Standing on the grassy banks of his trout pond, Eady had handed Klay a fly rod and a Bible. "Hold the book tight in your armpit. Keep your movement ten and one. Wrist straight, hard stops." Klay followed Eady's instructions while Eady went on about tippets and dry flies. He was finally getting the hang of it when Eady deftly turned the conversation to a topic Klay knew well: old-school boxing— Jack Johnson, Harry Greb, Ali, the Hitman, Marvelous Marvin. All of it a fishing expedition, Klay realized later. Eady letting out line, biding his time, monitoring Klay's response to each upstream twitch.

"You used to be pretty good in the ring yourself, they tell me," Eady said casually as he packed up their gear. Ruth Eady was standing at the top of the hill, calling them to supper.

"Who tells you?" Klay asked.

"People."

Klay shrugged. "I was South Broad good. Not North Broad good. There's a big difference in Philadelphia."

Klay told Eady what it had been like boxing as a teenager, working the bag in a rowhouse basement gym off Ninth Street in the Italian Market, the soppressata and capocollo drying on strings, swinging to the beat. **Bap. Bap. Bap.** Klay dreaming of winning those Golden Gloves. Getting told his feet were buckets of cement. "You no Primo Carnera," the old Sicilian barked at him. "You gotta mean. You gotta quick. You gotta fast." But the bodies stacking up said maybe his coach had it wrong. Maybe Klay was fast enough already. Maybe his feet moved so fast nobody could see them.

Then came the Fight.

His opponent was out of Joe Frazier's Gym on North Broad. Bryant "Lump" Sanders had the look of a heavyweight and a sledgehammer right hand. Klay had fought bigger men who hit harder, but in the fourth round, when Klay wasn't looking, Sanders's brothers had climbed into the ring with him. Maybe his sister, too. How else to explain that many gloves landing on him at once. Klay learned the meaning of the word "speed" that night. The doctor inspecting Klay's eye afterwards told him sure, he could keep fighting, but he was laughing. "We'll call you Helen 'the Keller' Klay."

"But you liked it?" Eady pressed, studying Klay's eyes.

Klay sensed he was entering a life moment. Here he was, a Philadelphia mortician's kid, standing in a Virginia country mansion, talking to the editor in chief of **The Sovereign,** a man who rarely spoke to writers directly and never invited them to his home. It all felt so unreal, so completely foreign, he decided to act against his instincts. He told Eady the truth. He didn't like boxing; he loved it. "No better feeling in the world than dropping a guy with a clean shot."

Eady took a moment before responding. "How about a shot that's not so clean?" he countered. Presenting the fly.

They were in the summer kitchen now, Eady standing over a small table covered in newspaper, working a fillet knife up a trout's belly, Klay seeing things he'd sensed about Eady come into focus.

"So—" Eady turned to face him. "Would you like a second job? It's called the CIA's National Resources Division, Tom. You'd work for me. Exclusively."

"Natural Resources Division?"

Eady laughed. "**National.** National Resources, Tom."

"I thought the CIA couldn't work domestically."

Eady ripped the fish's guts free, yanked them toward the fish's throat, then sliced them loose. He tossed the organs into a pail.

"We can. And we do. Most of NR's work is debriefing American business executives returned from overseas trips. College professors and scientists back from foreign conferences. It's light, informal. Maintenance, really. You would be something a bit more . . ." Eady searched for the right word. "Intentional."

A caddis fly—that's how Eady put it—a simple gatherer of information with antennae so long and slender as to be nearly invisible.

Eady turned on the deep well sink, rinsed his

knife, and began washing his hands under the tap using a bar of soap. "You'll be part of an unheralded, secret tradition, Tom. **The Sovereign**'s partnership with the Agency stretches back generations. Before CIA was CIA."

He switched off the tap, slid his knife blade through a towel, and hung it on a magnetic knife rack beside the sink. "The Brits got us started. They ran a propaganda shop out of Rockefeller Center, pumped anti-Nazi stories to the old **Herald Tribune,** the **New York Post,** the **Baltimore Sun,** trying to get the Americans to join them in the fight. Pearl Harbor sped things up, and the Brits handed their operation over to our OSS. Morale operations, it became. Many of America's best reporters, writers, cartoonists, and radio broadcasters served the war effort."

Eady opened a cabinet above his sink and took out a bottle of scotch. He poured two glasses and handed one to Klay.

"**The Sovereign**'s role was something special," he continued. "Richard Helms, future CIA director—who recruited me, incidentally—started out as a journalist with the United Press. Dick interviewed Hitler. Hitler was obsessed with America's eugenics programs. Wanted to know all he could about it. The American argument distilled, being that healthier humans meant lower taxes."

Eady opened a door separating the kitchen

from the main house, and three Jack Russell terriers darted into the room. "Ruth!" he called, ignoring the dogs. "Ruth!"

Ruth Eady, a petite woman with neat gray hair, a sad smile, and the hands of a persistent gardener, appeared in the doorway holding a plate of cheese and raw vegetables. She wore a bright yellow apron over a pale blue blouse.

"We'll join you in ten or so, darling," Eady said, accepting the snack plate.

Ruth looked from Eady to Klay and then down at the glass of scotch beside each man. She picked up Eady's glass, took a sip, and placed the glass back on the counter beside him. "I'll wait 'til I see the whites of your eyes." She smiled and picked up the dish with Eady's trout. "Come on, dogs."

"Find yourself a good woman, Tom," Eady said, topping off their glasses. "I could start with that. Or end there. Have you?"

Klay thought of Erin. "Not sure," he said.

"To the chase, then," Eady said, and clinked Klay's glass. "Where was I?"

"Hitler," Klay said.

Eady put his nose in his glass and inhaled his whiskey before resuming. "Hitler took the American eugenics effort further in every way, of course. Crucially, he extended his theories on the Aryan individual to the state. Germany made ill by her 'lesser races.' Jews, a disease; gypsies, an infestation. He used language to justify his savagery. It wasn't murder, it was cleansing. Immigrants weren't human beings, they were invasive species. Words made all the difference. Which is where we came in.

"**The Sovereign** had been reporting favorably on the American eugenics movement. 'Why should Hereford bulls and Rhode Island Reds benefit more from selective breeding than we humans?'—that kind of thing. Then an American intelligence officer discovered a reference to **The Sovereign** in a German eugenics journal. The Nazis' top scientists were reading us.

"That's when Bill Donovan came to us with a special request. You recognize that name?"

"Father of the CIA. They called him Wild Bill."

"Donovan's request was simple: double down. We agreed. We ran a feature on European architecture, praising Berlin. We followed up with a piece celebrating Germany's youth movement, those flaxen-haired scouts charging up the Zugspitze in short pants and brown shirts." Eady sipped his whiskey. "Mind you"—Eady took a square of cheese with a toothpick—"all along the Allies are using our maps to fight the war. We printed half a million for the War Department. Every soldier carried a map with our emblem on it. The Nazis considered it a victory to have the same **Sovereign** writing such positive things about their country. Goebbels especially loved it, praised **The Sovereign** publicly. That is when we dropped our bomb."

Eady opened a drawer, withdrew a magazine wrapped in cellophane, and handed it to Klay. The date on the cover was March 1942. It was the old format. No glossy cover photograph, just a silver atlas on a blue background in the upper left corner, and below it a table of contents. Eady pointed to an article halfway down the list. Klay read the title aloud, " 'Fallacies in Racial Hygiene.' "

Eady nodded. "In-house our people called it 'Operation Aryan Error.' " He tapped the cover with his finger. "We said German scientists were engaged in a massive cover-up. They knew their Übermenschen theory was poppycock but feared revealing it. Denial played. The important thing was Hitler's people had to eat crow one way or the other.

"Not a game changer, but a game influencer," Eady continued, returning the magazine to its drawer. "And I can tell you, Tom, that over the years, over the decades, of reporting hard facts, we have made a difference."

Eady placed a square of smoked Gouda on a cracker and offered it to Klay. "You'll be able to do what I did. Get those stories no one in the world is able to get. Prizewinning, world-altering stories because you'll have the Agency's reach and resources." Eady ticked off his long fingers: "Contacts. Intelligence. Access. Technology."

Growing up in a funeral home, Klay had learned early and better than most how to read behind people's eyes and words.

"Let me think about it, Vance," he said, turning to wash his hands in Eady's sink. He had a lot on his mind, he said. It wasn't the slight off note he detected beneath Eady's CIA sales pitch that caused him to pause. Nor was it journalistic ethics.

It was more personal. The FBI had worked its way into Klay Funeral Home, that undercover agent pretending to be an embalmer, standing shoulder to shoulder in the morgue with a teen-aged Klay, building his case. "Uncle Patrick," Klay had called him. Until his father's criminal RICO trial when "Uncle Patrick" took the witness stand and announced his real name and occupation: "Patrick Mulvaney, Special Agent, Organized Crime Squad, Federal Bureau of Investigation." Klay had a rule about law enforcement after that: fuck 'em. Didn't matter the agency, or the country. The CIA might not technically be law enforcement, but it was pretty damn close.

. . .

He found his answer to Eady hidden under the carpet of his new home, the redbrick Edwardian townhouse in the Eastern Market section of Capitol Hill. Erin was out of town for the signing, so he left the Prudential office, walked two blocks north, opened the door, and got to work. They had chosen the house for its gourmet kitchen, but the rest of the house needed work. The first thing he and Erin intended to do was to get rid of the ugly brown wall-to-wall carpeting.

He set his backpack down on the vestibule's slate floor, lifted a corner of the carpet, and pulled. He proceeded down the hallway, pulling up carpet as he went, until he reached the fancy kitchen's pale gray tile. He turned and continued into the dining room, then the living room. He pulled up brown carpet as he climbed the stairs, ripped and tore brown carpet from the guest room floor. He pulled his way along the upstairs hallway to the doorway of the master bedroom, which alone in the house had its original pine wood flooring exposed.

When he was done, he went back downstairs and started removing the tack strips and carpet padding. He'd asked his real estate agent why there was so much carpeting in an otherwise well-decorated house. "They had a dog," the agent replied, touching his nose with a silk handkerchief.

Klay doubted they had a dog. The couple who'd owned the house had died of AIDS. He bought the house from the second man's estate. As he explored their house, he could feel the couple's terror growing, the world around them alive with invisible enemies, the causes and cures of their illness still largely a mystery. He found unopened boxes of HEPA air purifiers in the attic and dust masks in drawers throughout the house. He spotted expensive filters under the sinks and behind the refrigerator. Blue rubber gloves sprang at him from the bottom drawer of the upstairs vanity. That was life for you: you erect all possible protections against the unknown, and what it looks like afterwards is panic.

He thought about Eady's offer as he worked. Even if he could see himself working for the CIA, doing so would certainly compromise journalistic ethics. He sat back on his heels with a snort. Who was he kidding? As a criminal investigator, he had never fretted over journalism's ethical lines before. Besides, lines implied a system. There was no system to the world. No handrails. What system of equality allowed a drunk behind the wheel of an automobile to go on living, while an innocent boy on his bicycle ended up dead? Life's only guarantee was that it didn't last forever, period. Lean on anything else for support and you might well fall forever.

The foam padding was old and dried and bore

a surprising number of staples per square foot. He began his carpet extraction in the afternoon, not considering that his new house had no overhead lighting, so by the time he was on to the carpet tacks, he was operating in darkness. It wasn't until the next morning that he understood why the previous owners had chosen to carpet so much of their home. Every room's floor had been patched with raw plywood. Instead of something out of **Antique Digest,** his exposed floors reminded him of the shuffleboard and hopscotch patterns in the attic of Klay Funeral Home designed to keep Klay and his brother quiet during funerals.

As he continued through the house on his hands and knees, prying up carpet staples with a screwdriver, he realized that his approach to journalism—his approach to life—was a lot like his approach to this house: he tore things up without regard to what lay underneath. He got to the bottom of things by whatever means necessary and then he moved on. It was the ripping and pulling he was good at. Until now Klay had always used a notebook and pen. Eady was offering him a jackhammer.

A week later, sitting in Eady's Watergate apartment, Klay asked, "How many do you have working for you already, Vance?"

Eady lit Klay's cigar. "You'd be my first, Tom."

"Bullshit."

"Truth is, I haven't ever needed to engage anyone formally before. As editor in chief I've been able to satisfy the Agency's intelligence needs quite effectively, and quietly, sending reporters on assignments of interest without risk to anyone but myself."

"My stories, too?"

"Some." Eady thought a moment. "Angola. We needed to know how strong the president's daughter was. She liked you."

"So, what are you telling me? Nobody knows? Porfle doesn't know?"

"I find the best way to keep a secret is not to tell anyone. But I don't need to tell you that, do I?"

"Are you threatening me, Vance?"

"No, son. I'm trusting you. If you should turn this down, you'd know my secret, you'd know the Agency's secret. I'm trusting that whatever your choice, you are a patriot."

Klay shook his head. "Where I come from, what you're talking about is a rat."

"That's a perspective you'll have to reconcile."

"So, why me? Why give me this golden opportunity?" Klay felt a sour taste grow in his mouth. He was probing like he hadn't already made his decision, like he still had a line he would not cross.

A smile wriggled loose from the corners of Eady's mouth. "Why you? Okay, Tom." He set his cigar in an ashtray. "Let's get down to brass tacks, shall we? Here's why you make sense: You are a loner. You make acquaintances easily, but you can't form lasting relationships. You're emotionally damaged, owing to a tragic incident involving your mother that we needn't recount, but some people—like you—know how to use the wounded parts of themselves to recognize wounds in others, and turn them to advantage. You drink too much, but you're not a drunk. Your father, Jack, ended up a senior member of the Scalise Mob, even though he's not Italian. He remains in prison, though he could certainly cut himself a deal. Nicky Scalise offered to bring you into the family. You didn't accept, but you could have. The underworld is in your DNA. You break rules frequently, but you have a sense of justice. You have, I believe, the need to do some real good, atone, correct the past. We all make mistakes, but rarely do we have the opportunity to counter their weight so profoundly. Thanks to the work I've given you, you're well traveled now, and reasonably well connected. You're a superb writer, and that's cover I need. You're a good criminal investigator, instinctively. I can make you better. You handle"—he paused— "unexpected adversity." Eady began relighting his cigar. "That do?"

Klay's pulse pounded above his left ear. His heart raced. In his mind, he pictured the old newspaper articles describing his mother's death. He'd read them a thousand times; now he saw Eady reading them, the old man studying the black-and-white photographs of his mother's mangled car. All of the articles had ended more or less the same way: "Two sons, age seven and nine, were thrown clear."

Klay locked eyes with Eady. "Don't ever mention my mother again."

Eady raised his snowy eyebrows. "We're thorough," he said. "I'm sorry."

Klay let the moment settle. "Then I should tell you there was an accident. In Indonesia," he said, watching Eady's eyes. "It will come up."

If killing the boy in Jakarta was what Eady had meant by "unexpected adversity," Klay couldn't tell. The old man listened to Klay's confession without judgment. "I want all of my Agency pay to go anonymously to the boy's family."

"I will see to it," Eady said.

Klay put out his hand. No one on earth had better intelligence than the CIA. He would use what they gave him to rip and tear his way to the bottom of better stories.

"Nothing you wouldn't otherwise do, Tom," Eady said, gripping Klay's hand. "That's my commitment to you. You'll be able to stand by every story. Every action." He refilled Klay's glass. "You have my word."

Klay had a different notion. The CIA worked for him now.

Like a rottweiler at the Palm Beach Kennel Club," Major Thomas said as Klay huffed to a stop his first day of training. The retired Marine checked his stopwatch. "If you ever gotta run for it, start early."

Klay was panting, hands on knees, sweating his blue T-shirt purple in the crisp mountain air. "I don't make a habit of running," he managed to say.

Morning workouts were designed to help focus his mind rather than to get him into any kind of shape. To his boxing skills, Major Thomas added close quarters techniques, reciting "Surprise, speed, violence of action" over and over as they worked hand-to-hand, blade and no blade, Filipino-style. Thomas chiding him for wanting to hit a man's skull with a closed fist when he could be just as effective using his palm, and still pick up a fork the next day. "Slow is smooth. Smooth is fast," he coached. "Good."

Klay would be an agent, Eady explained, but not an employee. An asset, "like the many brave men and women the Agency relies on around the world."

Eady insisted Klay be schooled in the same basic techniques a career intelligence officer would receive. "As much to give you a vocabulary for this world as to help with any specific skills," Eady said. "Besides, maybe one day you'll join us full-time."

Much of his CIA training mirrored what he did as an investigative journalist. For instance, showing up unannounced on a target bearing an extra cup of coffee and maybe some doughnuts—or a six of Carlsberg and a pack of smokes—was, in Agency-speak, "Always provide amenities." Klay laughed when his instructor wrote the rule on the whiteboard for him.

"What?" the man asked.

"Nothing," Klay said. "I'm from Philly. It's called not being a jerk-off."

The Agency's training, more tactical than academic, validated many of his methods, and gave new perspective to others. Still, more than once as he listened to the lectures, he felt the Agency's technique lacked an important second beat. Yes, you showed up unannounced on a target, but you were also quick to say you had to go. You had someplace else to be. That was the special sauce to getting something out of a bad guy. By signaling right out of the box that you were short on time, you put your target at ease. Maybe you even got them to expand on something from a prior meeting. But far more valuable was to get them curious about you. To get your target wondering, **Why aren't you asking me what I'm worried you'll ask me? Who are you to leave me!** Those were the questions you wanted your target to be asking. If you could accomplish that, you got invited back. Which was everything. Getting invited back was all you wanted. More interaction, more meetings, more Facebook messages, more WhatsApp texts. It didn't matter if the additional communications were porn shots (too often they were) or notes about a kid's football performance. More was everything. It meant you were getting in.

Klay kept his ideas to himself. It wasn't his job to give the CIA feedback.

His favorite class was weapons.

He'd touched his first pistol when he was five years old, standing on his tiptoes, feeling his way blindly through his father's sock drawer in search of Christmas presents. Over the years he got to know all of his father's hiding places for the handguns he kept stashed throughout the funeral home. His top desk drawer, the electric organ bench. Behind bottles of embalming fluid in the morgue. A pocket sewn into one of the curtains. His nightstand.

Major Thomas introduced him to a few weapons he wasn't familiar with, and it turned out Klay was still a good shot. His first time at the firing range, Klay put two in the silhouette target's body, one in the edge of its head. Thomas turned to him and said, "The Mozambique, right?" Klay nodded, pleased he could still pull off what he and his pals used to practice in the New Jersey Pine Barrens. Thomas raised his own weapon and delivered ten X-ring shots to the target's chest. After his third shot his bullets had no paper to hit. He holstered his Sig Sauer and looked at Klay. "You put your man down, son. Fire all you have at center mass, then fire some more. After that I don't care what you do. Got it?"

Six weeks later Klay was back at his desk, Porfle asking him how his hernia operation had gone.

Assignments followed. A drink with a Gabonese security minister. A quick sketch of a Malaysian politician's desk, dates read upside down from her appointment book. A visit with the chairman of the Djibouti Ports and Free Zones Authority to request dive permission. "Skimming the cream," Eady called it.

Their method for communicating was simple and effective. When "the public had an interest," Klay's early drafts, copied to Eady and more fulsome than normal, became his Agency reports. He and Eady communicated through the Comments and Track Changes features in Microsoft Word, just like any far-flung magazine writer and his editor. No need for a throwaway encryption system; no risk to the Agency's covert platform.

Eady's edits and comments were Klay's instructions: "Could use more detail here." "Get contact address for fact-checkers." "Do you have supporting documentation?" "Photos?"

Above all, nothing he wouldn't otherwise do.

THE CREVICE

Sovereign Headquarters
Washington, DC

The elevator door opened onto the tenth floor, and before Klay could exit, a long wooden tribal mask with grassy yellow hair and bulging eyes lurched into the gap. Klay stepped back.

"Hey, Charlie," Klay said, and held the elevator's door.

Charles Hawthorne, chief archivist at **The Sovereign,** peeked his soft face out from behind the Dan mask he held with both hands. "Oh. Hey, Tom. Sorry about that."

Hawthorne slid his generous belly and the tribal mask past Klay onto the elevator and set the chin of the mask on the toe of his shoe.

"Didn't expect to see anyone up here on a Sunday," he said, holding the door. "Where you been this time?"

"Bangkok," Klay said. He always said Bangkok. No one ever noticed.

"Must be nice."

"He in?"

"Much as he can be." Charlie hit the button for basement. It was a strange answer, but Charlie was an unusual guy. As the elevator's door closed, he stuck out his tongue and bugged his eyes, his impression of a tribal mask. Klay laughed. He heard hammering coming from the next room. Eady was updating the floor's exhibits. It was about time.

That it was Sunday made little difference for Eady. Sally would be at her desk until noon. Vance would be in his office well beyond that.

Klay rounded the vestibule into Eady's gallery and was nearly run over by two men carrying a zebra head.

"Coming through," said a workman.

Eady's great photographic collection lay stacked along the room's perimeter. In the middle of the room workers hammered a crate around the bathysphere. Like the belly of a gigantic housefly, Klay thought, wending his way among dozens of empty black support wires as he crossed to Eady's corner office.

Sally and her desk were gone. Her office was

empty. Inside his office, Eady was talking to a workman with his back to Klay. On his walls were dark circles and rectangles where his artwork had hung. Bubble Wrap spilled from half-filled cardboard boxes. His desk was bare. Lamps and end tables were gone.

Klay knocked on the door jam. "Spring cleaning, Vance?"

Eady looked haggard. He wore blue jeans, moccasins, and a plaid shirt. "Oh, Tom. Have a seat. I'll be with you in a moment."

Instead Klay walked to Eady's window. It was raining. A cold winter rain. Eady dismissed the worker and closed his office door. His globe bar had not yet been packed up. "Five o'clock somewhere," he sighed, and fixed them a pair of drinks. Klay crossed the room and sat on the old leather sofa. Eady's wingback chair was gone. He wheeled his desk chair to the couch, handed Klay a scotch, and took a seat across from him.

"I have good news and bad news."

"I like my good news first."

"I have cancer."

"Jesus."

"Treatable." Eady waved a dismissive hand. "I'll get through it. We're survivors, you and me." He leaned forward and clinked Klay's glass with his. "Lemonade of it is I finally get to retire. Always promised Ruth I would, then one of my wolves would bring home another terrific story, and round it would go again. Now the doctors tell me it's this place or my wife." He took a drink. "So, no contest at all."

"I'm sorry, Vance."

"It's been a good life, Tom."

"That bad?"

"No. It's not over for me yet. Not by a long shot. Just time for the more important things now." He sighed again.

They sat silently for a while. Klay assessing Eady's appearance, taking in the idea of **The Sovereign** without him at its helm.

"So, what's worse than cancer?" he said. A copy of the magazine's current issue lay on the floor beside Klay's boot.

Eady swallowed his whiskey and got up to retrieve the bottle.

"It's **The Sovereign** that's dying, Tom." He poured them another round. "It's been hemorrhaging for years while I was focused on other things. You know that, and the board has finally decided. We need to make a change, get a transfusion—"

"You're not the reason this place is in trouble, Vance." Everyone knew **The Sovereign** couldn't manage its finances. The institution delivered the exceptional. And paid for it. At every level.

On the cover of the magazine at Klay's feet was a photograph of a red bird of paradise perched on a tree branch taken in West Papua,

Indonesia. To get that photo, Snaps had hired a fixer-translator, a 4x4 and driver, a boat and pilot, forest guides, porters, a cook, and a float plane and pilot. He'd paid consulting fees to ornithologists in Indonesia, England, and the United States. He'd set up camera traps. He'd lived most of the year suspended 180 feet off the ground in a hammock blind specially built for his project holding a camera custom-designed by engineers in **The Sovereign**'s basement, waiting for the elusive bird to dangle its two tail wires just so. Three times during the year, he'd interrupted his work and flown back to DC to meet with a particular photo editor who insisted on reviewing his progress in person. All to get one exceptional photograph.

Start with the cost of publishing a hardcopy magazine in a digital age; throw in common excesses (print editors who characterized family vacations as fieldwork, staff scientists who approved research grants to themselves); toss in the odd whims of the Prendergast family ("Find me a giant squid!" "Locate **Endurance**!"); add to these the cost of such legitimate explorations as sending a custom-built titanium submersible to navigate Challenger Deep, the earth's deepest point; and you had a recipe for epic bankruptcy.

Eady smiled patiently. "You're not understanding me, Tom. It's not about me. They're selling The Sovereign."

"The magazine?"

"All of it."

"Fuck me," he said softly. "Why?"

Eady laughed. "Why does anyone sell? You'll continue to have a job, of course. They recognize quality. Unless you take a buyout. They'll be extending those offers soon, letting others go . . ."

"Who's the buyer?"

"The acquisition includes a billion-dollar endowment. That's the important thing. With that kind of funding we secure The Sovereign for generations. We've ensured this institution's mission, Tom."

"There's always a who, Vance."

Eady sighed. "The acquirer is Perseus Group Media."

"Perseus Group?"

"—Media."

"Terry Krieger," Klay said.

"I wanted you to hear about it from me, directly."

"Jesus," Klay said quietly.

"They had a piece of us already. It's nothing we made public, but PGM has had a twenty percent stake in The Sovereign for some time. It was the only way to catch up to Discovery."

"There must have been other buyers."

Eady swallowed his drink. "They tried. I tried. Google. Bezos. Disney. We screwed ourselves taking that early money. He wouldn't relinquish his shares, and nobody who could afford us wants Terry Krieger for a partner. We had no choice."

"How much is he paying you?"

Eady went cold. "Check yourself, Thomas. This was not my decision. Krieger pitched the board in Davos. I was brought in after. For appearances, I expect. The family wants to cash out." Eady cleared his throat. "In confidence, I did not support the sale."

A phone rang. "Excuse me." Eady reached into his jacket pocket. "I'll call you back shortly," he said, and hung up. "Wife worries about me day and night now."

Klay's sat in disbelief. Eady had cancer. **The Sovereign** had been sold to Terry Krieger and his mercenaries. From the corner of his mind he heard Bernard's voice: **Would you take Perseus Group money?**

Klay was about to stand when he remembered why he'd wanted to see Eady in the first place. "I want to go back to the Philippines," he said.

Eady sighed, and shook his head no. "I'm afraid that's not—"

"I didn't make the connection to Botha."

Eady shrugged. "Perhaps you were right from the beginning: he's not using the priest."

"No," Klay said. "He was there. I saw him in the airport."

"Saw who?"

"Botha."

Eady returned the nearly empty bottle of scotch to his bar. He stood with his back to Klay, looking out his window. "You saw Botha in the airport, are you certain?"

"Yes, Vance. There is definitely something more going on. The priest is a peace negotiator on Mindanao. Did you know that?"

"Was that in the file?"

"No. He had a photograph from the peace talks. I could come in that way. Do a story on the island's politics."

"No. First casualty of the new world order," Eady said, turning. "You're not going back there. Write up what you have on the priest. We'll run it online."

"I think it's worth—"

"Damn it, Tom! He won't print it! Krieger is a devout Catholic! Don't you see? Get it to me. I'll run it online before I leave. Sorry." Eady shook his head, regaining his composure. "A lot on my mind."

"Of course," Klay said. Eady rarely raised his voice. "You'll have it tonight."

"Good."

"Um." Klay pointed to the ceiling. "And the public?"

Eady shook his head. There was almost nothing left of his office to conceal a microphone, but

Vance Eady kept to his rule: no Agency talk in the office.

Eady got to his feet, "Sorry about all of this, Tom. I'm trying to get out of here before Monday, give my replacement an open field. Sharon Reif. She's the future, they tell me. I expect you'll find her . . . interesting. So, get the lay of the land and we'll talk again. Have a drink at the club. We have some things to discuss. There may be opportunity here . . ."

"Opportunity?"

Eady smiled.

It was, Klay thought, a crevice anything might hide in.

CHANGE, MOVE, OR DIE

Sovereign Headquarters
Washington, DC

It was several weeks before Klay was invited back to the tenth floor to meet Eady's replacement. He stepped off the oak-paneled elevator and was met by a glass wall. In the middle of the wall was a door with a metal handle. He pulled, but it was locked. The PGM security badge he reluctantly wore around his neck—one of many recent changes—did not seem to work, either.

A digitized female voice said, "Please look in the direction of the light. Speak your full name clearly." A red light appeared. Klay scowled at it and said his name. He pulled on the door handle. Locked. A moment later a thin young man wearing a wireless headset appeared. He opened the door and introduced himself as Timothy, Ms. Reif's personal assistant. "Sorry, you're not fully in the system yet," Timothy said. He wore a slim-cut light blue suit, narrow tie, and shiny black Australian boots. Klay followed him inside.

"I have Tom Klay," Timothy said to his headset.

Eady's labyrinth had been replaced by what looked like an Apple Store, a hive of hip young people moving among white desks topped with oversized computer monitors. On two walls enormous flat-screen monitors depicted a range of digital activity in real time. **The Sovereign**'s web pages were up on one, with graphs measuring followers, story impressions, engagements, likes, comments. Six more screens delivered news from dozens of other Perseus Group Media platforms. An electronic news ticker at ceiling level wrapped the room in green, like a neon anaconda.

Timothy opened a glass door. Sharon Reif rose from her desk. A politician was Klay's first thought. A TV news anchor. It was the razor-cut blonde hair set against black rectangular glasses. The instant, star-like self-assurance. "Tom Klay. Finally!"

Reif presented her hand half cupped, no thumb extended, as if she had a small bird she wanted to pass to him. Klay accepted her hand, then didn't know what to do with it. He held it for a moment and released it.

She wore an impeccably tailored cream suit, an Apple Watch, and a well-manicured smile. Her posture, Klay noticed, was as impossibly erect as Eady's.

Reif gestured toward her sofa. In place of Eady's worn brown leather couch was a spotless white upholstered sofa with a chrome frame, book-ended by armless white chairs.

She took a seat in one of the chairs and crossed her legs. Klay sat on the sofa, but found the seat too deep for him to sit back.

"How are you, Tom?"

He perched at the sofa's edge. "I'm good."

"Good is good." She leaned forward and patted his knee. "Did they catch the poachers?"

"From Kenya? No, not yet."

"Well, it's only a matter of time, right? With all the reporting we're doing, the government there is under a lot of pressure to bring those bastards to justice. We'll keep on it. It's been one of my priorities. We set up a hashtag for you, WhoShotTomKlay. It's getting a lot of traffic. Have you seen it?"

"No."

"Reader response has been absolutely terrific. You should check out the comments when you get a chance. It might make you feel better."

He didn't know what to say, so he didn't say anything. She was studying him, head cocked slightly like a chickadee, working on some theory about him.

"Okay, let's get down to business. We only have a few minutes before the press conference, but I wanted to take the time to meet you in person." She studied him again. "How are you?"

"Good," he said, puzzled. "Sharon," he added clumsily.

"Good is good. Okay, I need to lay some ground rules. No more violent crime. Legal says it's too risky—and metrics says it doesn't sell."

"Except that's what I do," he said.

She shook her head. "Change, move, or die."

While Sharon talked, Klay rubbed the pad of his thumb with the tip of his index finger, quietly spelling two words in one continuous script. It was a technique he used to remind himself how to handle moments like this. The words were "shut" and "up."

"You will adapt, Tom. I'm sure of it. We just have to set up a few new rules—of the house, as it were—and get you on your way. If you haven't guessed it yet, I love to say no. That's why I'm here. We're taking the magazine off line."

"It is off-line," Klay said. "It's a magazine."

"No, off line. Terminating it." She picked up an iPad from her glass coffee table. "We're going all-digital." She tapped the screen, sighed. "Your work is analog. I'm looking at your expenses. Twelve months for a single story?"

She swiped a finger up the screen. "You regularly miss your deadlines."

"I take the time the stories need."

"This goes back years," she said, paging through. "Extravagant expenditures. A pet store? You bought a pet store?"

The pet store had been cover for a piece on Mexican drug trafficking. Narcos love exotics, especially birds and white tigers.

"We got a good deal on it."

"Is that a joke?"

Klay had his own question: Who'd assembled this file for her? Porfle? Giovanni, the photography editor? Fucking photographers.

"We've had some good results, Sharon."

"When I need results, I call a plumber. We're in the news business here."

"That's funny."

"That's funny?"

"I thought we were in the insight business, not the news business—telling people why over what. At least that's what they told me my first day here. Vance Eady did."

"Vance." She narrowed her eyes and cocked her head, birdlike again. "The accountants are still trying to understand what he was up to."

"I'm sorry. I didn't catch that."

"What?"

He pointed to his left ear. "I'm a little deaf in this ear."

She raised her voice. "I said, the accountants have run into some irregularities when it comes to Mr. Eady. In the best light, they tell me, he took four steps—at four times the cost—to do what could have been done in one."

Klay laughed.

"Funny again?"

"You think Vance Eady was embezzling?"

"Probably not. No. But we're looking into it." She set her iPad down on top of a **Wall Street Journal.** "Nobody wants to kick a man when he's down. Certainly not a man who's meant so much to this institution. To the world."

She waved a hand and smiled brightly. "Let's not talk about the past, Tom. We wish him well. He was supportive of PGM hiring me. I appreciate that."

Klay was distracted by the smell of fresh paint and new carpet. What color carpet did Eady have? He couldn't recall. How could he not remember the color of the man's carpet he'd crossed a thousand times?

No whiff of desiccated tissue. No brittle animal fur. No sign Vance Eady had occupied this room at all. In place of his African masks, books, and zebra mount, a large painting hung on the wall above her glass-topped desk. A single blood-red brushstroke on white canvas. A mirror image of the Japanese painting using a black brushstroke hung behind his head.

"Do you know my background, Tom?"

"I saw the email. PR, right?"

He'd had Tenchant pull up some information on her. Married, forty-six. USC. Born in Chicago. Father, psychiatrist specializing in sleep disorders; mother, corporate lawyer; husband, reality television producer. She started in retail, then turned to advertising. Rose to partner at Aegis-Thompson in Los Angeles, which was subsequently acquired by Perseus Group Media. She was active on social media. Tenchant had pulled up her Twitter. "A bit of news: I'm heading to Washington as new EIC at The Sovereign. Psyched for a new PGM challenge! Big boots 2 fill. [Boots emoji]"

Klay told Tenchant not to bother digging any deeper.

"Public relations is selling, Tom. That's what we'll be doing now. Selling our information."

Klay found it hard to concentrate on what she was saying. Eady used to invite new hires to sit on his sofa and describe their futures for him. If they were nervous, which covered just about everyone, he would hand them his ivory walking stick with some line about how everyone needs a little assistance. They'd hold Eady's walking stick across their laps and tell him what they had planned for their illustrious careers, how they intended to tell stories in ways that refreshed the old and tired **Sovereign.** "Not your work, of course, Mr. Eady . . ."

Those he liked, Eady let in on his little secret. The rest he sent back to their desks, where they learned from their colleagues that they had nervously rubbed a walrus penis bone for half an hour while talking to God.

She was still talking.

". . . that's what I told the board about Prescott & Brower, which was one of my main accounts when I was a partner at Aegis. David Prescott founded P&B in 1892, selling pith helmets and elephant guns. Did you know that?" She paused. "Tom?"

"No."

"But you see the connection. It, too, was headed for extinction. Enter public relations. Packaging. Brand realignment. We identified P&B's core deliverable. It wasn't pith helmets. Or canoes. It was freedom. The African word for freedom is 'uhuru.' Did you know that? Of course you did. Our research told us people wanted the name, but not the musty stuff inside. Who needs a compass when we've got Google Earth, right? Well, nobody likes freedom more than teenagers. Our path was clear."

"Really?" Klay said, thinking it was tan of some kind, Eady's carpet.

"Really. We put P&B's logo on premium T-shirts, delivered low-cut jeans, gave out flip-flops with bottle openers in the soles to colleges across the country. Yesterday's pith helmets are the hoodies of today, I like to say. What do you think happened?"

Klay was looking out the window.

"What happened was our market cap jumped to six billion! Are you familiar with the P&B brand, Tom?"

His grandfather had had one of those pith helmets in the attic. Klay wondered if he'd ever used it. Chances were the shotguns in the attic had come from P&B, too. He didn't know. He had ventured into Prescott & Brower's flagship store on Fifth Avenue a few years ago. He walked in expecting to find fly rods and hand-strung snowshoes. Instead he'd encountered a world not that different from the sex trafficking markets he'd investigated overseas—teenage boys in tank tops and underweight girls in low-cut jeans spraying perfume on tourists.

"Prescott & Brower," Klay said. "With the pith helmets."

"Exactly. Change, move, or die, right, Tom? That's evolution. No one knows evolution better than **The Sovereign.** So, I ask you, do you want to be right and dead like the dinosaurs? Or alive and able to do your elephant stories?"

"Right and alive would be my choice, Sharon."

"I thought so."

Reif stood up. She put her hands on the back of her chair. "**The Sovereign**'s the most trusted media brand in the world. Did you know that?"

"I did."

"Not its most profitable," she continued. "That's for sure. But its most trusted. We're going to leverage that trust to get new products out. Do you have any idea how much money we've left on the table not patenting the discoveries our people have made over the years? New species? Tribal remedies? Genes?!" She looked at him. "Billions! I'd like you to stay on, be a part of this. Mentor a new generation. Would you like to?"

"I'm just a field guy with a pen, Sharon."

"That's content! We need content, Tom. It's our competitive edge, the piece our competitors would kill us for. Our challenge is to package our content better, to deliver it dynamically."

Klay didn't respond.

Reif gave him the chickadee look again. "So, what are you telling me, Tom? What? You want to leave us?"

Us.

The word echoed. It was true. He was an outsider now, evicted but invited to return as a Perseus Group tenant. He ground his teeth. It was the choice Bernard had been given as a ranger—**join Perseus Group or find some other way to support your family.**

He looked down at his security badge. He was collared now, too.

"I just want to do my work, Sharon."

She clapped her hands. "Excellent! We're agreed then. It won't be what it was, Tom. It will be better. Smells a little better already, right?" She waved a hand in front of her nose. "Whew! Right? Okay, I think we've covered everything for now. Any questions?"

"The obvious one," he said. "We've been taken over by a mercenary."

She raised an index finger, eager to respond.

"This is Perseus Group Media," she emphasized. "Different companies. Totally different! That's important to understand. Also, Perseus Group, our parent organization, will have no say at all on the editorial side. The board assures me of that. It's my team. But I'm thrilled to know you'll be staying with us."

She checked her watch. "Okay. Look, we'll be making a lot of changes. Which reminds me." She walked to her desk. "I know you and Vance were close. He was your mentor, they tell me."

"He was a good man." Klay corrected himself: "Is."

"And I don't want to intrude on that, but I

must ask that you eliminate all contact with him moving forward."

"I'm sorry?" he said.

"Bad ear again? I'm saying we've got some concerns, that's all. And I want us to get off on a fresh editorial foot. I'm sure you can understand that. I wanted to make the point to you in person."

"I appreciate that. But I'm not cutting off my ties to Vance. He's got cancer, for Christ's sake."

"It's a lot to process, I know. Okay, we'll put a pin in it for now. Oh, by the way, what's your take on Alexander Porfle? As an editor, I mean?"

"Porfle?" Klay said, steeling himself. "Extraordinary. Best editor I've ever had."

She nodded. "Good. Last thing . . ." She opened Eady's coat closet and removed the curved white stick with a knot at one end. Klay suppressed a smile. It was Eady's walrus baculum. She slapped the penis bone in her palm.

"An ivory shillelagh is what I guessed at first." She slid a hand along its curved shaft. "Turns out it's a walrus penis bone." She looked at him. "I can't imagine a man leaving his dick behind by accident, can you, Tom?"

She dropped it into her wastebasket. "We'll come back to Mr. Eady another time."

There was a knock at her door.

"Come!"

Timothy wore a smile that wasn't especially sunny. He tapped his Apple Watch.

"Timothy will go over what to expect this morning."

"What to expect for what?" Klay asked.

"Terry Krieger, Tom," Reif said. "We want you to meet him." She clapped her hands. "Chop-chop. Let's go!"

ONE BEAUTIFUL BATTLEFIELD

Sovereign Headquarters
Washington, DC

"Here's where you sit," Timothy said, pointing to an upholstered seat in the front row of **The Sovereign**'s auditorium, the kind with bottoms that fold up when not in use. A piece of paper with Klay's name written on it was taped to the seat's underside.

"I see that," Klay said. "What's the agenda?"

"Nope." Timothy shook his head. "We want you totally natural." He wiped a spot from Klay's gray T-shirt. "So, act totally natural. Do you have a suit jacket here . . . ? Of course you don't. You can wait in the green room until we're ready to begin—we've got snacks and water back there for you. When Sharon calls for you, walk out that door and take this seat." Timothy checked his watch. "We have about a half hour. We'll start letting people in in ten. On my way," he said into his headset, and hurried for the auditorium's rear door.

Klay left the auditorium. He took a service elevator to the basement and walked the old marble hallway to the staff cafeteria. When he first joined the magazine there had been two places to eat in the building: the basement cafeteria for staff and the males-only executive dining room on the eighth floor. Lunch in the jackets-only Humboldt Room included exotic main dishes inspired by explorations past served by tuxedoed black waiters. A shortage of space not prejudice led to change. When reality television emerged as the organization's bread and butter, the Humboldt Room was converted to TV producers' offices, and roast quail, raw oysters, and sauterne gave way to **Savage Swordfish. Young Men and Fire. Cave In!**

Klay had done a reality television pilot once. **The Investigator** the series was to be called, featuring Klay, pitched as the Anthony Bourdain of wildlife crime. He'd been surprised at the number of takes each scene had required. Fit young associate producers dressed in the latest adventure wear asked him to step out of a helicopter again and again, or to greet a tribal chief over and over, gesturing repeatedly for the chief to look at Klay and not the camera. Months after the scene was shot they called Klay and said they didn't like the way he had entered the chief's hut and were flying him back to the Congo to shoot it again.

"This is television," they admonished him, nod more for the reaction shots, and would he please look more anxious? He was tracking dangerous poachers! They wore him down over time so that eventually he'd even agreed to stumble while on a contrived patrol with Bernard's Green Guardians, Bernard reaching down to give him a hand, the way Bernard would later do for real on the last day of his life. It took nine takes for Klay to stumble acceptably, but by then his muddy clothes did not match the scene, and he'd had to change into identical clothes and do it again. The series was never made.

The basement cafeteria was **The Sovereign**'s only eatery now. It was empty at the moment, everyone reporting to the auditorium for Sharon's all-hands meeting. Klay got himself a prewrapped roast beef sandwich from the refrigerator, a bag of potato chips, and a cup of hot tea. He ate his sandwich alone, peeling off a bite at a time, thinking about the changes he'd witnessed during his career.

He returned to the auditorium a half hour later to find it full. Fox was sitting in a back row. He had his brightly colored stockinged feet up on the seat in front of him and was twisting a coffee straw in his teeth. He lifted his feet, and Klay took a seat next to him.

"So, if they make you an offer, will you take it?" Fox asked, chewing his straw.

"Haven't thought about it," Klay said.

"PGM's doing it every place they acquire—keeping the storefronts and using a single back-end for content. I think we'll get offers."

Klay's researcher, David Tenchant, paused to say hello.

"Good to see you, Tench," Klay said. "Join us."

Fox grudgingly lowered his feet to let Tenchant pass.

The quiet younger man with greasy black hair was dressed as usual in black motorcycle boots, T-shirt, and tight black jeans. Tenchant had been Eady's hire, a surprise to everyone because staff writers like Klay normally did their own research, but Eady said Klay's criminal investigations exposed **The Sovereign** to lawsuits in ways its other journalism did not. "Let me introduce you to your stitch in time," he said, introducing Tenchant to Klay.

Klay had resisted at first, but it turned out Tenchant was a wizard with a computer, and a great asset.

"I know, I know," Fox continued. "Where else do you get to do this stuff, right? But if it's good, you know? If it's Perseus-money good, maybe it's worth taking the buyout?"

"Maybe," Klay said.

"Hit a beach someplace, write a book."

"You want to write a book?"

Fox twisted his straw.

"Mintz quit," Fox said apropos of nothing. "Said he'd spent twenty years documenting the impact of warmongers and he wasn't about to work for Perseus Group. Made a big to-do. 'Blood on his hands.' Threw his Hydro Flask across the edit room. You know how he is . . ." Fox punched Klay in his good arm. "Hey, look at that!" He pointed toward the front of the room. "Isn't that your nemesis?"

Klay looked across the auditorium. Porfle was making his way to a seat in a front row. Walking beside Porfle was Raynor McPhee, investigative reporter for the **New York Times.**

"What's Raynor McPhee doing here?" Fox asked.

Klay watched as Porfle ushered McPhee into the second row. McPhee was physically unremarkable—short, pudgy, balding, wearing what looked to be his grandfather's cardigan—but his reporting was legendary. His recent series on human slavery in the seafood industry had him embedded on a Thai fishing boat for five months, and had won him a Pulitzer.

"Is he coming here?" Fox asked. "Do you think?"

Klay didn't have time to think. The lights dimmed, and Sharon Reif strode to center stage wearing a wireless headset mic. "Change, move, or die. That's evolution, I like to say," she began. "And no one knows evolution better than **The Sovereign . . .**"

Erin arrived. "Sorry I'm late." She swatted Fox's toes, and he shifted to let her into the row. "I miss anything?"

"She's doing a TED Talk," Fox said.

Erin leaned across Tenchant and said, "Nice piece on the Philippines, Tom."

"It's still up?" Klay was surprised. He turned to Tenchant. "I thought Sharon pulled it?"

Tenchant nodded and with exaggerated concern said, "Her people told Admin to take it down. For some reason they can't do it." He shrugged. "Computer glitch, what I heard."

"Jesus," Klay said, studying him. "The talents hidden in this crew."

"No Jesus in that story," Erin said. "Speaking of, I heard Terry Krieger's making an appearance."

Fox chucked his straw into the aisle and sat up straight. Klay heard his name and looked up. The row in front of him had turned around. "Shit," he said.

Sharon was squinting into the audience. "Is he here? Tom?"

Timothy appeared, looking down at Klay with disapproval. Klay sighed and followed him to the stage.

"Okay, now stand there." Sharon pointed to a small red sticker on the stage. "And voilà!"

Lights flickered, and suddenly Terry Krieger rose from the floor and was standing on stage. "Hello, Tom."

Krieger wore a sweat-stained Chadwick Elephant Orphanage T-shirt, cargo shorts, and sandals. The billionaire was fit, five ten or so, tan, with a short Ollie North–style haircut. "I'm sorry we can't actually shake hands, Tom. Soon, I hope . . ."

Hologram Krieger turned and faced the audience. "Good afternoon, ladies and gentlemen. I'm sorry I can't be with you in person. But I'm pleased to have this opportunity to say a few words, using Perseus Group technology, to offer a hint of what we have in store as the new owners of this amazing institution. But first, I have someone with me who wants to congratulate Tom Klay on his recent work."

Hologram Krieger stepped back, and a baby elephant bounded across the stage, its little hologram trunk swinging loosely with joy. The baby stopped at Klay's feet and reached its trunk toward his face.

"Awww!" Sharon clapped. The audience clapped and marveled with her. Then the tiny elephant turned to the audience, waved its trunk farewell, and vanished.

"You are doing unparalleled work saving elephants, Tom," Hologram Krieger continued. "Thank you."

Klay stood motionless until he realized this fiction, and his colleagues, were awaiting a response. He nodded. The hologram nodded back and then turned to the room. "Now, Tom, let me demonstrate how the Perseus Group family of companies can take your work and the work of everyone at **The Sovereign** to a whole new level . . ."

A large movie screen descended at the back of the stage. Timothy appeared at Klay's elbow and quietly led him offstage. The room grew still.

WE HEAR: Deep tribal drums.

WE SEE: Tall grass, endlessly lush—day.

VOICE-OVER (deep male bass, James Earl Jones–like): "Dungu, an ocean of green in the heart of the Democratic Republic of the Congo. Ancient home to . . ."

FADE IN: Elephants.

". . . ELEPHANTS!"

A herd of elephants walking through tall grass transitions to giraffes running, hippos yawning, storks rising. Then an African village, shot from above, its red clay alleys swept smooth.

Ground-level clichés begin: The happy-children-chasing-a-soccer-ball scene/The river-washing scene/The basket-of-heavy-charcoal-on-the-head scene/The stoic-men-tending-emaciated-cattle scene/The small-motorbike-carrying-an-entire-family scene.

Then, WE HEAR GUNFIRE.

WE HEAR EXPLOSIONS.

CUT TO: Fire. Rebel militia. Terrorists. People fleeing, screaming.

More gunfire.

VOICE-OVER: "In a land ravaged by terrorist groups—Mai-Mai, M23, the Lord's Resistance Army. In a country without governance, sharing borders with war-torn South Sudan, Uganda, and a lawless Central African Republic. On ground plundered by rapacious outsiders for centuries—there is WAR."

CUT TO: Burning grass. Skeletons of houses. Hacked bodies. Tearful faces. An amputated black forearm lying in the dirt.

Then . . .

CUT TO: Muscled men in cool sunglasses and short haircuts arrive. Out of helicopters. In armored vehicles. On foot. Private military contractors with Perseus Group logos on their shirts. They erect guard posts. They hand out food. They apply bandages. They build a church.

VOICE-OVER (Terry Krieger's voice): "**The Sovereign** has celebrated the world's indigenous people and its wildlife for nearly a hundred fifty years. Perseus Group is committed to protecting these lives using the world's best technologies, best equipment, and best people—so that a hundred fifty years from now, our descendants will be able to enjoy the natural and cultural heritage we have preserved for them."

CUT TO: Mothers washing laundry in a river look up. Children pause their soccer game and look up. Fathers tending cattle look up. Cattle look up, too. A flock of birds appears. The flock moves as one, then breaks into two, then three clouds, rolling over and around itself, a joyful murmuration. The birds sail above a herd of elephants. Then a car appears on the horizon. A portion of the flock peels off to examine the incoming vehicle.

The birds are Askari drones, perfect house sparrow replicas. One drone flies to each of the car's windows. The faces of the car's passengers appear in boxes on the screen. Below each face is a full name, identity card serial number, biodata, and criminal history. An individual bird darts away from the vehicle and peers directly into the camera. It is inches away from the camera lens. Its eyes look REAL.

The Sovereign audience appears on the large screen. An actual Askari drone is in the auditorium now. Then more. A dozen. The sparrowsized machines hover above the stage, waiting. Faces from the audience appear on the screen along with employee IDs, home addresses, social media IDs, and birth dates with the years blurred.

A drone approaches Sharon, who is standing next to curtains at the edge of the stage. She waves an embarrassed hand in front of her face. It is captured on the screen. People laugh and point. The birds respond. Each pointed finger or raised hand, every head that turns, calls a drone to it. The drones move quick as hummingbirds. They dart over the audience, taking in data, projecting it onto the screen. Then something in the birds changes, as if some communal decision has been reached. The drones whisk over the heads of the audience and disappear.

The movie screen fills again.

CLOSING MONTAGE: Black schoolchildren at tiny desks eagerly raise their little hands. A massive elephant herd strides calmly through green grass. The images turn global: An orangutan swings through trees. A toucan turns its eye to the camera. A humpback whale breaches for the heavens.

MUSIC SWELLS.

PULL OUT. Mother Earth. Home. Above, a satellite keeps watch. The satellite turns. Its dish bears **The Sovereign**'s silver globe logo, intersected by a Perseus Group sword.

Krieger's hologram returned to the stage, hands clasped. "From the beginning, my companies and I have focused on the task required. On 9/11 our job was to respond to the worst terrorist attack in history on American soil. In the years since, we have come to see instability expanding the world over. You know the locations. You've told their stories.

"Beneath all of us lies one beautiful battlefield," Krieger said. "Earth. As I've told the president, conservation of this planet must be an essential part of America's defense strategy. We don't hire botanists to police drug trafficking even though cocaine comes from a plant, and we shouldn't put biologists and scientists in charge of policing crimes against nature. We need people who understand conflict and protection. Thirteen months ago, Perseus Group selected three of the worst hotspots in Africa and sent our people and technologies there with a simple mission: to add placekeeping to peacekeeping."

He ticked off the results of securing three African parks: Elephant and rhinoceros poaching down 70 percent. Kidnappings down 80. Theft . . . rape . . . murder—all reduced. Communities stabilizing. Class attendance up.

"Response times to emerging diseases are falling and will continue to fall," Krieger said, "making it less likely that Covid-19 and other zoonotic diseases hiding in the forest will make it to our shores. Scarce resources produce famine, corruption, violence, war. We know how important this is now. By starting at the beginning—with nature—we believe we can prevent not only the next terrible pandemic, but also the next global conflict. We are proud to include **The Sovereign** in the Perseus Group family. Together, we will uncover secrets of the natural world and use them to protect this planet for all of us. Thank you."

A smattering of applause filled the room. Sharon returned to center stage and said there was time for a few questions.

The Sovereign's chief ornithologist pointed out that sparrows hovering was not natural at all and asked what testing had been done to determine its effect on community bird behavior. Someone from television said if drone birds could follow an elephant herd, like bodyguards, with park rangers wearing GoPro cameras, **The Sovereign** might want to do a film about it, "Through the Eyes of Sparrows" or something.

"What's in it for you?" someone shouted, causing some uncomfortable laughter.

"Let's keep this civil," Sharon said.

"No," Krieger said. "It's the right question. What's in it for me? A lot. How many times have we heard, 'We should protect a rainforest or a coral reef because we don't know what benefits might lie hidden inside'? The technology you witnessed this morning was brought to you by hummingbirds. We attached sensors to hummingbird wings and let machine learning algorithms train our drones how to move. Among elephants, our drones fly like the sparrows they resemble. Other environments require the mobility of hummingbirds. We have built a UAV capable of both. By flying naturally we can get closer to wildlife, and protect it better. By flying faster we can protect it more quickly.

"Nature is full of dual-use secrets," he continued. "Hypertension medicine hidden in the poison of a Brazilian viper. Anticancer drugs locked inside Madagascar's rosy periwinkle. Blood thinners coursing through Brazil's tike uba tree. Adhesives under gecko pads. To unlock nature's secrets, we first need to protect them. Not through charity, which demeans the recipient, but through markets, which enable nature to earn her keep. At Perseus Group we are disrupting legacy conservation to deliver the world a highly profitable conservation dividend."

A young woman in the middle of the room raised her hand.

"The new hottie," Fox whispered to Klay. "Tanya Something. Grantee. Works on sharks."

The shark expert asked why, based on his history, they should trust Krieger to continue **The Sovereign**'s mission—"Not just your history in Iraq as Raptor Systems," she said, "but your more recent history, as Perseus Group Media, buying up newspaper and television stations and either closing them down or turning them into platforms for racist, misogynistic demagogues . . ."

"Ouch." Fox snapped at the air with his teeth. "Girl bites shark." He shook his head gloomily. "I loved her, Tom. I really did."

"You don't have to trust me," Krieger responded. "Trust your own eyes. Trust the communities we've already supported. A year from now I'll be back here on this stage and we can look at our results together."

Porfle got to his feet. "Terry, you stated in your presentation that your company is empowering the natural world to protect itself. Beyond teaching drones to flap like hummingbirds, could you provide us further examples?"

"Certainly, Alex. You've just witnessed our drones' flocking response to crowd movement using transition algorithms inspired by starling murmuration. Does anyone know what procto-deal trophallaxis is?"

"EAT SHIT!" someone yelled out.

Sharon scowled.

"Exactly right," Krieger said. "Termites exchange food and information anus to mouth, enabling them to move forward relentlessly without asking their queen for directions, inspiring our people to develop an information-exchange algorithm that enables our surveillance devices to respond autonomously while staying on mission. Our drones communicate using these markers, digital pheromones, if you like, and work as a unit.

"These are just a couple of the nature-based technologies that together offer us a force multiplier and enable us to follow poachers to their homes, study them, and take them down as a network."

The screen behind Krieger filled with a final image of armed Perseus Group rangers frisking a row of shirtless black African men, the prisoners' chests pressed against a concrete block wall, their hands zip-cuffed behind their backs. One of the prisoners had his face turned to the camera.

Klay raised his hand.

"That's all we have time for," Sharon said. "Let's give Terry a warm round of applause. I'm sure we can agree we have much to do and many fresh stories to tell as a result of this fabulous new relationship. Thank you!"

Krieger's hologram dissolved into the stage.

"Well, he seems committed," Fox said. He turned to Klay. "What were you going to ask?"

Klay turned and made his way up the aisle into the lobby.

"Tom?" Fox repeated.

The auditorium emptied around them.

"Tom Klay," a voice said.

Klay turned and Raynor McPhee emerged from the crowd.

"Raynor," Klay said.

The two men shook hands.

"Sorry about Kenya," McPhee said. "You doing okay?"

"Thanks," Klay said.

Fox put out his hand. "Mitchell Fox. I respect your work very much, Raynor."

McPhee shook Fox's hand without noticing him. His attention was with Klay. "You know why he's doing this wildlife shit, right?"

Klay didn't answer.

"Are you leaving the **Times**?" Fox asked.

"You think you're not part of a strategy?" The crowd jostled McPhee, and he had to work to stay in front of Klay. "This glimpse today," McPhee continued. "You know what he's doing with these drones. They're already in western China. The technology they're using to imprison Uighurs is coming here next. You see that, right?"

"I see it," Klay said. "I don't see what to do about it."

Porfle appeared at McPhee's side and clapped the **Times** reporter on the shoulder. "Ah. Good. You know Tom already. Excellent."

For an uncomfortable moment no one spoke.

"Well. Raynor," Porfle said, leading McPhee toward the elevators, "shall we continue our conversation upstairs in my office?"

McPhee left with Porfle, but after a few steps the **Times** reporter shrugged off Porfle's hand and returned to Klay. He pointed toward the auditorium and said, "Our job is to recognize when history is about to repeat itself and sound the alarm. It's not enough just to expose bad actors among us. We have to force the public to respond. You know what he is."

Klay was only half listening. He was thinking about the final image of Krieger's presentation, the accused poacher looking toward the camera. The man had been bleeding from the scalp, and he had lost a good deal of weight, but Klay had recognized his face and the raised coffee bean tattoos covering his torso. The man was not a poacher. He was Goodson Ltumbesi, the Green Guardian who'd saved Klay's life.

CANDY FOR A WHALE SHARK

Manila, Philippines, and Cebu Strait

The day after making his hologram presentation to **The Sovereign,** Terry Krieger strode into the Champagne Room at the Conquistador Hotel in downtown Manila. Dressed in an open-collar Turnbull & Asser gingham check shirt and blue blazer, Krieger appeared less formal than most of those tucking into the hotel's famous salad niçoise. The décor of the dining room in the city's second oldest hotel could not have been less to his taste. French provincial chairs and tufted banquettes, white-clothed tabletops, tasseled chandeliers, gold curtains. Worse, it was very likely, given how many diplomats in Manila favored the Conquistador, that someone would recognize him with his host, the man at the far corner of the room who was now rising to welcome him, wearing a white jacket with gold epaulets, his obese arms spread wide.

"Terry!" Anthony Gatt beamed.

Krieger halted before Gatt could embrace him and took a seat with his back to the restaurant. Fat Anthony smoothed his pale blue ascot with his hands before retaking his seat opposite Krieger at the four-person table set for two.

Krieger looked at Gatt. Half Filipino, half Chinese, and somehow as big as two men, Fat Anthony was president and CEO of the number one in-port ship-servicing company in the South China Sea, the one to go to for everything a visiting warship or submarine might require. His company, Core F Services, operated tugboats, managed port authority and customs fees, sent divers down to demine harbors, provided food and fuel, hauled away trash and sewage, and shuttled crews into town for R&R.

Fat Anthony was also Krieger's fixer, a wharf rat who knew every latrine, mess, frayed line, and flag officer in the region. Every whore and every bloodied knife, as well. Port service was a competitive industry. To stay on top, Fat Anthony oversaw a network of moles throughout the world's armed services that ensured he won the contracts he wanted. A man like that was both useful and dangerous.

It galled Krieger to be in the same room with

Gatt, but Gatt's message had been urgent, and Krieger had too much riding on him to ignore it.

Krieger ordered the Dover sole. Waiters brought Gatt's meal to their table as if they were supplying an expedition. Foie gras terrine . . . black truffle soup . . . goto congee . . . rock lobster salad . . . osetra caviar . . . pan-seared duck liver with pear and sunchoke . . . A5 Kobe Wagyu . . . Krieger watched it all disappear into Gatt.

"Mindanao City Port," Gatt said finally, letting the words slip from his mouth syllable by syllable, while chewing the end of a lamb chop he held in his fingers. His extra-long thumbnails were manicured, coated in clear nail polish, and cut to a point. Like cockroach feet, Krieger thought, watching them flash over his food.

"As I predicted, that one was not easy to acquire. It required many months of negotiations. Many greased palms. But it turns out Moros can be capitalists, too." Gatt smiled and reached for his napkin. "It surprised even me when suddenly it became possible. Do you remember the priest I told you about? The one who opposed our offers?"

Krieger did not respond. "The problem is a priest," Gatt had said. "A peace negotiator who is trying to expand the Muslims' territory to include a port, the same one you have your heart set on, I'm afraid . . .

"Well," Gatt said, shaking out his napkin, "no

matter. He decided to remove himself from our world and join our Father."

"So. Why am I here?" Krieger said, and waited.

Gatt looked up from his pot de crème. "Yes, it is about the money, Terry. You have your deep-sea port now. I have provided you the other services. Now it is about the money."

"We have a schedule for that," Krieger replied.

His assistant, Mapes, had suggested this as a likely reason for Gatt's urgent message, but Krieger had resisted accepting it. Gatt knew better. Or should have. He wasn't just a fixer. Gatt was an investor. Krieger got to his feet. That was the problem with wharf rats: you had to either get used to them or kill them.

Later that week Krieger sat in his office on board his superyacht, **Raptor.** He closed his laptop and looked through the ship's sliding glass doors onto the Sulu Sea. The Philippine sky was crystal clear. A light breeze caressed the curtains. If things went as planned, he could have his meeting this morning and still join his family, who were on nearby Cebu Island, diving with whale sharks.

To **Raptor**'s west was Palawan Island, and beyond that was the strategic heart of the maritime Orient: the South China Sea. Unless he was wrong, man's next civilization-altering conflict would take place not in the deserts of the Middle

East, or in the skies over North Korea, but out there on Asia's most strategically important body of water. When the great conflict would kick off was very much up in the air. Maybe it would start tomorrow. Maybe it would not begin until after Krieger was dead. Tomorrow was too soon, and dead was too late. It was coming, and if it was coming, he wanted it to happen on his watch. History, he decided, needed scheduling.

In some ways he had already accomplished the hardest part. He had secured China as a client. "China can build overseas, Terry. But she cannot yet put her boots or weapons there," China's general secretary, Ho Jianming, had confided during a visit to Krieger's hunting property in Africa.

"The longer your reach, Mr. President," Krieger had replied, "the more vulnerable are your fingers." Perseus Group was now China's overseas security firm, the billion-dollar glove to protect China's trillion-dollar fist.

Both men agreed on the importance of the South China Sea to China's future. Beneath its waters lay more oil and natural gas than was possessed by any single nation on earth, as well as important deep-sea channels for China's ballistic missile submarines. Unfortunately for China, above those resources rumbled the second most trafficked military and commercial sea-lane in the world. Day and night, half the world's merchant tonnage and a third of its sea traffic, including tankers, freighters, warships, and fishing vessels, traversed the sea's waters. The South China Sea was a marginal sea, surrounded by seven other countries so that it was more of a lake, each of which claimed rights to exploit the waters. Extracting wealth from such an active sea was like hunting for a lost contact lens in Tiananmen Square.

China was not a friendly neighbor. It claimed nearly the entire South China Sea and all that lay beneath it. To enforce its claims, China deployed its maritime forces to sail the waters, seizing most any visible rock or reef, onto which it promptly dumped tons of old concrete and debris, transforming maritime features into artificial islands it then fortified and armed. Rock by rock, reef by reef, China was adversely possessing the South China Sea. It was an approach that invited conflict.

Krieger had competition for the waters, too. A Russian, Dmitri Yurchenko. Yurchenko's paramilitary company was lobbying the Vietnamese to let Russian state oil giant Rosprom drill Vietnam's oil claims, forcing China to either relinquish its claims to Vietnamese waters or take on Russia. Yurchenko was courting Malaysia with a similar deal, both arrangements bait awaiting a switch. For the right price, Krieger knew, Yurchenko would reverse his arrangements with Vietnam and Malaysia in favor of

China. Once Beijing stepped in, Yurchenko's Amur Tactical Resources would have a direct pipeline to Chinese leadership, and the most valuable military-services contract on earth. Krieger could not allow that, of course.

The Americans had their own interests to protect. The US Navy's Seventh Fleet was sending destroyers, fighter jets, and surveillance aircraft through waters and airspace claimed by China, reasserting claims of the Philippines, Vietnam, Taiwan, and others while demonstrating its own freedom to navigate the South China Sea—all the while bringing the world closer to war.

Krieger wasn't ready for war yet. He offered China a businessman's solution to its growing South China Sea problem.

"Don't seize islands," he told Ho. "Buy the far shore."

Krieger presented Ho with a plan to acquire the region's strategic ports, bury the ownership, and take control of the entire South China Sea without conflict. They started with Orviston Wharf in Darwin, Australia, a simple purchase in Australia's forgotten north. For China, buying up foreign ports meant improved access to resources in the South China Sea without increased friction. For Krieger, it meant laying a snare around the world's most valuable body of water.

. . .

His laptop buzzed. Krieger looked down at an image of his daughter, Blaze, in a corner of his screen. She was on board a dive boat, in her bathing suit, scowling. He hit accept. "How are the whale sharks?" he asked.

"They feed them whale shark candy on Cebu," she said. "It makes them forget to migrate."

"What's whale shark candy?" he asked.

"Shrimp."

"Isn't that what they eat?"

"That's not the point and you know it," she said. "I'm not going back in the water."

"Stand by." He muted their conversation and turned to his assistant.

"Donsol," Mapes said. "We can fly them there in about an hour."

He returned to Blaze. "Pack up. You're going to Donsol. They don't bait them there."

"Can you still meet us?"

"Before dinner," he said.

"I'll take that as a promise," Blaze replied.

He had to laugh. **Fortune** called him "the world's richest security guard"—but the real boss in his family was his seventeen-year-old daughter. He closed his laptop and moved it to the corner of his desk. He checked his watch, leaned back in his chair, and interlocked his fingers.

"Okay. Bring him in."

Mapes shut down her digital tablet and headed for the door. She was tall and lean, half Thai, half

African-American, with a shaved head, dressed today in black pants and black jacket over a high-collared white blouse.

"And Mapes," he added, "have the chopper ready by noon."

Mapes closed the door behind her, conversation not her strong suit—but then conversation was not why he'd hired her. Sex was not the reason, either. Truth was he was afraid of what Mapes might come up with in bed. Chances were a bed would have nothing to do with it.

Mapes returned to his office, and Krieger got to his feet.

"Admiral," he said, rounding his desk and putting out his hand. "Thank you for making time for me."

Admiral Everett Tighe, commander of the US Navy's Seventh Fleet, wore his service dress whites. "Any friend of the Navy, Terry," he said, surveying Krieger's office with barely disguised contempt. It was the same with all these old salts, Krieger thought. He could practically hear the adding machine spinning inside Tighe's head, the old man calculating **Raptor**'s cost, taking it all personally, as if every dollar Krieger spent over the price of a Boston Whaler were an act of treason.

As treason went, **Raptor** possessed some Benedict Arnold–level amenities. The 190-foot Abeking & Rasmussen superyacht included dual helipads, belowdecks hangar, drive-in tender bay, and a custom submersible. Her zero-speed stabilizers allowed Krieger to slip into a ripple-free lap pool at speed or deliver his signature backhand drop on the midships squash court. All of the important areas, including this office, were armored and containable. His supervillain yacht, Blaze called it.

Tighe added, predictably, "It's your dime."

"Indeed," Krieger said. "Please."

The admiral glanced toward the sumptuous white leather lounge chairs in the room's aft section. By contrast, the single wooden chair in front of Krieger's desk had the look of a dunce seat. Krieger circled his desk and sat down behind it. He had plans for this meeting, and they did not involve the admiral's comfort.

"Coffee, Admiral?"

"Does a bear shit in the woods?" Tighe replied.

Krieger smiled. **Does a bear shit in the woods?**

"My grandfather used to say that," Krieger said. "That right?"

Gerhardt Krieger used to say a lot of things: "Never burn a bridge." "Never trust a man with a mustache." "Lips that touch liquor shall never touch mine." "Clean your fuckin' rifle, boy." His grandfather had been a gem, the multimillionaire inventor of the Krieger Strip. "God gave me the idea while I sitting on the can," he liked to say. "I guess he knew he couldn't trust me with much, but it was a good one." The Krieger Strip was about as simple an idea as a person could come up with, except no one ever had: aluminum trim to protect the edge of a car door. It was enough to make the Krieger family rich for generations. "Because Detroit produces a lot of cars with doors on them," his grandfather said.

Krieger's father, the Colonel, had been an entrepreneur, too. He invented a synthetic shoe sole that was lighter and lasted longer than Vibram. Madison Avenue hated the material, but the US Army loved it and the Krieger Boot Company further compounded the family's considerable wealth. "Because," as the Colonel said, "the Army produces a lot of soldiers with two feet."

Krieger was not invited to work for either of his family's businesses. It was a family rule, started by his puritanical grandfather and passed down: Kriegers accept no charity. You make your own way or you get nothing. After the Academy and the Marines, Krieger's first invention was Raptor Systems, a privatized army to fill the gap between what Washington politicians promise and what they do. Raptor Systems had been an extraordinary success. "Because," as Krieger liked to say, "Washington produces a lot of politicians with two moving lips."

Then came Iraq.

"I said, beautiful ship you have here, Terry . . ." Tighe held up a cigar. "You mind?"

"You're my guest," Krieger said.

Mapes returned with a silver pot on a tray and poured Tighe's coffee. Krieger watched, expressionless, as Tighe cut his cigar.

"Here you are." Tighe dropped his cigar cap into Mapes's open palm. She accepted it, but glanced at Krieger deliberately. Krieger smiled, knowing what she could do to Tighe with that open palm.

"Let's get down to business, shall we, Admiral?"

Tighe chuckled and considered his cigar. "This is just a passex, Terry. A courtesy call out of respect for all you've done for the services."

Krieger caught the condescension in Tighe's voice. It was brass like Tighe who'd torpedoed Raptor Systems. Raptor Systems had gone in when the US military wouldn't, protected Americans when the government couldn't, given diplomatic cover to their military and military cover to their diplomats, and had gotten them out alive. Not some of them out. All of them. Not a single American client was lost on Raptor Systems' watch.

Instead of awarding him a medal, they crucified him. Dragged him to Washington and strung him up before the House Committee on Oversight and Reform, where that overfed hedgehog called him a war profiteer . . . a mercenary . . . a paid assassin. The secular libtards wanted to make America safe again—no more

9/11s—but they didn't want to pay for that retasking. They wanted it done, but they didn't want to know how it was done, he told the committee.

"The battle for America was won by mercenaries—like me," he argued, and recited the names of the Revolutionary War heroes whose statues filled Lafayette Park directly across the street from the White House: "Von Steuben, Kosciusko, Rochambeau, Lafayette—German, Polish, French—each a foreigner hired by General Washington to fight for America's freedom." He concluded his congressional testimony with a single question. "In Baghdad, on your CODELs outside the wire, when your delegations ventured out into that violent unknown, who did you ask to protect you? Was it an overworked soldier on his third deployment? Or was it Raptor Systems?"

The answer they gave him was Never Again. Never Again would Raptor Systems be awarded a US government security contract. Terry Krieger would have to go elsewhere for his supper.

Thrown into the briar patch by men and women like Tighe, Krieger had emerged with an idea that made him more powerful than ever.

He called it Perseus Group.

Blackballed by the world's biggest military and its government, stripped of his access, Krieger had needed a new business model. His years operating in conflict zones taught him that when it came to combat there was one resource that was more important than personnel, plant, or even firepower.

Fifteen years later, peel back the complex network of Perseus Group enterprises—security services firms; high-tech and military design companies; surveillance systems providers; media and entertainment properties; logistics, insurance, and transport enterprises; even Krieger's conservation and community stabilization efforts—and you would find one powerful idea. It was an idea as simple as car-door edging and as necessary as army boots: intelligence.

Strategically useful information has one significant shortcoming when it comes to the individuals who possess it: intelligence is very difficult to trade. An individual with secrets to sell has to engage in a very risky process: identify a buyer; secure an audience; negotiate a price; arrange payment; make the handoff; and conceal sudden, unexplainable wealth. At each node, the seller is exposed, and the cost of a mistake could mean one's life.

Krieger established a series of funds to compensate an elite group of people for the secrets they carried. Membership in a fund was by invitation only. The minimum buy-in was 20 million dollars' worth of intelligence, valued by Krieger alone. In exchange, an investor received a percentage of their fund's performance.

His fund system was more art than science, he told his investors. Often the Fund, as he referred to the collective, identified value where none had seemed to exist. Pakistani salt has little to do with Sri Lankan life insurance, until you look at the shipping lane that runs from Gwadar Port directly past Colombo, Sri Lanka, and take into account which families control the salt and insurance industries there. Tin is hardly as valuable as gold unless you can access it in quantities sufficient to monopolize its supply to the world's makers of smartphones and rocket launchers. On it went. The algorithms Krieger's people used to price intelligence ensured that investors got what they wanted, which is to say, ensured that they got more. And if one didn't always receive top dollar for specific information, one did receive ongoing payments that were secure and reliable. For traitors, that was more than fair.

Most of his investors were senior officials privy to top secret intelligence. Others had a single golden egg to sell. Like Fat Anthony Gatt, not all worked for a government. The Lockheed Martin engineer who stole plans for the F-35, the world's most expensive fighter jet, needed both cash and an exit plan. Krieger's people spent two years advising her on her investment portfolio, including a tip on a company that was about to fail disastrously. She shorted the stock and came out rich. Meanwhile, Krieger's people laid a trail to Chinese hackers and sold the jet's blue-prints to the Saudis. The engineer still worked for Lockheed. The best exits didn't require one to leave.

By pooling intelligence and providing a return, Krieger incentivized his investors' behavior. By compensating them for their transgressions, he bought their silence. Anyone who invested with Krieger understood the cost of betrayal. To say that you invested your life in the Fund was not an understatement.

Krieger controlled a network of highly placed informant-investors around the world, making him constructive director of a meta-spy agency he used to package and deliver strategic op-portunities to his extremely powerful clients. Commodifying intelligence worked. "Because," Krieger liked to say with a modest smile, "I have more of it."

Krieger looked at his guest. Admiral Everett Tighe was neither an investor in one of Krieger's funds, nor a client. Tighe was a fool. Krieger was about to make him useful.

When Krieger did not respond, Tighe shifted in his chair. "All right, Terry, all right," he said, fingering the scales of the Lady Justice statu-ette on Krieger's desk. "Have it your way. Shall we . . ." He waved Mapes away.

"Shall we what?" Krieger asked.

". . . do this in private?"

"This is private, Admiral."

Tighe blew out his cheeks, then gestured with his cigar for Krieger to proceed.

Krieger leaned forward, placed his hands on his desk, and laced his fingers. He spoke calmly. "Admiral, the Seventh Fleet has been giving preferential treatment to Core F Services. That will no longer fly."

"Not sure I care for your tone, son," Tighe said, coming about. "However, I'm not familiar . . ."

Krieger looked at Mapes. His expression said, **I have to put up with this?**

"Core F, Admiral."

Tighe's expression remained blank.

Krieger pinched the skin between his eyes. "I will indulge you because this involves embarrassing issues for you. Anthony Gatt. Fat Anthony."

Mapes placed a photograph of Tighe and Gatt standing together in a grip-and-grin in front of the Terror Club in Singapore, the British Navy's watering hole.

"Husbanding?" Tighe said through his cigar. "You're talking about husbanding contracts, Terry? Chit? I didn't realize Perseus was in that sector." He picked a flake of tobacco from his tongue. "That's oh-fives, oh-sixes. Your people should know that." He looked at Mapes. "But I can tell you, if you have a beef with one of our contractors, one of your competitors, you file a bid awards protest with FLC Yoko. Off the record, in case you're thinking of filing such a challenge, I'll advise you that it's my understanding Core F has provided the Navy excellent product, soup to nuts."

Tighe looked for a place to ash his cigar ash. He ignored the crystal ashtray Mapes had set before him and ashed his cigar on one of Lady Justice's scales.

As Tighe performed his little display of power, Krieger smiled to himself. Gatt had indeed come through. It was some twenty-five companies deep, but Krieger now owned Mindanao City Port. He would present the port to China, along with a rather sizeable bill. **Another pearl for your string, Mr. President.**

"Admiral, I don't care about you and your officers overpaying for port services in order to take a skim. Your men protect the Pacific flank of the Western Hemisphere. You offer your life to your country. I recognize that. I don't care about a little graft. What I do care about is the national security of the United States."

Tighe set down his coffee cup and got to his feet, motioning for Mapes to open the door. "You've been in the sun too long, Terry. We're done here."

"Sit down, Admiral. You've been passing Fat Anthony fleet movements, transit maps. Advising him in advance of your schedules, and those of our allies, in the Seventh AOR."

Tighe paused. "I don't know what you're talking about."

"Admiral," Mapes said, stepping forward to take over, as planned. "You have a first-class petty officer emailing classified ship movements directly to Fat Anthony for you." She placed printed copies of the emails on the desk next to Tighe's coffee cup. Tighe ignored them, still standing.

Krieger was thinking, **Now's when you say, "Do you have any idea how many sailors are under my command?"**

"Do you have any idea how many sailors are under my command?" Tighe barked.

Mapes touched a button, and a screen descended to Tighe's right. The office lights dimmed automatically. Another touch and a video began. It was a scene from the MacArthur Suite at the Manila Hotel. The video quality was excellent. Three slender Asian girls naked on a king-sized bed. Tighe naked, too, except for his admiral's cap. The underage girls expressionless as they worked on Tighe. A girl on her knees allowing Tighe to do things to her. "Allowing" too strong a word . . .

"All right. Point taken," Tighe said, returning to his seat. "Turn that garbage off. Fat Anthony. Yeah, I know him."

Krieger could not get over how easily power-ful men, men who should be leaders, could be led. Tighe had been altering the itineraries of the Seventh Fleet to patronize ports operated by Gatt, who then compensated Tighe in sex. Not millions of dollars and sex. Not hundreds of thousands of dollars and kilos of coke and sex. Just quality girls any creative petty officer could have secured for his commanding officer, no strings attached. The **George Washington** to Phuket when she should have been in Singapore. The **Blue Ridge** to Kota Kinabalu instead of Kuala Lumpur. Tighe moved the entire Seventh Fleet, including submarines, around the triangle that was the South China Sea all for a slice of high-end trim.

Being a man was about learning to channel one's drives, Krieger thought. Sure, he'd done the Four Floors of Whores in his day. But he'd been young then. Business was his woman now. To spread the world's legs and assert himself was his objective. When he needed to blow off extra steam, he didn't whore; he picked up his rifle and hunted.

Tighe was wounded—Krieger could see that—but wounded was not enough. "I don't judge your reasons, Admiral. Men have appetites. But when your business conflicts with mine, yours must end. And so, beginning today, you will cancel all outstanding contracts with Core F. You will control your appetites."

"You little punk. You think you can jerk my chain?" Tighe gestured toward the screen. "A little fucking R&R. There is not a single—"

"Anthony Gatt," Krieger interrupted, "was selling your ship movements to the Russians. To the Chinese! Don't tell me you didn't know. That's treason, Admiral."

Mapes laid a sheaf of papers in front of Tighe. "Comms between you and Gatt," she said.

Tighe glanced coolly at the top document, recognized something, and began thumbing pages, increasingly unnerved. Krieger knew it wasn't the content of the emails that shook him. It was the emails themselves. Tighe had communicated with Gatt using CAINA, the Pentagon's network for communications among leaders in times of war. No one but the intended recipient could read comms sent in this way—or so they had no doubt told him. But Krieger had his Gatt emails. Tighe's eyes moved through the pages. He had internal NCIS reports, too.

Krieger watched comprehension dawn on Tighe's horizon: Perseus Group had hacked the top secret communications channel of the head of the Seventh Fleet.

"Treason, Admiral. So, starting today, this little sex ring of yours is over. Tell everyone involved you've found religion. Understood?"

"What about . . . ?" Tighe pointed his cigar at the screen.

"Taken care of."

"How do you know? If Gatt has copies—"

"He doesn't."

Gatt's task had been to reserve the hotel rooms, select the girls, order the foie gras and Cristal. Mapes oversaw the cameras.

Gatt had been a valued Fund investor. He had delivered critical intel on Australia's finance minister in advance of the Darwin deal; on a Pakistani salt baron in secret control of Gwadar port; on the wife of a Malaysian sultan who would now be happy to allow arms through his state. But Gatt had been double-dealing. While gathering compromising information for Krieger, he had been simultaneously selling that same intelligence to the Russians. Not to the Russian government. Worse. To Krieger's rival, Dmitri Yurchenko. Krieger wasn't sure how much Yurchenko knew yet, but that was a separate issue.

Mapes touched a button, and the screen filled with the image of Anthony Gatt, all 409 pounds of him, naked on a morgue table, his gigantic body swollen and pale after three days at sea. The commander of the Seventh Fleet ran his eyes over Gatt's corpse. Fish had started on him. His eyes, fingertips, and most of his nose and lips were missing, a chunk of his thigh. His thickened tongue filled his mouth.

Appetites, Krieger thought. The Fund depended on them. But the Fund had rules.

Tighe glanced at the cigar ash that soiled his pant leg, but did not seem to see it. His eyes roamed the room, unfocused, calculating his exposure. Krieger gave him time, waiting for two words that took some men longer to come to than others.

"And me?" Tighe said finally.

Krieger got to his feet. He circled his desk and waited for Tighe to stand. "You, Admiral," he said, walking Tighe to the door, "are exactly where I want you to be."

Moments later a helicopter lifted clear of **Raptor** and flew Tighe back to the **Blue Ridge.** A second chopper, bearing Krieger, took off in the direction of Donsol and Krieger's family.

ON ICE

Sovereign Headquarters
Washington, DC

Sharon didn't send Klay into the field. She put him on ice. He spent his days reorganizing his office, attending conferences, reading. He labeled and filed the hundreds of documents that overwhelmed his tiny office. He wiped off his whiteboard, though some of the ink had bled in and refused to go. He opened a desk drawer and exhumed the pile of voice recorders that had accumulated over the years. They were nearly all Olympus brand, little black or silver jobs that ran on two AAA batteries. At fifty bucks, it was easier to buy another one than to upload, label, and file what was on them. He smiled as he spilled two dozen recorders across his desk.

It had started as a grade school English project, going out with a cassette recorder the size of a schoolbook and recording family and neighbors' oral histories. Klay began recording people the way a photographer might snap shots of strangers. He loved the rhythm of people communicating across geographic or ethnic space, between social classes, over generations of time. Funerals were a time of gathering. A dead person's diaspora returned. He met mourners from Paris, Sicily, Nigeria, Staten Island. He took snapshots of their voices and studied them. He was writing short stories then. Ear was good, but not enough. To get sound onto the page, you had to be perfect.

He continued the practice as a journalist, well aware that secretly recording a subject carried risks, not admitting he had recordings unless Legal pushed back on something in one of his stories. In those cases he might say, "You know, my phone might have been on during that exchange," or some other excuse that didn't make sense, but would nevertheless be accepted if his material was juicy enough, everyone compromising just enough to go to print.

Klay picked up recorders at random and began listening. He was surprised how much he'd forgotten. He couldn't recall many of the people he'd taped, or even be sure of the country where some of the recordings had been made. After a week he looked at the list of audio files he had created—manager, voodoo market, Togo, 2004; dry goods and dog smuggler, Mongolia, 1999; colonel, AU-RTF, Central African Republic, 2014—and realized none was likely to be of any use to him in the future.

He looked at the pile of Olympus recorders he had yet to upload and decided his memories, whatever they might be, weren't that important, either. He snapped a few in half and tossed them into his trash, felt bad about it, plugged in his headphones, and listened some more.

Suddenly Bernard's laughter filled his headphones. They were hiking, Klay realized. He heard the crunch of gravel, the swing of his pack, his breathing. On the recorder, he asked Bernard whether he thought the land was a living thing. "You don't understand at all," Bernard replied. He heard the scratch of rocks clicking together, his own rough voice saying, "It's a long way down, brother." He remembered that moment. Bernard had done a back flip off the cliff edge into a river three stories below. On the tape, Bernard called up to him inaudibly. Klay repeated his words for the recording: "Come. Celebrate the land." The recording ended. Klay hadn't jumped.

He removed his headphones and texted Bernard's mother, asking about Goodson. Goodson had been roughed up, she responded, but he was safe. The Green Guardians had been disbanded. It was just Perseus Group rangers now, she wrote, "flying drones, rousting up villagers."

He got more emails reminding him to set up his Twitter account. He was headed to the gym one afternoon when a rep from Development dropped by and reminded him about the fundraiser that night. She handed him a card with the names of three couples printed on it. "Chat with them. Make them feel welcome. Charlie Peterson is oil. The Merricks, too. Root is that Root. They've all been to Africa. They'll love talking to you . . ."

It went on like that.

Meanwhile, each time he asked Porfle for a new assignment, Porfle would shrug and say he hadn't heard anything. Klay tried to be patient, to follow PGM's new procedures, but boredom and frustration were closing in on him. He did not do well bored. For the first time since he'd joined **The Sovereign,** he wondered if it might be time to move on.

One afternoon, desperate to get out, he decided to visit an animal shelter. His days "on the beach," which is what the Perseus Group people called their unassigned hours, had him thinking he might get a dog. He would just be looking, he reminded himself as he hailed a cab. If he were actually going to get a dog, he wanted a Chesapeake Bay retriever.

Still, it wouldn't hurt to look at the strays. Just

the idea of getting a dog made him feel a little better. The taxi pulled away from the curb and a text appeared on his phone.

"Confession at 11," it said.

It had been three months since he'd heard from Eady.

THE CONFESSION CLUB

Washington, DC

Two blocks from the White House there is a large brick townhouse with black shutters, a mansard roof of chipped slate, and a green front door so dark it might be mistaken for black. To the building's left is a branch office of the General Services Administration, and on its right an office building owned by PEPCO, the electric utility. Countless government employees trudge past the townhouse each day, though few, if asked, could pick it out of a lineup. For more than 130 years, the Confession Club has hidden in plain sight. The tall, ground-floor windows, originally sized to let a dead body out without having to remove the front door, are always curtained. There is no number on the building to confirm its address. The club's sole intercourse with the outside world is a marble front step, the color of an old tooth, worn in the center so that a doorman must sweep a puddle from the step after each rain.

Klay felt uncomfortable in his jacket and tie, but he was pleased with what was about to take place. In a few minutes, in a quiet room upstairs, Eady would tell him their Agency relationship was over. He was more than ready to hear it. And if that was not why Eady had invited him tonight, then he had something to tell Eady. He was quitting. And not just the CIA. **The Sovereign,** too.

He knew what Terry Krieger was. He had witnessed his work up close, in Congo. It had been the dry season, maybe eight years ago—he could not be sure of the year, only the season and the victims. Klay had been on assignment, doing a story on the environmental impacts of minerals mining. Bernard was his fixer. They stayed in Kisie, a remote mining town in North Kivu. A South African mining company owned the rights to the area's tin ore.

Perseus Group had a training camp nearby. The camp was supposed to be training Congo's military to fight the rebel groups that popped up around every mine, taxing commerce in and out. In reality, Perseus Group was security for the mines. He and Bernard had been in Kisie two days when rebels attacked, butchering their way through the town before seizing control of the country's most profitable tin and cobalt operations. More than three hundred people—men, women, children—were slaughtered. Klay got a good look at the rebels' weapons. They were PG-15s, Perseus Group's version of the AR-15.

Six weeks later, Krieger's people rode in on big South African armored personnel carriers called Mambas, firing PK machine guns, and wiped the rebels out. Two hundred more people died. As ayment, Perseus Group took a half share in Kisie's mining operations, which Klay was sure had been Krieger's strategy from the beginning. No one reported either of the massacres. He had not reported them. Kisie was just another African insurgency put down. Perseus Group was outside of scope. And now he worked for the man.

Ever since Krieger's hologram event, Klay's nightmares had become more frequent and more intense. He had been reliving the accident in Indonesia on and off for more than a decade. Bernard's murder had twisted itself into that nightmare. And both of these deaths were threads woven into the formative tragedy in his life, which had shaped him and his dreams since he was a child. A child who had witnessed his mother's murder.

No. He would not work for Terry Krieger. His work for the CIA was over, too.

He pressed the small black doorbell.

By the time he left this building, he'd be free to press the reset button on his life. What that meant, he didn't yet know. He could always become an embalmer, lay people out in a box again instead of on the page. He could write obits—charming little tales about men and women who'd led surprising, underappreciated lives. Buy a house "down the shore," as they said back home, finally get that Chesapeake Bay retriever, find a lover, lead a charming, underappreciated life of his own.

The door opened. An older black man in a waiter's uniform greeted him.

"Hello, Arno," Klay said.

"Good evening, Mr. Klay. Mr. Eady's expecting you upstairs."

The club's charter hung just inside the door.

> To foster mutual improvement, education, and enlightenment, convivial men the world over find pleasure and recreation in association with others like minded to relieve the spirit of what some call the monotony of domestic life and the routine and toil of business. The Club provides its members with a place to confess what they would not share with wives or family . . .

"No women then," Klay said, reading it on his first visit to Eady's club.

"They say Pamela Harriman made herself an exception, but no," Eady said. "No women." The lower hall and stairwell were lined with portraits of the club's past members. Eady pointed some out as they walked. "Theodore, not Franklin," he said of the Roosevelts. "The man himself," introduced Major General William J. Donovan. Brown Brothers Harriman, the Goldman Sachs of its day, was well represented over the years. "Some of the Wise Men," Eady continued, indicating Harriman, Acheson, Kennan, Bohlen, and John J. McCloy—"another Philadelphia man and a friend." Eady winked. "Ford—no, by the way," he said of Nixon.

"A lot of old white men," Klay said.

"That's true," Eady said, "but we're changing. That's all I can say. I can't talk about living members."

Klay scanned the gallery. The portraits were not only all white men, he realized, they were all dead white men.

On his next visit Klay arrived early, so Arno Tyne had directed him upstairs to wait. As he climbed the stairs, he heard the local NPR station blaring Bill Clinton's scratchy drawl. Upon reaching the second floor he was surprised to find the ex-president sitting forward in a wing-back chair, that big red nose, puffy white hair, and confident smile working cheerily on a dour William Rehnquist. Clinton was taller than he'd expected; Rehnquist was frailer. "If you like those Hush Puppies," Clinton was saying, patting the chief justice's bony forearm, "the chukkas with arch support will completely change your life."

The second floor was dark and empty tonight, so Klay continued up the stairs to the top floor. He heard voices as he climbed and recognized the cadence of Eady's low murmur set against loud, unfamiliar bursts. Klay hesitated. He had thought he'd have Eady to himself tonight. He stepped quietly, and arrived at the doorway without drawing attention.

Eady sat in an oxblood leather wingback, on the opposite side of the room, beneath a small painting. He held a pipe in one hand, and had one leg crossed over the other. He was talking to a stranger who looked to be about Eady's age, but instead of sporting thick white hair like Eady, the man's head was bald and dotted with liver spots. The man wore a brown suit, white dress shirt, and cowboy boots. He had a big, hard gut that looked like it could take a punch. Something about the man told Klay it had.

Still unobserved, Klay tried and failed to get a bead on the men's relationship. Eady wore his enigmatic smile, and there was something slightly off in his companion's loud laugh. The stranger grabbed a fistful of mixed nuts from a dish on a table between them. He raised a hand in the air and called out, "Alfred!"

Which is when they noticed Klay.

"Well, here he is," the stranger said, dusting salt from his hands.

Klay shook Eady's hand, reflexively making his mortician's assessment. It was something that happened, growing up in a funeral home, working as a door greeter. Most people die of old age, and their mourners tend to be elderly also. Shake enough elderly hands and you develop an ability to intuit a person's state of health. The grip and musculature of a handshake could give you an idea of how many years a person had left.

Klay felt a reasonable hump of muscle between Eady's thumb and index finger, and solid musculature among his metacarpals. The creeping in the skin on the back of Eady's hand was normal, too. Things must have been going well with his treatments, Klay thought. Or maybe it was still early. He'd never asked Eady what form of cancer he had or its stage. If he didn't hear the details tonight, he promised himself he would call Ruth later in the week.

The stranger's grip, by contrast, was firm and calloused, the hand of someone who did more than he appeared to do.

"Have a seat, son," the stranger said. Klay didn't like it. He didn't like sitting with his back to the room, and he didn't like this stranger. Most unsettling of all, he didn't know why. His father used to have a saying for people who rubbed him the wrong way, "I don't like that guy. I got to get to know him better." Klay sat down.

"Sir?" Arno said to Klay.

"Wonder what he'll have," the stranger said.

"Sorry," Klay said. "Who are you?"

The man raised a glass to his lips, chuckling, and sipped his drink.

Eady put a hand on Klay's sleeve. "We'll get to that in a minute, Tom." He arched an eyebrow. Arno was waiting.

"I'll have a bourbon."

"Vance and I are sampling a fine Japanese single malt," the stranger said.

"Bourbon works for me," Klay said. "Booker's if you have it."

The stranger looked at Klay over the rim of his glass. "This Yamazaki's worth twice that Kentucky mash, and I'm footing the bill."

"Double then," Klay said.

Arno nodded.

Klay waited.

It was nearly midnight. They were the club's only guests. The room's silence was broken only by the sound of scratching clocks. There were clocks throughout the club, on walls, on top of tables and shelves. More than one corner held a grandfather clock. Eady's fingers strummed the armrest of his leather wingback chair. The stranger leaned forward, took two olives from a dish, and popped them into his mouth. Wedding ring, single-button cuffs, Bulova watch. He fished the pits from his mouth and added them to a small pile on a cocktail napkin. Agency, Klay concluded.

"Ah! Here we are," the stranger said, accepting two scotches and Klay's bourbon from a silver tray Arno held.

"Thank you, Arno," Eady said. "We'll be about an hour."

The guest shook his head. "Less," he said, and tossed a cocktail stick onto Arno's tray.

Less? Nothing took less to say than what Klay wanted to hear: "It's over." "We're done." Klay looked the man over. Maybe he should get to know this guy better after all.

Arno scooped up the olive pits with a napkin. "Yes, Mr. Eady."

"You got any real food, Arno?" the stranger said. "Some wings or something?"

Eady closed his eyes and pursed his lips in both apology and permission for Arno to exit.

"Okay, okay," the man said. "No food then."

"So," Eady began.

The man's left hand shot up, and Eady fell silent. The man held it in the air and together they listened to the hiss of Arno's hand descending the stair rail. When the hiss stopped and what sounded like the bottom step creaked, the stranger lowered his hand, picked up his drink, and offered a toast. "Name is Will Barrow. Joke if you like. Cheers!"

Klay sat without touching his drink.

"What's the matter?" Barrow said, raising an eyebrow.

"I like to know what I'm toasting," Klay said.

"Not what I hear."

"I'm sorry?"

"From what I understand you'll drink to your breakfast."

"What does that mean?"

"It means you don't always meet your deadline because a story's gone cold. It means I can smell it on your breath, Mr. Klay, and you haven't had your first sip. It makes you vulnerable. Same way sending money to a family of stick-poor Indonesians makes you vulnerable."

Klay resisted the urge to turn to Eady. His payments to Adri's family had been the secret within his secret. Eady had shared it with this man.

"Logistics, Tom," Eady interjected. "Necessary. Now that I'm gone, I wanted you to meet Mr. Barrow. Mr. Barrow is—"

"I know who he is."

"Maybe," Barrow said. "Maybe not. Are you going to drink that?"

Klay looked at the brown liquid in his glass. "A drink's about the company."

"The company," Barrow echoed. He leaned

back, pulled an ankle onto his knee, then laced his fingers behind his head, and stared at Klay.

"Tom," Eady said. "I'd have preferred to introduce this proposal to you myself, one-on-one, the way we've always communicated. But . . . well . . . my situation has forced me to accelerate things. Sitting behind a camera most of my life made me a patient man. Too patient it turns out. I'm having to learn to change that. What I have to say is something I hope you will accept and understand and, whatever your decision, that you will keep it confidential. Among us. Here."

Eady was babbling. Eady didn't babble.

Klay studied the painting above Eady's chair. It was a Monet, it turned out. The simple painting consisted of a large black rock shrouded in mist. What made it powerful was Monet's decision to emphasize the mist, not the rock. The curtain, not the stage.

"I won't beat around the bush, Tom. **The Sovereign** has a long-standing, symbiotic relationship with the Agency because of the work we do as—"

"For Chrissake." Barrow turned to Klay. "It's simple. With Vance out, we're out."

"I understand," Klay said.

"No," Barrow said. "You don't."

"I'm fine with it," Klay said.

"We're not. We don't care to be out."

"We can't, Tom. Not now," Eady agreed. "I've

been in place most of my career. So long I don't know which came first. I'm proud of my service, and I want—"

"Not interested," Klay said. "It would be inappropriate for me, for the work, to continue given this material change in circumstance, without you in place, Vance."

Jesus, Klay thought. It came out sounding like Luca Brasi's wedding speech.

"Tom—"

Barrow laughed. "Would it be inappropriate? Because I would hate to be goddamn inappropriate when it comes to the work." Barrow raised his fingers and put air quotes around the word "work."

"Excuse me?"

Barrow tossed another handful of nuts into his mouth.

Eady said, "Tom, we have a mission for you. It's more than you've done for us in the past. You'd be in a complicated and potentially—"

"Vance," Barrow interrupted, chewing, "why don't you and I go around on this again. I'm not sold on this horse."

"We are out of time, Will. I said I'll handle this."

"And I said we have another way into it," Barrow challenged.

"We have no one positioned the way Tom is, and you know it."

"You want to go on the record with him, then?" Barrow asked.

Eady looked at Klay. "I do."

"With this man here?"

"He is our best chance. Tom, this is about Ras Botha. A chance to take down Botha for good."

Klay sat back in his chair and waited.

"A South African prosecutor has gotten her hands on a cache of documents which," Eady explained, "could unseat South Africa's president. We want the prosecutor to succeed."

Klay laughed. "You want to prosecute Gabriel Ncube?"

"We do," Eady said.

"I thought Ncube was your lackey?"

"Predictability is what we value," Barrow said, taking over. "Gabriel Ncube has grown less so."

"You want regime change?" Klay said.

"We support the constitution of our long-standing ally," Barrow replied.

"By unseating its democratically elected president?"

"Tom—" Eady interrupted.

"Vance, nobody fucking likes Ncube. He's destroyed the country and the ANC. But what's this got to do with Botha?"

"Botha's been arrested again. Rhino horn this time. The same prosecutor has both cases—Ncube and Botha. It's too much for anyone to handle, and too important to us. We need your help."

Klay laughed. "You want to take Botha and Ncube down using South Africa's courts? Are you out of your minds? The South African judicial system is a joke. Ncube owns it," Klay said. "You take a solid case to one of their prosecutors, and chances are he'll sell it to the defendant. Hell, you can hire a prosecutor to bring charges if you want. To take down the president of South Africa, you don't need a prosecutor, you need a superhe—" Klay felt his pulse accelerate. He sat up and narrowed his eyes. "Who's the prosecutor?"

Eady smiled. "Hungry Khoza."

"Hungry . . ." Klay let out a breath. "Hungry is going after Ncube?"

"She's been appointed special prosecutor in the Office of Public Protector," Eady said. "She is therefore—"

"—constitutionally protected," Klay said.

"Yes. Fully insulated from politics. Ncube can't stop her. And as you well know, the NPA can't corrupt her. If she's got the goods, she's untouchable. But she's also got Botha's case. Now that she's got him, she can't let go of him. Her task force is under tremendous international pressure to prosecute Botha. You haven't heard of it?"

Klay shook his head. His mind raced, appreciating the significance of Hungry's appointment.

Constitutionally protected or not, if she was prosecuting the president of South Africa, she was in very real danger.

"Ncube is using Botha's case to delay Hungry," Eady said. "He's demanding, 'as a South African rhinoceros lover,' that she prosecute Botha fully and immediately."

The old man patted Klay's knee. "Help her, Tom. Behind the scenes. Free her up to pursue Ncube full bore." Eady's blue eyes twinkled ever so slightly. "Embed with her."

Klay glanced at Eady sharply. Just because he was thinking of that possibility didn't mean Eady could. Barrow remained silent. Barrow knew of his relationship with Hungry, of course. They wouldn't be bringing this to him otherwise.

Eady shrugged. "Your goals, ultimately, will be consistent."

Klay's eyes returned to the Monet. The dark rock in the painting was shaped like a beckoning finger.

"Botha . . ." Klay said, considering Eady's proposal.

"This is a real chance to bring him down, Tom. Consider it my last act as your handler." Eady's smile closed. "A gift."

Klay looked hard, holding Eady's eyes, seeing before him the mist and the rock. "Cache of secret documents," he echoed skeptically. He turned to Barrow. "Any chance it was the

Agency that happened to leak these secret files to Hungry?"

Barrow crossed his arms. "In a perfect world, can't say I wouldn't mind. But no, sir. I expect if we had those files ourselves, we wouldn't need you. She got them on her own."

"We don't know what she has, Tom," Eady said, shifting in his chair and folding his hands. "That's your second objective. We need to know."

"I won't undermine Hungry."

"Wouldn't ask you to," Eady said.

They knew they had him at Botha. But he sensed something else. These two old spies breathing out their pale fog were obscuring something.

"And Sharon?" he asked. "I don't work for you anymore, remember?"

"I'll have a quiet word," Eady said.

"She's had me on ice."

"Of course she has. You were mine. She wants hers. I will take care of it."

A harpoon hung lengthwise above the room's fireplace. The plaque beneath it read, "Whale iron carried on board the **Essex,** 1820."

Man hunting whales—that's what Eady and Barrow were counting on.

"I have a condition," Klay said.

"See a doctor," Barrow grumbled.

"My condition is, I do this job and I'm out."

Files destroyed, he continued. No record of his work with or for the CIA. Tabula rasa.

Eady turned to Barrow, who shrugged, leaving it to Klay to decide who to trust and what to hope for.

Klay had a rule about trust and hope. He trusted people to act in their self-interest. It was his responsibility to figure out what that was, not theirs to tell him the truth. Hope did not figure into it because hope was not certainty. Hope was certainty's flirtatious cousin. Yet here he was, sitting with two men trained to lie, watching one of them study his hand and the other one shrug his shoulders, hoping he could trust them.

Eady started to wrap up their powwow. "You'll go in as a knock, of course." NOC—nonofficial cover—the Agency's standard disclaimer. "But **The Sovereign** will support you. As always."

Klay laughed. "Terry Krieger's **The Sovereign** now, Vance. Are you speaking for him?"

Eady cleared his throat. "I was assured PGM will continue my policy of protecting any journalist in the field regardless of circumstance." Eady paused. "Nevertheless, let's not fuck it up."

TWO-MAN TEAM

Arlington, Virginia

Klay stood in the kitchen of Tenchant's home. A black SUV was waiting outside. He rinsed his coffee mug and set it in the sink. Eady had not only cleared the assignment with Sharon; he'd gotten Tenchant approved, too. Tenchant had often asked to work with him in the field, but Klay had always found a way out. He preferred to work alone. But Eady was right. This trip was records-based, and he could use Tenchant's computer skills. The man had a gift.

Maggie Tenchant straightened the front of her husband's new Patagonia windbreaker. "You take care of him."

"I will," Klay said, amused.

The tags from Tenchant's jacket had been

lying beside the sink in the powder room. It was Andes blue, made of ripstop nylon with a waterproof finish, half-elastic cuffs, and a draw-cord hem. The hood adjusted with one pull and was guaranteed not to block the wearer's peripheral vision. The whole thing was capable of folding into its own breast pocket. All the protections, Klay thought, as he washed his hands.

He'd told Tenchant they needed to be inconspicuous in the field—none of his usual biker jewelry, no motorcycle boots—and he guessed the jacket was his effort to comply. Tenchant's hair was washed, his boots were good for hiking, and his silver skull ring was gone, leaving only a black wedding band and a runner's wristwatch. Klay was surprised Tenchant had gotten through personnel. Beyond his clothing, Tenchant's sinewy arms were tattooed shoulder to wrist, each sleeve featuring a Japanese Nio, a wrath-filled, muscular guardian of the Buddha. Tenchant's guardians were Agyo and Ungyo, protectors of Todai-ji temple.

"I mean it, Tom," Maggie continued. "I've been reading about the white farm murders. Women set on fire, children decapitated—"

"Mags—" Tenchant said.

"Don't let him do anything stupid."

Tenchant cocked his head and looked at Klay as if stupid was what he liked to do.

"We're headed out on a paper trail, Maggie,

not a jungle trail," Klay said. "Besides, I thought our man here was taking karate."

Tenchant took a piece of cinnamon raisin bagel with cream cheese from his wife's plate and popped it into his mouth.

"Taking it?" Maggie said. "He's a black belt!"

Klay was surprised. He'd assumed Tenchant was just a beginner. A blue belt, maybe.

Tenchant shrugged.

"Well, maybe it will be Tenchant protecting me," Klay said.

"It's a good sign," Maggie said. "Isn't it? Sending him with you. They'll keep him on, don't you think?"

"She's worried about the acquisition," Tenchant explained. He picked up a napkin and wiped cream cheese off his fingertips. "Rumor is big layoffs are coming."

"It's a good sign, Mags," Klay said.

Outside, their driver honked his horn. Tenchant placed a hand on his wife's belly. "I'll be back soon, little fella."

"You text me every day," Maggie said.

"I'll text you every day," Tenchant said.

They kissed goodbye.

"Not one bent hair," she said, smoothing her husband's unruly mop. Tenchant rolled his suitcase toward the door.

Klay put out his hand to say goodbye. Maggie took it and gave Klay a peck on the cheek. "I mean it, Tom," she whispered. "Please be careful. For my family."

Klay picked up his duffel bag. "I'll have him back in ten days. Promise."

I wonder if you could help us," Klay said to the woman at Delta's business-class ticket counter. She was glancing from her screen to Klay's passport, clicking computer keys. Klay had used his miles to upgrade to business. Tenchant was in economy.

"My friend has never flown overseas before," Klay said and began making a case for upgrading Tenchant. Midway through he realized how weak his arguments sounded. "He is an organ donor." Klay smiled weakly.

She glanced at Tenchant in his new Patagonia jacket and returned Klay's passport. "I'm sorry," she said, in that way.

"It's okay," Tenchant said, handing her his passport. He pushed up his sleeves, flashing his Japanese tattoos, and placed his hand on Klay's shoulder. "We're taking my father to the impotency clinic in Johannesburg," he said. "He doesn't really like to talk about it." He turned to Klay, "It's okay, Dad."

She glanced at her screen and then back at Tenchant. The corners of her mouth quivered.

Smiling, she clicked more keys and handed over their boarding passes.

"Thank you," Klay said.

"Don't thank me. He has almost as many miles as you." She winked at Tenchant. "You should get to know your son better."

Klay turned to him, surprised. Tenchant shrugged. "Visiting Maggie's mom."

Would you care for champagne, sparkling water, juice?" their flight attendant asked.

"I'll have a bourbon manhattan on the rocks," Tenchant said.

Klay had orange juice. Ever since Jakarta he took care where and when he drank. At home. Eady's office. The Gray Pigeon. Places where accidents didn't happen.

With regard to their assignment, Klay had shared only what Tenchant needed to know: They were embedding with a criminal investigation underway in South Africa. The goal was to tell the story from the inside. The prosecutor's name was Hungry Khoza. "An old friend," Klay said. "Her target is Ras Botha."

"An old enemy," Tenchant said.

"Yes."

"Can she get him on the Kenya murders?"

"Maybe," Klay said, and closed his eyes.

Tenchant was on his third manhattan when Klay felt a tug on his sleeve.

"I never said it, but sorry for that grapefruit thing."

"What grapefruit thing?" Klay said.

"Tanzania."

"The albino story?" Klay shook his head. "Wasn't your fault. That's just the editing process, Porfle-style," he added.

"As it turns out, I do bear some responsibility."

"It happens," Klay said, trying to brush Tenchant off.

"How'd it start, anyway?" Tenchant asked.

"What?"

"The grapefruit thing."

"Forget it," Klay said. Klay caught a flash of disappointment in Tenchant's eyes, and it occurred to him how little he knew his researcher. They rarely interacted socially, not even for lunch. Tenchant ate with the copy editors and fact checkers. Klay ate at this desk. He didn't know about Tenchant's martial arts. Today was the first time he'd been in his home. It had taken years before he and Snaps had found their groove in the field, and Snaps had been an experienced field photographer. Tenchant was a computer nerd.

"Excuse me?" Klay said to the flight attendant. "Another round for us? Bourbon for me. A phone call," he said, turning back to Tenchant. "Snaps had taken those incredible pics. Remember?"

"The albino with her hand cut off."

"That one. The dug-up graves. The muti rituals. I called to give Porfle an update, just the usual, I'm about to hang up when this buffalo walks by. Huge animal, balls swinging around his knees. I say, 'Holy shit, those are some big fucking balls.' I wasn't talking to Porfle. I was talking to myself.

" 'Explain,' Porfle says. Explain what? Just some bull the family keeps. Balls the size of grapefruit blowing in the wind. Right?"

"Right," Tenchant said.

"So, I'm hanging up and Porfle says, 'Don't forget to give me the bull balls.'

"I ask what does he mean. He says, '**The Sufferin'** needs to grow some of its own.' Says he wants the 'balls blowing in the wind,' just like I said it. Because it's Porfle, I ask him directly, 'You want the whole balls as big as grapefruits . . . in the story?' He starts shouting he's the goddamned editor, leave it to Tweedledee to take it out. 'We'll test their mettle,' he's yelling. You know how he is."

Tenchant sipped his drink. "Uh-huh."

"So, that's what I did. I wrote it up with balls as big as grapefruit blowing in the wind. It was completely irrelevant to the story. When he got my first draft, he said it's about time the bloody **Sovereign** wrote with brio." Klay shook his head.

"He hates you," Tenchant said.

"No, he doesn't."

Tenchant shrugged.

"Hates?" Klay asked. "Really?"

"What did you think?"

"I don't know. I figured he was a little hostile. He sits at a desk and I run around the world. I'm no fan of his, but he hates me?"

"Says you're an arrogant prick."

"Does he?" Klay said, narrowing his eyes. "Okay. Well, then, I'm glad we had this little chat."

"Aw, come on. Tell me the rest. I'm the one that ends up paying for this, you know."

Klay took a drink. "All right. So the first draft comes back. Porfle writes 'balls size of grapefruit blowing in wind' would be better as 'testicles like grapefruit blowing in the wind.' I say okay. Then I get another email marked urgent. 'Urgent! Tom, worried about testicles in wind. Please respond ASAP!' I write him back. He wants to know was there actually a wind on that day and was it strong enough to move such large balls? Or, 'more likely, were they not in fact swinging because of the bull's gait? Possibly there was only a breeze,' he writes me. 'So, not blowing.'

"I turn in my draft, he writes in the margin, 'Tom, there are several varieties of grapefruit and we don't know which one you're referring to.' He asks me to be more specific, 'as with navel oranges, for example.'"

"Yeah," Tenchant said. "We'd just done that evolution-of-citrus story. I asked him if he wanted a specific variety for your story. I didn't know it would become a thing. I just—"

"So, I write back, 'Readers know grapefruits vary in size. The point is they were unusually large fucking balls, which "grapefruit" connotes.' I say navel oranges might be familiar to readers, but the balls on the bull I saw were definitely larger than navel oranges, which is why I called them grapefruits."

"That's probably when he called me to his office," Tenchant said. "Er, cubicle now."

"Cubicle?"

"Sharon's moving the magazine staff into cubicles."

"That's going to suck for you," Klay said.

"You, too. Don't you read your emails?"

"Fuuuck." Klay sighed. For a moment he'd forgotten this was his last assignment. He wasn't going back to the magazine. **You're quitting, remember?**

Tenchant said, "So, I walk into Porfle's office, and he's on the phone. He points at your manuscript with his pencil. 'Check into this,' he mouths to me."

"Check into grapefruit?"

"Yeah," Tenchant said. "So, I start researching grapefruit. It was pretty interesting. The American grapefruit started out in Malaysia. Spanish missionaries brought pomelos over here, and grapefruits grew out of that. The originals were all white. Then one day this Texas farmer finds a red one. It's sweeter than the white ones. Americans go crazy for them. All of a sudden, grapefruit farmers start making money—this is the Great Depression. They patent a version and call it Ruby Red. It's sweet and dark red. They make it the Texas state fruit."

"Fascinating." Klay sighed.

"Yeah. I thought so. Then one year there's a huge storm and all the Ruby Reds fade to pink. Taste just as good, but the growers have this big ad campaign going about how delicious an apple-red grapefruit is, and now they're gone . . ."

Klay told himself to stay engaged in Tenchant's story. Teamwork, he reminded himself, might be important on this trip.

"So, this scientist in Texas named Henks—or Hacks? He packs up three thousand grapefruit buds, flies them to the Brookhaven nuclear lab on Long Island, stuffs the branches into a nuclear reactor, and fucking nukes them with thermal neutrons."

"Is that true?"

Tenchant laughed. "He grafts irradiated buds onto healthy rootstock, comes up with something five times redder than the Ruby Red. You know what they call it?"

"No."

"Me, neither. I mean, I forget what it was. I never fucking wanted to know any of this. But that's what I get paid for: to figure out what variety of grapefruit could possibly swing between a bull's—Rio Reds! That's what they called them. It goes on and on for weeks like this with Porfle trying to decide which reference to use. Maggie and I stop eating grapefruit. I can't stand looking at them."

"You were Porfled," Klay said.

"I was Porfled!"

Klay was pleased. He and Tenchant were laughing together. His little bonding mission had been a success. It was the most basic spycraft: nothing brings people together better than a common adversary.

"So, in the end, the sentence Porfle came up with—and God help me—I agreed to it—was—"

"Wait," Tenchant said. "Wait! I remember it verbatim because it came back to me to fact-check. The final sentence was 'A bovine, probably of the zebu or Sanga variety, with prominent male features walked in front of me.'"

"Which . . ." Klay prodded.

"Tweedledee excised."

"Circumcised."

"Castrated."

"So that's the grapefruit story," Klay said. After a moment, he leaned forward. "So, Tench, one tip I can offer before we get into this is, no matter what the data looks like, drill down to find individuals. If you start to get distracted, keep in mind there's always a who. If you get off track, or the information seems overwhelming, come back to that, okay?"

" 'There's always a who'?" Tenchant echoed.

"Yeah. You know, I find it helps me."

"Okay. Thanks, Tom. Yeah. I appreciate it."

"Any questions?"

"Just one."

"Shoot," Klay said.

Tenchant sat up. "It's serious, though, okay?"

"Sure, Tenchant. Okay."

"If you add it all up on that story, from the very beginning, I mean, what would you estimate is the total time you spent with your balls in Porfle's hands?"

REUNION

Pretoria, South Africa

K lay raised his glass, drinking in Hungry's deep-set brown eyes. "To catching up on four lost years."

"Five," she corrected, not lifting her glass from the tablecloth.

"Ah," he said. "And to your new appointment. Congratulations."

She smiled. "Thank you."

Their eyes remained locked as they touched glasses. Hungry had come to the restaurant from her office. She wore a red jacket over a black dress and the trademark pearls her grandmother had given her. "The Crocodile in Pearls," the newspapers called her. She wore her hair natural now.

It had been straight when they met. Time had added a few more lines at the corners of her eyes, responsibility weighing on her in a way that made her even sexier somehow. Another layer he'd like to take off, he found himself thinking.

"Now that you've surprised me, what is it that brings you to South Africa?"

"You." Klay smiled. "I heard you were short on staff."

"Always." She nodded. "But I know you, re-member? You're here for Botha. Am I right?"

"I am."

"I read about what happened in Kenya. I was very sorry about Bernard. I texted you, but no response. Not a surprise, really . . ."

"I'm sorry, Hungry. It was a bad time."

"Was he behind it—Botha?"

"That's what I want to find out. Do you have enough to hold him?"

"Oh, he threatened me in the courthouse, in front of the judge. So, we're holding him without bail. We can do that for years, frankly. But no, there is not a lot to the case, legally. Politically, it is a different matter . . ."

"I heard."

She sighed and tapped a crouton with her salad fork. "As usual, we've had more attention from the West over a handful of rhino horn than we have for the people here, the children . . ." Her voice trailed off.

He nodded. "You're investigating Ncube."

She glanced to her left, where two men at a table across the restaurant were staring at her, pretending to chew. "It is not a secret."

Klay had noticed diners looking in her direction and whispering since she'd walked in.

"I can help you with Botha," he said, taking a bite of his roll. "It doesn't have to be just a magazine assignment. I know him. I could take him off your plate. I've got staff with me."

Hungry studied him. " 'Off my plate'?"

Klay shrugged. "Off your hands. Act as your investigator—unofficially."

Hungry chuckled and shook her head. "Always ready to cut a corner," she said disapprovingly.

"Bernard was my friend."

Hungry sighed. "It's unethical, Tom. Ordinarily, I'd say impossible. But I have a chance to do something important for this country. It requires all of my attention. Botha's not officially my mandate. He's an accident of fate, I suppose. I saw the case and I knew it would be problematic, but I took it anyway. Let me think about this."

"Define 'this,' " he said, and smiled.

She smiled, too. It was an old joke between them. Back when they were dating he used to ask her, "Can we make this work?"

"Define 'this,' " she'd reply.

But he never could. And the years had passed.

Still, one thing had always worked between them.

He signaled for the check.

Standing in a hotel room, Klay let his eyes linger on her face, momentarily overwhelmed as he considered this singular, brilliant woman, the one he felt he was meant to share his life with. He pulled her towards him more roughly than he intended, but she pressed her mouth just as fiercely on his. He unzipped her dress, felling himself rise as she undid his belt. She shrugged off her dress. He kicked off his shoes and stripped off his shirt. In a single motion she undid her bra and stepped into him, pressing her full breasts hard against his bare chest.

He cupped her ass intending to lift her, but she spun away from him, stood beside the bed and faced him, hands on her thighs, legs apart, challenging him with her eyes to remember, watching him as he did. He came to her then, put his mouth to her breasts, then dropped to his knees and pressed his face into her, drawing her thong down, taking in the smell of her, the taste of her. He lifted her and she wrapped her legs around him. The room dissolved and the past returned, and locked together, they fought and fucked and loved. And then it was over and they were themselves again, looking up a ceiling fan making its rounds, sweat cooling their damp skin.

He used to tell himself that being dishonest about the CIA was the best thing he could do for their relationship. If he was honest in every other way, then eventually, when he did share his truth with her, they could weather what came next. **This time,** he told himself each time they kissed hello. **Next time,** he vowed each time they said goodbye.

Now he'd crossed a line. Hungry was his mission. Yes, he was after Botha, but everything else was deception. He had to manipulate Hungry into giving him her files. It was true that they were on the same side, so success for him should mean success for her, but targeting her suddenly made him feel sick.

Hungry turned to him. "Botha," she said.

"Who knew he could be a force for good?" Klay smiled.

A shadow crossed her face and she looked away.

He touched her hand. "My new editor loves your life story. She wants to send over a documentary film team once I'm done. Says you're a brilliant woman."

She forced a smile. "I did go to Harvard."

"No, you didn't."

"I might have."

When she was twenty-six, she'd turned down a full scholarship to Harvard Law School to stay home and help draft Mandela's post-Apartheid constitution.

"You might have," he agreed. "But then you'd be eating black cod at Nobu with your future ex-husband instead of lying here with me sweaty and satisfied."

"Possibly." The shadow returned and she kissed him lightly. "Principles have kept my standards low."

He ran a finger down her arm. She lay back. Soon his finger retraced itself and found a more distracting path. She had fingers of her own, of course. She kissed his chest, and then slowly moved her lips to investigate what they had discovered.

Klay felt the familiar pressure, their time together always less than enough.

Hungry sat up first and pulled the sheet to her chest. "You can't embed, not officially. If anyone even suspected we'd given foreign journalists access to our files, we'd be finished. Our enemies are everywhere, Tom."

"Wait a second," he said. "When exactly did you make this decision?"

She smiled. "I'm a multitasker, remember?" She turned to him, her face serious. "You'll visit our office. Meet our people. You are journalists doing a story on Ras Botha. That's fine. You have a track record investigating him, and everyone knows **The Sovereign.** I can share things with you quietly and point you in the right direction. Anything concerning our investigation into the president, you cannot be present for, not even in the building."

"Chinese wall. Understood."

"If you want to share what you find with me, that's your decision. You're under no oblig—"

"I'd do it anonymously."

She waved away his interruption. "You're under no obligation," she continued. "Nothing you learn from my office goes public before his trial."

"Understood."

"You trust this person you brought with you?"

"He's good with computers. I'm taking this beyond rhino horn, Hungry. I want Botha to pay for what he did."

"Of course you do," she said. "They fired Vance?"

"Why do you say that?"

"You said you have a new editor."

"Right. Vance retired. He has cancer."

"Oh, I'm sorry, Tom. I know he's meant a lot to you over the years. He's been like a father, hasn't he?"

"Thanks. Not exactly a father. But a good man. He seems to be doing all right so far. He did most of his work here back in the day. Mandela is his hero."

"And now you have a new owner now, I read."

"We do," he said. "Perseus Group Media. You're well-informed."

"Terry Krieger has done a lot of damage in this country. Have you met him?"

"Not exactly." He told her about the hologram presentation.

"Does he know you're here?"

"I wouldn't think so. He wouldn't know any more than I've told Sharon."

"Which is?"

"The minimum: 'I'm investigating Ras Botha, a South African kingpin I believe is behind the killing of my friend, not to mention attempting to murder me.' She was salivating so much over a 'revenge piece,' she agreed. But I made clear my safety depends on total secrecy."

"She's close to Krieger?"

"I'm not sure, to be honest. She came on as an acquisition in the PR space. He's pursuing nature-based technologies, militarized conservation, but he didn't need a magazine to do that. The rumor around the office is he bought **The Sovereign** to please his daughter."

"So you promise me you're not working for him."

"For him? No." He looked at her. "What's with the third degree?"

"Two prosecutors investigating Ncube have been murdered. PGM outlets covered the stories. They were mouthpieces for Ncube."

"Jesus."

"I have to be extraordinarily careful."

"You're going to need a silver bullet, Hungry. Something that takes down Ncube on your first shot."

They lay back and watched the ceiling fan turn.

"Do you have it?" he asked. "A silver bullet?"

Hungry sighed. "I have a bullet, I'm not sure yet what it's made of."

"You want to tell me about it?"

"You shouldn't even be asking that." She rose onto an elbow and poked a finger into the scar below his shoulder. "Does this hurt?"

"Ow. No."

She smiled. "And you think it was Botha's people?"

"I do. He denies it, of course. The weird thing is he says he got me my surgeon."

"Lord, that man." She shook her head. "And he told you this how? When?"

"I bumped into him in the Philippines. Must

have been just before you arrested him. He was with his son."

"Hmm," she mused. "How would he know you needed a surgeon?"

She got up and started to dress.

"See! We're a good pair. That's a question I didn't ask."

"Well, we've got him at New Lock. You're free to ask him anything you like." She reached for her dress. "I have good investigators. Three South Africans to speak truth to power. You'll like them."

"I'm looking forward to meeting them. But I'm hoping . . . I'm hoping there's time for more us . . ."

"For us, what?" she said. When he didn't answer, she cleared her throat. "Tom, I'm not sure we'll get to be like this again," she said stepping into her shoes.

Klay was pulling on his pants. "Are you telling me something?"

"The president's got me under surveillance. And Botha's people may be watching you . . . if not already, then soon."

"We'll figure it out, Hungry. Sharon wants me close to you, which I said is a hardship."

He noticed she didn't smile.

"How long are you here?"

"I have to get Tenchant back in ten days. His wife's pregnant."

"Not long," she said.

"No," he said, facing her, "but I can come back."

She turned for the door. "We should go."

Something was bothering her. There'd been something in their lovemaking, too. Not something more. Something less.

BLOODING A KRIEGER

Kimber Conservancy, Zimbabwe

Krieger handed his daughter his binoculars and pointed toward an outcropping. The male lion lay in the shadow of a boulder. The big cat yawned, exposing impressive canines.

"He's perfect, Dad," Blaze said. She took out her iPhone and started a video.

They were hunting Kimber Conservancy, 2,496 square miles of electric-fenced, raw Zimbabwean bush, just over the border from South Africa.

"That's Cyril," Pete Zoeller said.

Blaze studied the lion another moment, then turned. "We don't name wild animals, Mr. Zoeller. Names are for people and pets."

Krieger smiled—he had taught her that.

Zoeller, the senior professional hunter on the Kimber for going on fifty years, smiled, too. He had taught Krieger. "You're right about that, miss," Zoeller said.

Blaze handed the field glasses back to her father. "I only have one dart for a lion his size."

Krieger put the glasses on the seat. "Then don't miss."

Zoeller smiled quietly. In more than three decades hunting the Kimber, Krieger had never seen Zoeller other than the way he looked right now: faded safari vest over a massive bare chest, brief shorts, boots, and a necklace bearing a single lion's tooth. He had been a bush bodybuilder all of his life, lifting tires, fuel drums, cargo chains, even curling the children of his clients, a young Terry Krieger included. "Old Pete" still had silky yellow-white hair that reached to his broad shoulders and a mustache that extended well off his square chin.

From his outfit and what appeared to be recently acquired dentures, one might mistake Zoeller for a has-been circus act. But Krieger knew better. Not so many years ago, Krieger had invited a famous Hollywood actor to Zimbabwe to hunt elephant. The guy's movies had done a great deal for the defense industry, and Krieger had gotten to know him. Zoeller found them an elephant, but the actor with the veins running down his famous biceps had ignored Zoeller's whispered advice to wait. He'd fired too soon and too high, and the enraged bull elephant, already in musth, had charged.

Zoeller stepped in front of the actor and was able to get off a shot from his double, but the elephant was in a hormonal fury, too fast for a second shot, and Zoeller had taken the animal's charge fully in the chest. The impact launched him skyward, his body sailing like a blond rag doll up and over a huge termite mound. Fortunately, the elephant drove its tusk deep into the concrete-like termite mound, where it wedged, offering Krieger time to make an easy kill shot.

That night, Zoeller had appeared dressed for dinner as if nothing had happened. He had sustained six broken ribs, a fractured skull, and a crushed spleen. But that would not be discovered until a week later. The only sign that anything out of the ordinary had occurred was that Zoeller asked Krieger if he and the boys wouldn't mind a quiet dinner together, apart from the famous actor and the other guests. While the action hero toasted his conquest of a raging bull elephant, Zoeller had eaten his braised kudu and watercress salad, finished his Tusker, and had a bite of honeyed pie. Afterwards, as the hunter retired to his tent, Krieger overheard him talking to himself, quietly repeating the same line over

and over. "I always wondered would I stand," he
said. "I always wondered."

Krieger never watched the action hero's films
again.

Hunting was not for everyone, and that applied
not only to Hollywood actors. Krieger had seen
an Iraq veteran with two dozen confirmed combat kills get the shakes so bad he couldn't pull
the trigger on a zebra. But for Krieger, hunting
was a kind of walking meditation. His first wife
used to make fun of him for his after-deal hunting trips. She would leave the house while he
packed his gear, jealous that he needed a blood
sport to satisfy him, angry that hunting filled a
void she couldn't.

How to explain it? Every significant business
deal seemed to move a pendulum inside him, his
most sophisticated deals ratcheting that pendulum so far in one direction that instead of feeling satisfied, he felt supremely out of balance.
Hunting was his very soul demanding something primal, a blood conquest to match his
intellectual victory.

He'd shared his pendulum theory with China's
president during their hunting trip together on
the Kimber. Ho's broad, lineless face had broken into a knowing smile. **"Wu ji bi fan."** He'd
nodded, stepping over a fallen log. "When things

reach an extreme, they must move in their opposite direction." Ho patted Krieger's shoulder. "Yin and yang, Terry. We need a calm to have the storm."

The Seventh Fleet was in Krieger's pocket now—the entire Seventh Fleet of the United States Navy. He hadn't closed the deal yet, but his tactical success over Admiral Tighe had ratcheted the pendulum inside of him to a point that demanded release.

Blaze held up a vial of tranquilizer. She was filming the hunt for her college applications. "I need to adjust this," she said into her iPhone. "Because he's way above average male weight."

He couldn't believe she was headed to college. To him Blaze was still the little seven-year-old girl who had taught Krieger's brother what a liberal was. It had been Christmas at the Montana ranch. James, a dermatologist from San Francisco, was tucking Blaze into bed when Blaze said, "Uncle James, Daddy says I shouldn't talk politics with you because you're a liberal."

James had been amused. "What's a liberal, Blaze?"

"Daddy says if I get an A on a test and a lazy girl gets an F, a liberal will take away my A and give it to the lazy girl so she gets a C and I do, too."

That was Blaze. She had politics in her future. Or maybe even Perseus Group—if she could step up today.

"We'll need to bait him, Tots," Zoeller said, looking up at the lion. "He's breeding age and nothing's going to get him off those females."

"Who's Tots?" Blaze asked.

Krieger smiled. "It's my bush name. Ras Botha gave it to me when I was a boy. Tots because I was the baby Krieger when your great grand-father hunted here. If you do well, maybe Pete will give you a bush name."

Blaze gave a short laugh. "I think I can live without one, Tots."

While Zoeller set up a blind, Krieger sat in the passenger seat of the open Land Rover, closed his eyes, and breathed in the warm air. Behind him, Blaze was looking at her phone. Their trackers, a father and son named Njovu and Isaac, went off to find a zebra to use as bait.

Krieger could feel Ras Botha's presence on the Kimber. Even when they were boys, Botha had been something out of mythology. He'd been there for Krieger's first lion. Krieger's father and grandfather had painted Krieger's cheek with the lion's blood, but Botha had cut out the big cat's testicles and handed him one for him to swallow. Botha was a little younger than Krieger, but only in years. In the bush Botha was an ancient, a true Boer. Unfortunately, a true Boer in more ways than just hunting: Botha couldn't avoid trouble in an empty room. For as long as Krieger could remember, Botha had been on his way into, or out of, prison. "Recruiting trips, Tots," Botha called his frequent incarcerations. The man was indomitable.

It had been a criminal trial that had inspired Botha to sell him the Kimber. "Tots, my bru," Botha's phone call had begun. "Lekker investment opportunity for you . . ."

Krieger had laughed when he heard Botha's scheme. Botha proposed to sell him the Kimber, quietly and off book, in order to plead poverty to his judge. "If I'm so poor, how can I be the head of a fokken international crime syndicate? Right, Terry?"

Krieger would have paid whatever Botha asked for the property. He had been sending Botha money to support the Kimber for years. The Krieger family had hunted the Kimber for generations. The black rhino above the mantel in Krieger's Missoula ranch had been shot by his great-grandfather on the Kimber, mounted by taxidermist Carl Akeley himself. If Botha wanted to turn over the extraordinary property, Krieger was more than happy to oblige. "I'm South African," Botha had said, always overselling. "What do I want with Zimbabwe?"

Krieger brought in the House of Saud as a minority partner in the purchase. He didn't need their money; he gave them a piece of the Kimber to cement a business relationship. The Saudis loved to hunt. They built a new main lodge and upgraded the airstrip, extending it and paving it in order to handle their larger aircraft. They erected mini luxe villas in various spots across the property. They added a warehouse-sized refrigerator with butchering tables large enough to handle multiple elephant carcasses. They built facilities for caping and salting skins, installed a freezer, and added a taxidermy studio with an apartment for their preferred artist. All the usual and appropriates throughout. But Krieger forbade them from touching the lodge and huts where he stayed. The old stone-and-wood structures had been used by his grandfather. He liked the camp as it was.

Along with its animals, what Krieger treasured most about the Kimber was its guaranteed privacy. According to the Kimber's partnership agreement, there would never be more than two hunting parties on the property at a time. When Krieger was visiting, no one else was permitted. He and his family would be completely alone.

Still, he missed Botha. The plan had been to keep him around, use him as the lead PH, maybe even find him some investments, but Botha could not keep his scheming in check. By the time he got out of prison he had acquired land on either side of the Kimber, intending to turn the conservancy into a smuggling route. When

Krieger asked him what he thought he was doing, Botha said, "I opened the Kruger park fence. It's trophy-quality Big Five all the time now, Tots!" Botha pretending the expansion was to make the Kimber a better hunting property.

But Krieger could read a map, too. Through his acquisitions, Botha had created a banana-shaped corridor stretching from Zimbabwe's Marange diamond mines south to the port at Maputo.

"That's diamonds like my fist, Tots," Botha had exclaimed when Krieger confronted him. "Russians right there to take it out. Or the Chinese if I want. Dig it up on Tuesday, I'll have it under a jeweler's loupe on the weekend."

Krieger had laughed out loud. He'd caught Botha leveraging the Kimber to traffic diamonds and God knows what else, and Botha's defense had been to pitch him an even bigger deal.

Krieger sighed. When it came to business, Botha was just too African. He'd trusted Krieger to sell the Kimber back to him when the time was right. Big mistake, "Never hold another man's dick" being one of Krieger's rules. A rule he'd now have to modify for Blaze.

The trackers returned with a zebra, already parted. Isaac shouldered the zebra's legs while his father, Njovu, lugged buckets of offal. They carried the carcass to a tree at the edge of the clearing, upwind of the lion's promontory. Krieger watched them hook a chain into the zebra's Achilles and haul its flanks into the tree. The African boy looked to be about Blaze's age, but Njovu could easily have been a grandfather. The old man was having difficulty doing his job.

Krieger got out of the truck. He looked at his daughter. "Come on, Blaze," he said. "Let's help them." He started toward the tree, and she followed him.

He reached into the gut bucket and scooped a handful of intestines. "Think of it as mucking the stables for Nefertiti and Marigold."

"Yeah," Blaze said, "like I would know."

She reached into the bucket.

The old man was struggling to secure the free end of the chain. His son did it for him quickly, then turned to Blaze. "Let me," he said. He put his hands into the gut bucket with Blaze's. "You're too pretty for this. I will do it."

Blaze smiled, grateful. "It's not that bad once you get started. But you don't—"

"Boy!" Krieger barked.

Isaac jumped, nearly spilling the bucket.

But Krieger wasn't addressing Isaac. He was talking to Njovu. The old man turned, saw his son, and leapt forward. He seized Isaac by the shoulders and jerked him backwards so hard they both fell into the dirt.

"Jesus, Dad," Blaze said. "It's okay."

As if nothing had happened, Krieger reached into his bucket of zebra guts and tossed a length of intestine underhand into the tree. The gut wrapped a low branch and dangled like sausage.

Blaze glanced across the clearing. Njovu and Isaac had moved off to the blind, the father instructing the son in something, Isaac furtively looking in her direction.

Blaze hurled two fists of grassy stomach content as hard as she could into the air, but throwing grass is difficult.

"Goddamn it, Blaze!" Zebra shit covered Krieger's shirt. It was in his hair. His face. He quick-checked to see if she'd done it on purpose.

"Sorry." Blaze laughed.

"Oh!" Across the clearing Isaac stifled a shy laugh. Krieger swiveled and glared at the young man. Why didn't these people just do what they were told, he thought.

The bait tree was ready.

"Like a Christmas tree from the Apocalypse," Blaze said into her iPhone.

"So now you like baiting animals," Krieger interrupted.

Blaze turned. It took a moment to see his point. Concern flashed across her face. The whale sharks. The trouble she had caused him. "It's different here," she said. "This is for science. And we're not affecting the lions' long-term behavior."

He smiled and stepped back to let her continue.

"Like a Christmas tree from the Apocalypse," she repeated, and began to circle the tree as she narrated her video. "But it will be worth it to dart this lion. His pride has never been collared before, so we'll be able to start a completely new study group. This is very exciting," she said. "We will take blood and hair samples. Check and photograph his teeth. Address any injuries, and collar him with this." She reached into the back of their truck and withdrew a lion collar. "This is a Total Information Project collar, designed by Perseus Group." She zoomed in on the collar. "The collar gives the lion's location, which we track using the TIPP app, first designed for elephants. We can also monitor testosterone and other hormone levels, as well as brain waves," she said, and focused on a patch of silver metal inside the black collar.

After an hour waiting in the blind without success, Zoeller sent Isaac to the truck. The young man returned with a small equipment bag, a rope, and what looked like a radio. Zoeller set the box on the ground, plugged in a pair of headphones, and scanned through stations, pausing occasionally. He found the one he wanted and removed his headphones.

"We're going to use a bait box now," Blaze

whispered into her phone. "What's a bait box, Mr. Zoeller?"

"That's one right there," Zoeller said, pointing to the box.

Blaze rolled her eyes and turned her camera to her father.

"What's a bait box, Dad?"

"It's a digital representation of a prey item used to attract study animals," Krieger replied.

"Thanks, Mister Robot. We will be editing this." She spoke directly to her camera. "I've never heard a bait box in action before, so we'll all be seeing and hearing this for the first time."

Zoeller handed the bait box to Isaac, who flashed across the clearing and up the baited tree. He tied the device to a high branch. In moments he was back, his chest barely moving.

"You're very fast," Blaze said. The boy smiled.

Using a remote, Zoeller switched on the machine, and the quiet low of a calf rumbled from across the clearing. Zoeller slowly increased the volume. Sitting on a folding stool beside Blaze, Krieger listened to the recording and tried to imagine the animal. He pictured the calf with one hind leg staked to the ground standing beside its mother. He heard curiosity in the calf's calls, no doubt confused to have its neck free but one leg anchored. Then he heard the long question it asked as it realized its mother was being led away. The calf issued a higher note to alert her it was trapped and unable to follow. It cried louder, after she'd probably gone out of view, eager to help her locate it. Then the calf grew quiet.

Krieger watched Blaze.

The calf found its voice again as it saw two men approaching. Clearly the calf recognized the men. **I'm safe now,** its quiet tone said. **Why did you leave me?** Krieger knew this moment. It was the same with men and animals. Everyone wanted to believe they were home.

He heard the calf cry out in surprise, then terror, as it experienced pain beyond its understanding, pain that would not end. Krieger had been with men as they made this same journey. He'd designed and manufactured tools to help them get there in a predictable way. In the end he'd discovered it cost almost nothing to transport a man to the same place as this calf, twenty dollars at a CVS.

Krieger looked at his daughter. She was breathing rapidly. Her cheeks were flushed red. "Relax, Blaze. It's just a recording."

"What are they doing to that animal?" She was filming him.

"Turn that fucking thing off."

She blanched and stuffed the phone in her pocket just as a young male lion emerged from the bush sniffing the air, and slowly circled the clearing. More adolescent lions appeared, followed by adult females. Krieger was surprised there were so many. Finally, the big male lion arrived. Cyril did not look at the bait tree. He ignored the female lions, too. Cyril focused on the humans in the blind. Their blind was little more than a sheet of canvas and some tree branches. Zoeller flicked off his safety.

Blaze raised her dart gun.

Krieger placed his hand on the barrel and pressed it toward the ground.

"What are you doing?" Blaze whispered.

He held his rifle out to her.

"No."

"You are a Krieger, Blaze. Hard decisions are what we make. You kill that lion or I will."

That evening, Krieger relaxed in a camp chair facing the firepit, his rifle across his lap, a scotch and a cleaning kit on the ground beside him. He'd showered and changed, exchanged his khaki hunting clothes for olive green trousers and a sharply pressed white shirt. He wore his elephant-hide slippers.

His phone buzzed with a text. The text contained only two words. "Mischief Reef," it read.

Krieger ran a cleaning patch through the barrel of his father's rifle, a single shot .416 Rigby. Great white hunter Harry Selby had carried the venerated rifle into the long grass, and Krieger's father, a sometime client of Selby's, had purchased it from him. A double rifle gave you a second opportunity—good for the animal, good for the hunter—but Krieger's father believed that having only one shot intensified a man's concentration. "Puts your heart inside the bullet, Terry," his father used to say. Krieger found that to be true, and he applied his old man's philosophy to other aspects of his life. He pursued one-of-a-kind business deals. Deals with genuine consequences. Deals that, if he missed, could turn and gore him.

He intended to use the rifle on a big buffalo in the morning. Zoeller claimed it was a legendary animal. "He's called Minotaur, Tots. Very grumpy." All the big animals had names now, apparently.

Krieger looked at the big male lion carcass hanging by its Achilles tendons from a skinning rack. Blaze would not be joining tomorrow's hunt. In the end, he had been wrong about her.

THE PURGE

Pretoria, South Africa

The next morning, Hungry drove Klay and Tenchant to an industrial stretch on the outskirts of Pretoria, empty at this early hour of all vehicles but one. "Ncube's spy," Hungry said, pointing to a white Corsa van parked along the curb.

Klay saw the driver's face in the van's side-view mirror as they passed. He was asleep.

"Fortunately, they do not like to exert themselves." She circled the block and parked in the back. "We'll go in another way." She led them to a brick building next door. A sign beside the entrance read, "WhiteOut Industro Laundry."

Inside, Hungry nodded hello to a man holding a pad and pencil, recording stacks of folded

bedsheets. "Abby. My radical friend," Hungry said
as they passed. "We grew up in Soweto together."

She pushed a laundry cart out of their path,
then opened a heavy door and ushered them into
the building next door. "Welcome to the nest,"
she said. "Sorry for the . . . everything. The building used to be a garage for diesel trucks. We're
up there." Hungry pointed to a lighted doorway
at the end of a catwalk that ran along the second
floor's back wall.

The garage was two stories of open space to ac-
commodate trucks, illuminated from above by a
row of filthy windows. A graveyard of greasy old
truck parts and big jointed tools filled the floor.
It stank of motor oil.

"Watch your step," she said, taking hold of a
metal pipe railing. As he climbed the bar grate
stairs, Klay heard snippets of voices arguing.

A man's voice said, ". . . for your own good,
Miss Edna . . ."

A woman replied, "When I need another man
telling me what's good for me, it won't be you . . ."

"Goodness," Hungry said under her breath.

At the far end of the catwalk was a massive
stainless steel door more than four inches thick,
with recessed locking bolts along its edges, the
kind of door found on a bank vault or, Klay rea-
soned, a safe room. Klay smiled. Someone had
propped the impregnable door open using a floor
mop and a couple of bricks. All the protections . . .

Inside, the argument continued: ". . . slipping around those clubs has brought sin home with you . . ."

Hungry grasped the mop and slid the bricks away with her toe. "Please," she said, ushering Klay and Tenchant inside. Behind them, the steel door closed with a hush.

"It's my kota he has, mum," a large woman said. "He has taken it for himself. In his desk drawer."

"Untrue," the man said. "I do have it in my desk drawer, but I have it for your own good. You have your daughter's wedding to think of . . ."

Three people were seated at desks in what resembled a mini squad room. Whiteboard. Steel filing cabinets. Computers. Each had their breakfast laid out in front of them, none appeared to have started eating yet.

Hungry cleared her throat. "Mr. Tom Klay and Mr. David Tenchant of **The Sovereign** magazine, this—I am rarely embarrassed to say—is my task force. They think we call them the Wild Dogs because they are three of our nation's finest criminal prosecutors. But you will find, as with so many things in South Africa, the truth is much more straightforward."

Hungry gestured toward a large, light-skinned woman in a bright dress and ornate headscarf. "This is Miss Edna Sebati, who," she said sharply, "is in charge of this office when I am away."

Miss Edna nodded.

"Miss Minenhle Mthembu—Minnie—my junior prosecutor," Hungry said. Minnie smiled. She was slender, in her late twenties, wearing a dark business suit and white blouse.

"And last, Officer Julius Sehlalo, our investigator, formerly of the Hawks."

Sehlalo was handsome and fit, and as dark-skinned as Tenchant was pale. He wore a tailored navy-blue jacket over a black T-shirt. A gold medallion on a gold chain hung around his neck.

Klay and Tenchant smiled hello, but that didn't help much. They were outsiders, and tension in the room was thick. As he reached forward to shake Sehlalo's hand, Klay noticed a holster under Sehlalo's jacket, a reminder that this special prosecutor's office came with special powers.

Hungry walked behind Sehlalo's desk. She opened a drawer and removed a large sandwich wrapped in foil. "This kota is the property of the state now. I will dispose of it according to the rules of eminent domain, affording just compensation to its owner in the form of mineral water and raw vegetables of her choice."

"State capture!" Miss Edna shouted.

"Back to work," Hungry said, stifling a smile. "I believe you have some."

Hungry led Klay and Tenchant through a doorway into her windowless private office. As she closed the door, Klay glimpsed Sehlalo offering a yogurt to his coworker. That was good. A team that stuck together was important.

Hungry indicated her office's two wooden chairs, placed the sandwich on a bookshelf, and took a seat behind her desk. She withdrew some papers and a laptop from her briefcase. "We refer to Miss Edna's weight problem as her daughter's wedding," she explained. "Her daughter Rosie's been married four years now and lives with her husband and two children in Cape Town, but sometimes we must find a way to express the things we dare not say." She looked briefly at Klay. "Shall I give you a bit of background, Mr. Tenchant? This office—"

"Tenchant's fine."

"Tenchant. Okay then. You are here to do a story on our investigation and prosecution of the wildlife trafficker Ras Botha. Naturally, this is a sensitive situation. It is not generally appropriate for us to discuss our work with outsiders, especially foreign journalists, and never a case in progress. But Tom has written about Botha in the past. **The Sovereign** is respected throughout our country, and my superior is aware of your presence. There are certain limits you will have to abide by, but I have also instructed my team that you are here to support our investigation, and we, your story. We believe in your magazine, and we believe your work can help us."

"Any publicity is good publicity," Tenchant said.

"No. Good publicity is good publicity, Tenchant." She looked at him sharply. "Let me give you a bit of background on who we are and what else we're doing. Three years ago, our president, Gabriel Ncube, appointed his son-in-law, Justin Franklin, to be our country's public protector. Franklin is now in prison, arrested for bribery by Officer Sehlalo." She nodded in the direction of her doorway. "Our president saw opportunity in his son-in-law's arrest. Gabriel Ncube's entire career has been marred by criminal allegations, including murder, the rape of an underage girl, and selling off mining, defense, and other state interests to line his pockets. He saw a way to cleanse himself politically. He appointed the esteemed advocate Angela Mabaso to replace his son-in-law as public protector, and he very publicly encouraged her to create a new anti-corruption task force to rid his government of wrongdoing. She accepted his advice and created this ad hoc anti-corruption unit. But she did not accept his suggestions on how to staff it. Against the president's wishes, she chose me.

"The public has nicknamed our unit the Wild Dogs after the animals' reputation for biting and eating their victims while on the run. Somehow, we have sometimes become the Hungry Dogs. Which I am afraid is also true . . .

"We have a man sweep the office each morning," she said, noting Tenchant's eyes roaming over documents stacked on the floor and her shelves. "We can talk freely here."

Her eyes were still on Tenchant, assessing him, Klay realized. "But of course, nothing is ever certain so we do take basic precautions with our phones and other communications. Our internal communications are air-gapped," she said, and nodded at a computer monitor on her desk. "My staff will brief you. Questions? No? Okay," she said. "My team has seen you. They know who you are. They know you're here to help. But they are not happy about it. Journalists are a great risk for us. If Ncube discovers I'm helping you, or that you are helping me"—she glanced at Klay— "we're through. That is just how it is."

"Thank you, Hungry," Klay said. "I briefed Tenchant on the security parameters we agreed to, and on the compartmentalization of our efforts. He understands you have a corruption investigation underway and that we are to stay well clear of it. We're here to tell the story of Ras Botha. Exclusively. Any help your people can give Tenchant, of course, would be much appreciated. He's ready to get to work. We both are."

"Okay," she said. "Good. Let's bring you back out there and try this again . . ."

. . .

Tenchant was on his hands and knees under a spare desk in the Wild Dogs' office, his blue button-down shirt riding up his bony back. His tattooed arm emerged from under the desk. "Can somebody help me plug this in?" He was holding the universal travel adapter he'd brought from home.

"That won't work here," Miss Edna said. She dug through her desk and found a South African adapter. "Give this to him, Minnie, please."

Tenchant plugged in his laptop and took a seat at the desk they had found for him. "What's your Wi-Fi?" he asked.

"Use your own phone for the internet," Sehlalo said.

"Hush!" said Miss Edna. " 'Laundromat' is the network, Mr. Tenchant. The password is 'Phambili!Kenako.' " She spelled it out for him.

"Thank you. Just Tenchant."

"Use a VPN, please," she said. "Choose outside South Africa. If you need to go on the website of target individuals or companies please let us know. We use Tor, but some things require a search from another location."

"Okay," he said, typing rapidly. "I'm on the Companies and Intellectual Property Commission website. Do you have an ID or passport number for Botha . . . ?"

"Exit that," Sehlalo said. "I want a list of every site you intend to search before you go online."

Klay was leaning against a wall, watching. He called across the room to Sehlalo. "How do you like that weapon?"

Sehlalo turned. He glanced down at his shoulder holster, then back at Klay. "Gits 'er done," he said affecting a cowboy twang, a hostile edge in his voice.

"I was thinking it goes with your suit," Klay said, taking a step forward.

Sehlalo opened his jacket and drew his weapon, slowly but confidently, and placed it on the corner of his desk. He gestured for Klay to take a look. Klay picked it up. Klay preferred a Glock—short trigger pull, super reliable. But as appearances went the sharp-edged Glock looked and felt like it had been designed by Lego.

Tenchant joined them. "Wow. Looks like something Batman would use. What is that?"

"Vektor CP1," Sehlalo said. "Nine mil."

"The pride of South Africa," Klay said, handing it back to Sehlalo. "Don't drop it, right?"

Sehlalo accepted his gun and holstered it. "They fixed that over here."

"Glad you trust them," Klay said. The two men glared at each other. Klay said, "Tench, you good?"

Tenchant went back to his desk. "I'm good, boss."

"Okay." His team stuck together too.

Minnie dropped a stack of documents on

Tenchant's desk. "Our Botha case files." Tenchant opened the top file and got to work.

Klay didn't see him again for two days. On the third day, Tenchant knocked on Klay's hotel room door. Klay was dressed in old gym shorts and a T-shirt. Tenchant was wearing shorts, flip-flops, and a Sovereign T-shirt with the silver globe on the chest. He was holding his laptop.

He let Tenchant in and went back to doing some sit-ups on a bath towel beside the bed. "Did you know every computer in the South African government, every single one, is compromised?" Tenchant asked, taking a seat at Klay's desk.

"Be done in a minute, Tench." Klay grunted.

Tenchant opened his laptop. "They used pirated software to save money, and now the entire country is Swiss cheese."

"Hungry's office, too?" Klay asked.

Exercise wasn't pleasant for him anymore. He'd thickened in the years since his time as an amateur boxer. He was less wiry now, he liked to say, more kitchen appliance. Even in his thirties, exercise had been easier. He was pretty sure he used to bend at a different part of his stomach, and he knew push-ups didn't used to sound like old barn doors on rusted hinges. He remained a powerful man, but his shape varied. Fitness ebbed and flowed from him, improving when he was home, declining in the field. He'd spent most of his professional life abroad.

The Sovereign was famously generous when it came to travel expenses. His colleagues flew business class, stayed in four- and five-star hotels, sought out countries' premier chefs and unique entertainment. But Klay, who measured himself by his work, secretly feared that failure might lurk around the next corner, and he might not get his story. He used his travel money to buy more field time. He flew coach, unless he had the miles, and slept in his bivy sack or in cheap motel rooms. He ate modestly and relied on Malarone dreams and his own dark thoughts for entertainment. He stayed in the field and reported—allowing his body to soften, his lungs to weaken—focusing his mind ever more firmly on his target.

Klay did some leg raises, then flipped over for more push-ups. When he got home, he'd hit the gym again. This was his last assignment, after all. Last for the Agency, last for **The Sovereign,** too. Once he nailed Botha, he was going to clean up his life. Eat more vegetables. Get healthy.

"Hungry's system is a mess," Tenchant said. "I pentested their internal system. Scanned the machines with Nmap, checked for vulnerabilities. Turns out their general network connects to the Public Protector's office. They haven't updated anything in months, so vulnerabilities everywhere. I fired up Metasploit-Framework using auxiliary scanners. First thing I checked for was BlueKeep and instant remote system shell. Bluekeep got leaked from the NSA, but you'd be surprised how—"

"Sorry. You did what?"

"Ah. I forgot. You're illiterate. Nmap is a port scanner, but people have added a few vulnerability scripts so it can do double duty, at least on the more common problems." Tenchant looked at Klay. Nothing. He waved his hands above his head. "I used some craaaazzzy computer code to perform a colonoscopy on the office's general system—I don't have access to their air-gapped machines—results were cancerous. Polyps everywhere. That help?"

Klay paused his push-ups. "Thanks," he said dryly.

Tenchant smiled. "Point is, I'm staying off-line as much as I can in case there's something devious lurking in their system. That's why I took a cab over to the Companies and Intellectual Property Commission today. Botha has sixty-eight companies registered in his own name in South Africa. Nineteen in his wife's. There's a little of everything. Mining. Real estate. IT. Safari camps. Game breeding. Three golf courses. An arms manufacturer of some kind. About thirty companies called Alphan Investments. Alphan Investments 1, Alphan Investments 2 . . . He's got websites set up for some of these, which will help me. I searched a few and found links to other companies outside of South Africa. Hey, how do you know so much about guns?"

Klay lay on the floor, his forearm over his eyes. "Tom?"

"What?"

"The other day, with Julius. You knew all about his pistol. I asked him later, and he said you were right about the recall. Something about the early model firing when you dropped it. He said the Vektor's not a very well-known gun."

Pride, Klay chided himself, **your fucking pride.** He had fired a Vektor during his training with Major Thomas, part of his foreign weapons module. "I did a story on guns once," he said. "Mechanical evolution of firearms. Blunderbuss to AR-15s, I think it was. That one was so futuristic it just stuck up here." He pointed to his head.

"Yeah," Tenchant said, "that's what I figured. But when I searched online for gun stories by you, I didn't find any . . ."

Relentless fuck.

Klay got to his feet, turned his back to Tenchant, and switched on the television with a remote. "Did you do a search on memory? Because mine's not as good as it used to be. Must have been back when I freelanced. I did all kinds of stories back then. Happy to forget most of them."

"Yeah, no doubt. Anyway, tomorrow I'll start data mining, run transforms on the companies and names I came up with, and generate a link analysis we can look at. It's going to be a helluva spiderweb, I'll tell you that."

Klay wiped his face with his T-shirt. "Do you have anything juicy I can use to surprise Botha? I'd like to disrupt his world tomorrow."

"Not yet. What time's your meeting?"

"Eleven."

"Not enough time. I could hack it."

Klay looked at him. "Hack what?"

"The Dogs' air-gapped network. I have the feeling Sehlalo's not giving me everything, you know? If we go early, you'd just need to have everybody in Hungry's office for a few minutes with the door closed. Or get them outside somehow . . ."

"No. Out of the question. We're not hacking Hungry's internal system."

"Okay. I was just throwing it out there," Tenchant said and went back to reading his email.

"Out of curiosity," Klay said, "could you do it?"

Tenchant's eyes stayed on his laptop. "Yep."

Klay sighed. "The answer is no." For now, he thought.

"Got it. Maggie says hello," Tenchant said. "She wants to know if I've seen an elephant yet. Do you think we will?"

"No. We're on deadline."

Klay heard himself and paused. When he was starting out with **The Sovereign,** he had resisted getting emotionally involved in his stories' victims. His interest was limited to how and where animals or their parts were being trafficked. One day Eady had pulled him aside. "You have to see the animals in the wild, Tom. Get to know what you're working to protect." The old man had handed him a plane ticket to Tanzania. One evening during that trip, driving back to camp, Klay noticed a lone elephant standing among the trees. The light had fallen and the gray matriarch was nearly invisible among the trees' bare branches. Something caught his eye. He turned in his seat and realized an enormous herd of elephants was lined up shoulder to shoulder along the road, just one tree deep in the bush. An entire society had been watching him, just a few feet away, and he'd almost missed it. Over the years, when he needed reminding why he did what he did, he thought about that evening.

Klay looked at Tenchant. "Tell Maggie we'll do a quick game drive."

"Excellent," Tenchant replied, typing.

"It's important to see what you're working to protect," Klay added, but Tenchant wasn't listening. He was focused on his note.

Under a hot shower, Klay thought about Hungry. He thought about truth and lies, and who he was and who he hoped to be. Maybe she could handle the truth about him—or, more accurately, the lie. She'd hate him for his dishonesty. Dishonesty was betrayal—he knew that—but maybe she would see his lies differently after he told her what he'd been working to protect . . . No. He could not put her at risk like that. Their only chance was for him to quit. Once he was out, they could start over. He didn't know the outcome, but he did know the sequence. Quitting came first.

He was drying himself when he heard Tenchant exclaim, "Holy shit!"

He poked his head out of the bathroom. "What?"

"Look at this!"

Klay pulled on the hotel bathrobe. "What is it?"

Tenchant spun his laptop around to show him a photograph of a large group of people standing on the steps outside **The Sovereign** building.

"We missed the staff photo," Klay said, getting dressed. "No big deal."

"Look."

Klay buckled his belt and looked again. Sharon Reif was standing on the third step, in the middle of the photograph, wearing a white safari shirt. Porfle stood below her, grinning feverishly.

"The fuck are they all wearing?"

"Safari Fridays," Tenchant said.

"Safari what?"

Everyone in the photograph wore a safari shirt complete with epaulets and a blue chest patch. Journalists wore tan, support staff dark green, management brown. Only Reif and two people Klay didn't recognize wore white. They looked like a troop of Cub Scouts.

"Sharon had the shirts designed by one of her old clients. They wanted your size by the way. I said extra-large. Don't you read your email?"

"Where's Erin?" Klay said. "And Fox?" He searched faces. "Where's Ernst? And Charlie from Archives?"

"They're all gone."

"Gone?"

Tenchant read aloud an email from Fox: " 'Well, it fucking happened. For those of you not present, and for my lawyers, I'm writing this down. Last week, as you know, Sharon sent out an email notifying everybody to be available at ten a.m. Friday for a meeting with their department head. No exceptions. Here's what happened. They lined us up and called us individually into our boss's office, where we were either fired or handed a fucking safari shirt. Correction. They fired everyone, then those they wanted back, to work for Perseus Group Media, they gave a fucking safari shirt. It took all morning. There were lines all through the building.

Then around five that afternoon Sharon called the department heads back into her office, same ones who just did the firing, and she axed them one by one. Some got rehired. Fucking Russian roulette. Bodies everywhere. I'm looking for work. Any ideas, let me know.'"

Klay was not listening. He was searching faces. "They fired Erin?"

"I don't know."

"What a fucking place. Jesus." Klay stood for a moment, rubbing his forehead with one hand. "What do you want for dinner?"

"I ate already," Tenchant said.

"What did you have?"

"You didn't ask about our status."

"Our status?" Klay was confused. The possibility of being fired took a moment to register. He'd assumed, as he always had, that changes in personnel wouldn't affect him. But Klay worked for Perseus Group now. "You're right. What's our status?" he asked.

Tenchant read another email. "Porfle says decisions on anyone currently in the field will be announced Friday—Fridays are designated kill days apparently. Travel is rebooking us to come home. But he says not to worry."

"Don't respond to any travel emails, Tenchant. We're not available. In fact, don't respond to anyone. We're in the field, bad comms."

"Okay, but Porfle said not to worry."

"Porfle said that?" Klay said.

"Yeah. So, that's good, right?"

"Porfle did?"

"Shit," Tenchant said.

Klay looked at the expectant father. "Don't worry, Tenchant. I never leave a man behind."

FLUKE

Pretoria, South Africa

Thanks, bru," Klay said, handing the room service waiter a tip. "Touch up the minibar, would you?"

Klay sat down on the edge of the hotel room bed. On the cart in front of him was his dinner: a roasted half chicken, French fries, three bottles of Castle Lager, a cup of rice pudding, and a salad. He hadn't asked for the salad. He poured ketchup on his plate, switched on his laptop, and opened up his email. His screen filled with unread messages, nearly all from Porfle. They began two days ago, he noted, before the office shake-up.

The subject line of the oldest message read, "URGENT!"

He opened it.

"TK. Call me. Porf."

Then another. "T. Need to speak ASAP! Personnel! Send time. A.P." Klay looked at the time and date: an hour had passed since the first email.

Then, a third, just hours from the last. "URGENT!!!!!! Tom, I have tried repeatedly to reach you. Urgent personnel matter. Sharon requires response IMMEDIATELY! Pls. provide times for a conference call! Alexander Porfle."

Klay ate a piece of chicken, dipped a French fry in the ketchup.

He opened an email from Erin. "Hi Tom. Well, they cut me. Legends had to Fall. Hahaha. Don't worry. I'm happy to go. Grant and I may move to Denver. Thought you'd be interested in the below."

She had included a link to a **New York Times** article. Klay clicked on the link and read the headline: "**Times** Journalist Struck in Hit-and-Run."

He scanned the story. Raynor McPhee had been returning to his apartment around one a.m., crossing Berry Street in Brooklyn, when a car struck him from behind. No witnesses. Nothing caught on neighborhood surveillance cameras. Raynor suffered two broken legs, a concussion, and a broken wrist. Police were investigating.

Beneath the article was a box with links to three of Raynor's most recent articles. The latest was "The World's New OK Corral." Klay clicked on it.

The story opened with an anecdote about the widow of a slain Mexican investigative journalist whose phones had been tapped by the Mexican government. The source for the surveillance technology was not Mexican, however. It was Perseus Group. Raynor's story described a battle for supremacy for global strategic services taking place between Perseus Group and a Russian company called Amur Tactical Resources. The article suggested a personal rivalry between the companies' CEOs. Klay had heard Dmitri Yurchenko's name but knew him only as an oligarch tied to Putin. Yurchenko, Raynor wrote, was a traditional mercenary, interested in winning government and rebel group military contracts. Perseus Group was more sophisticated. "It's not just about selling instruments of war for him [Krieger] anymore. It's about risk attendant to conflict and the return he can get from manipulating both," a former Perseus Group executive was quoted saying in the story. There was only brief mention of **The Sovereign,** listed as one of several recent high-profile media acquisitions, ". . . moves industry analysts consider part of an effort by Perseus to control its image by acquiring targeted media and entertainment properties."

Klay logged in to Signal and sent Raynor a quick message. "Sorry to hear about your accident. These boys play rough. Overseas at moment. Let's chat on return. Meantime, get well. You're needed. Tom K."

He drank a beer and finished his chicken. His fries had gone cold. When he first started traveling for **The Sovereign,** he'd eaten fearlessly, the more exotic the better. Late stage balut— duck embryo—the beak and feathers filling his mouth. Pig's blood soup. Decomposed sardines recovered from a buried pot, served by a grinning ex-headhunter on Sarawak. Sometimes, he ate foods he abhorred in order to get into his targets: Tiger blood with a Siberian trader. Raw whale meat with a trafficker in Shizuoka. The hands of a Cameroonian gorilla he'd known by name. He vomited that last meal afterwards. It felt worse than cannibalism.

His favorite among his weird meals, not for the taste but for what it signified, was koi pla— raw fish mixed with live red ants—first enjoyed from a rusting hubcap while motoring up the Mekong River on the border of Laos in north-eastern Thailand. That trip—the distance he traveled to get there, the smells he encountered— the sweetness of lemongrass and coriander, the pungency of dried fish and durian. The soft, melodic rhythms he overheard in markets and on buses. Heat so damp and thick you could swim in it. All of it evoked images of his father's generation off to a land many would not return from, to a war that would forever change those who came back. Mourning veterans of the Korean and Vietnam Wars passed through Klay Funeral Home so often during Klay's childhood that he came subconsciously to consider travel to Asia to be an important passage on the way to becoming a man. Thailand was his first Asian trip, and though he would later travel the world, that trip marked a break for him, a flag planted in the dirt of his life that said, **I am no longer in Philadelphia. I am not Jack Klay's son. I am free.**

He opened another beer. Years later, he no longer experimented when it came to food overseas. No still water. No unskinned fruit. No raw vegetables. Nothing washed. He ordered the same meal every place he went anywhere in the world.

Fluke. That's why he'd stopped eating exotic local meals, why he insisted on the same reliable chicken and fries no matter where he went. Years after that first trip, he went back to Thailand and reprised that first meal right down to the hubcap. He ended up in the hospital. It turned out, koi pla carries a parasite, a fluke that causes liver cancer and kills tens of thousands of people every year. You are very lucky, the nurse in Chiang Rai told him. His ailment was merely food poisoning. It wasn't the risk of liver cancer that made him change his diet, though. It was the day and a half he spent kneeling in a tiled bathroom. He vomited through an appointment with a government official and nearly lost his story. Joyriding street food wasn't worth it.

He opened ProtonMail and composed an update to Eady. There wasn't much to say. He and Tenchant were in place. He would be interviewing Botha in the morning. He hit send.

A response appeared immediately, surprising him.

"Investigation window closing," Eady replied.

Closing? He'd just arrived.

Klay replied with a question mark.

Eady wrote: "She's got a leak. Botha secondary. SECURE HER FILES."

Eady had sent him to investigate Botha. "A gift," he'd said. "My last act as your handler." Now his number one priority was Hungry's files?

Klay stared at his computer screen. Eady had spelled it out in an email. Encrypted or not, Eady would never include such sensitive details in his correspondence. Something was wrong. Flukes happened in raw seafood. They did not happen with Vance Eady.

YOU WERE THE GUN

Kgosi Mampuru II Management Area, Pretoria, South Africa

The woman with short auburn hair and deeply lined skin tore the cellophane off another pack of Camel cigarettes, unwrapped the foil, and dumped the contents onto a pile she had created on the wooden bench beside her. Between her feet was a large woven polypropylene bag filled with bulk packages, including toilet paper and Dial soap.

"They get nothing here," she explained, not looking up.

"It's unbelievable," Klay agreed.

He was sitting opposite her in the waiting room at the notorious Kgosi Mampuru II prison, formerly Pretoria Central Prison, renamed for the nineteenth-century king (kgosi) who fought colonial domination and was hanged on the prison site—twice. The benches had welded rebar for legs, screws in the wood soldered tight, everything smoothed to a gloss by generations of visitors.

The woman got out a box of plastic baggies and began filling them with loose cigarettes. She worked steadily, taking each baggie to its limit, two rows wide, stretching the plastic to near breaking before sealing it. She set each filled bag aside and started on another.

"You're getting faster," Klay said.

She looked up. "What're you, some kind of packing engineer, timing me?"

"I'm looking to enter you in the cigarette Olympics, if you're interested," Klay replied.

"Yeah, right."

She kept at it. The hard part, he saw, was sealing a full baggie without crushing its contents.

"You want some help?"

"Wouldn't say no."

They worked together. Camels. Peter Stuyvesants. Marlboros. More visitors arrived, taking seats on benches around them. The newcomers each with their own items they'd brought, their own rituals. The smell of home cooking filled the room. A man tapped his foot. A woman began to knit.

"They get nothing," the woman said again.

"The noise is awful. There's no sleeping at night. He can only sleep in the daytime when the doors are open. But they're always looking in at you, you don't know what they want, so you can't sleep then, either."

Klay thought of his father. Jack Klay was currently at USP Coleman in Sumterville, Florida. He wondered how he slept at night.

After an hour they called everyone up to a window and handed each of them a large blue card sheathed in plastic bearing a prisoner's name, date of birth, and two fingerprints. At the bottom of each card was a list of charges and court dates.

"When I was a girl, they gave me a card to check out library books," the woman said. "Now it's my husband." She lit a cigarette. "Maybe mine knows him," she added, and stole a glance at Klay's card. She drew a quick breath. Without looking at Klay again, she gathered her things and hurried away. Klay looked down at his blue card. Ras Botha's charges filled the card front and back and were scrawled vertically along the card's edges in print too small to read.

Klay followed the other visitors and got in a long line for a metal detector and body search. The cigarette woman was three people ahead of him. When their line turned a corner Klay looked up, intending to catch her eye again, but she stared out a small window instead.

A hand touched Klay's shoulder. "You don't have to wait in line, Mr. Klay," a guard said. "He's expecting you."

The cigarette woman shot him a last, appraising look as he walked past her, around the metal detector, and into the prison. The guard, whose name was Jacob, was about Klay's size, dressed in a brown uniform, olive web belt, and black laced boots, but he was in poor condition and breathed heavily on the long walk, which took them up and down poorly lit stairwells and through long hallways whose walls were painted lemon yellow.

They passed men in orange prison uniforms stamped with "corrections" in circles, like leopard spots, working brooms and mop buckets. Several, he noticed, had the number twenty-six tattooed on their right hands. The prisoners paused as Klay approached, checked out his shoes, his watch, and his size. Some gave him chin juts and eye fucks. Others looked right through him.

"Anyone famous in here?" Klay asked as they walked.

"Some."

Jacob named a few prisoners. Klay looked them up later. An Apartheid-era assassin. A billionaire mob boss from the Czech Republic. A pair of murdering twin brothers.

"All his friends," Jacob said.

Jacob led Klay into an office marked "Warden." The warden was not in, a receptionist declared. Jacob looked at Klay. "Botha flu," he said, and opened the warden's door.

Inside, Ras Botha was seated at a small conference table. Jacob indicated for Klay to sit at one end, across from Botha. Then he pulled a chair out for himself, took it across the room, and sat down behind Klay, against the wall.

"So, you do have some balls of your own," Botha said. "I'm glad to see it."

Botha wore blue jeans and a black golf shirt, a dive watch, and a gold wedding ring. On the table in front of him were two oranges loosely wrapped in a paper towel. **He's lost weight,** was Klay's first thought. Lines in Botha's forehead had grown deeper than Klay remembered, and there was a cut over his left eye.

"I'm here to get your side of things," Klay said.

"That right?" Botha licked his lower lip in a way that drew his cheeks in so far Klay wondered if he was missing his bottom teeth. Maybe he was. Klay hadn't noticed before.

"I'm a big man in here. Privileges," Botha said and nodded toward his feet. He wore hiking boots. "No prison shoes." He gestured to his clothes. "No fucking jumpsuit." He looked over Klay's shoulder at Jacob in case Jacob was thinking of making him wear a fucking jumpsuit. Klay turned, too. Jacob didn't appear to be

thinking about Botha's clothing. He was studying a magazine.

Botha rolled an orange across the table. "For
you," he said.

Klay watched the orange roll toward him. It
stopped beside his notebook.

Botha waited, but Klay did not touch the
fruit. "You want to know about me? Okay. I
made good money mining. Did you know that?
Not really mining, but stealing from diamond
mines. I like animals," he said, "which is what
gave me the idea for it." He sucked his lower lip
and launched into his story. "I met a black boy
on the gravel ramp. He sees some big diamonds
coming through. Big as this." Botha indicated
the end of his thumb. "So, I asked him, what
do the gates look like? The building? How many
guards? Where do they stand? Does he know any
of the guards? Tell me the schedules . . . what . . .
what . . . what . . .

"The boy says it's wrapped tight. They x-ray
coming out and they metal-detect both ways. He
tells me he can't even get out a window. They're
little windows in the hallway, like on a ship, too
small to climb out. I been on some big yachts.
Big. Adnan Khashoggi hunted with me on the
Kimber, did you know that?"

"Didn't know that," Klay said and tapped his
pen. His notebook was open in front of him. At
the top of the page he'd written Botha's name,

the date, and the interview location. The page was blank.

"That's right, counselor. Russians. Putin. Some big Americans. Names you would know."

"Like who?"

Botha studied Klay. "Yeah, but I was telling a story. I told the boy, open one of the hallway windows. Not open it, just unlatch it. That's all he had to do." Botha began peeling his orange. He did it slowly, chipping off pieces while he talked. "I'm telling you so you know how my mind works."

Klay gestured with his hands. "Please."

Botha continued. He said he drove out to the young mineworker's house with some men and some lumber and had them build a pigeon coop behind the mineworker's house. Then he bought a flock of homing pigeons.

"You're a pigeon racer now," he told the young man. He pointed to the pigeon trainer he'd brought. "He's going to be living with you." Botha eyed Klay. "You ever raised pigeons? Birds only fly so far at a time and come back, like eight kilometers a week. We didn't want any mishaps, so we took our time." He tapped his temple with a finger. "Six months later, the birds were ready. I gave the boy a four-inch section of PVC pipe, sealed on one end, and told him to put a bird in the pipe and take it to work in his lunch pail.

"Pigeon pipe goes through the metal detector,

little cloth sack on his foot, diamond or two in the sack, out the little window. Skips the X-ray." He popped an orange slice into his mouth. "Millions, I made that way." Botha picked his nose. "They arrested me on sable that time, but you probably read about it. We moved them in bakkies kitted out like farm trucks." He raised a hand over his head. "Stacked with vegetables up to the sky. Secret compartment inside. Moved them from red zone to green zone. All we had to do. Millions on that one, too."

"What's red zone to green zone?" Klay asked.

"Hoof and mouth," he said. "Sable in the green zone, certified. Worth five or eight times red zone sable. Just had to cross that border. Do you see what I'm saying to you?"

"Borders don't matter to you."

"Ach, that's one way to tell it. Another is, borders are where the money is. You should remember that."

"Thanks for the lesson. How 'bout if we talk about Kenya."

"Kenya?"

"I don't have time for your bullshit, Botha."

"You don't have time?" Botha sat back and smiled. "You want, you can borrow some of mine." He broke off a large section of orange and took his time chewing it.

"I'm talking about your elephant poachers. The two men you murdered."

"Hey!" Botha called out. Klay heard a magazine crackle. Botha reached into his pocket and slapped a few bills down on the table. "Jacob, my friend, why don't you go get yourself a Coke?"

Jacob took the money and left.

"So, counselor, you have something you want to say to me?"

Botha wasn't wearing handcuffs. He was shorter than Klay, compact.

"Tell me about your shooter."

Botha sat back in his chair and grinned. "I told you before. Elephants are property. What people do with them is their business."

Klay thought of Bernard. Klay might be built bigger than Botha, but Botha was meaner—he could see that. There was no question, no uncertainty in his dark eyes. Botha was a killer.

Botha's eyes narrowed. "You're thinking too much, counselor," he warned. "You want to get emotional? You should be thinking about that little poes you got right here. Advocate Hungry Khoza. That skirt is property, too. How long you been fucking the very special prosecutor?"

Klay came out of his chair, his fist in the air. Suddenly he was down, his face slammed into the tabletop, Botha leaning all his weight on Klay's locked arm. Botha put his mouth against Klay's ear. "Know your target, Tom. Didn't they teach you that in Assessments?"

"Assessments" was a CIA term.

"Take your fucking hands off me." Klay rose from the table, lifting Botha off the ground with him. His chair crashed to the floor and the office door opened. Jacob entered with his nightstick drawn. Botha stepped away from Klay. He raised a hand and Jacob paused. Botha tilted his head toward the door, and Jacob backed out of the office and closed the door behind him.

Klay wiped blood from his nose and lip.

"You were the gun," Botha said calmly, retaking his seat. "Not me, counselor."

Klay spat. Botha wiped Klay's blood and spit off his cheek with the back of his hand.

"I was the gun? The fuck are you talking about?" Klay said.

Botha looked at Klay's untouched orange. "I have a client. American. Very powerful guy. I been to the States many times. Many, many times. Did you know that? Miami. Dallas. Vegas. This guy's got a big place in Zim, bigger than the King Ranch. Beautiful fucking place. Used to be mine until I sold it to him. The Kimber, it's called. Anyway, this client, he wants a hunt. Always does after a big deal goes off. And he makes some big fucking deals. This time he's blooding his kid. Wants a good lion for her and then something bigger for himself. Gets off on it. My PH tells him he knows a buff. Great big dagga boy I been saving for myself." Botha spread his arms above his head to indicate the buffalo's wide horns. "Minotaur. Client says he wants to get his daughter her lion, take Minotaur, then out. Boys set up camp for him, bait up the lion. Only she can't take the shot, wants to tranquilize it for a school project. Client shoots the lion, then snotklaps her. Pop!" Botha swung his hand. "Put her on a plane home that night. Next day, my trackers locate his buff. Jump in the bakkie. There he is. Bigger than God, and not enjoying his age. Isaac sets up the shooting sticks. Njovu gets the truck ready."

Normally Klay would give a guy like Botha all the time he wanted to tell his stories. He would come back again and again and listen as long as his target would talk, letting the guy unleash his ego. Rope-a-dope him with innocuous questioning; then, when the target was worn out, Klay would wade in with his real questions. But this time he didn't have that luxury. Unchaperoned time with Botha might never come again. He needed to move Botha toward something Hungry could use to prosecute him. **Investigate Botha so Hungry can take down Ncube—that is your mission,** he told himself. **And control yourself.**

Still, something about Botha's story smelled funny. Something about the man said, **Wait.**

"You listening to me, counselor?"

"I'm waiting for the movie to come out."

Botha shook his head. "You know," he said,

wagging a finger, "you are some fucking crazy fucker. You remind me of me. So the fucking client waves the shooting sticks away. Wants to free-hand his shot. Now, he's carrying a .416 Rigby. But it's a single, and if he misses—? I have a motto for my camp: never leave a wounded animal behind. If it's shot, we kill it."

"Your camp? I thought it's not your property anymore."

"Yeah. We'll see. Client asks Old Pete Zoeller for a range check. Pete carries my Holland and Holland double rifle in five hundred nitro express. If anything goes wrong, he's there to second him with two. Pete's making his check when the client fucking shoots. Misfire. Round's a dud. No time for a second with his fucking single shot. It's on, and it's no joke. Minotaur is no fucking joke, I'm telling you. They got a locomotive coming down on them. Now here's the part—client doesn't sweat it. He pushes Old Pete out of the way, takes a step to the side, pulls a .45, and wham, shoots the boy."

"The boy?" Klay said.

"Shoots Isaac, dead. Confuses 'em," he tells Pete. "Says his lads did it with the hajjis in Afghanistan. Called it a Crocodile Dundee. He was right, too. Minotaur stopped mid-charge. 'Send me the funeral bill,' he tells Pete."

Botha wiped a few drops of Klay's blood off

the tabletop with his paper towel. He looked at Klay.

Klay's mind was spinning. He scanned Botha's eyes, his breathing, his posture, and was startled to find no clue whether the man was lying.

"You know a lot of fucking assholes. That your point?" Klay asked.

Botha leaned forward. He punctuated his words carefully. "My point, counselor, is that boy never knew he was fair game. My point is, you take care with your assumptions. Didn't they teach you that at the Farm? No? Maybe things have changed."

Jacob put his head into the room and Botha nodded. He gathered bits of orange peel into a pile and scooped them into his palm with his paper towel; then he pushed back in his chair and stood. "You work for him now," Botha said.

"I work for who?"

"The American. Terry Krieger. You work for him now." Botha picked up Klay's untouched orange. "I'm in here because of you. You ever think of that? Your girlfriend's looking on the wrong tree branch."

He dropped Klay's orange and his peels in a wastebasket near the door. "She's got her hands on some dangerous documents. Ask her where she thinks they came from."

He nodded to Jacob and left.

THE UNRAVELING

Office of the Special Prosecutor
Pretoria, South Africa

The big steel door was propped open with a mop handle and bricks again. It was the same everywhere, Klay thought as he entered. You can erect all the defenses in the world, but if it's not convenient, it's not safe at all.

"What does 'gatvol' mean?" Tenchant was asking.

"Fed up," Miss Edna answered. "As in, 'We're gatvol of that tsotsi.'"

"Yeah," Tenchant echoed. "We're gatvol of that tsotsi. Oh. Hey, Tom." Tenchant put down his file. "I might have something."

"In a minute."

"I think you'll be interested: Botha and

Ncube's wife share a post office box," Tenchant said. "It's in their company registrations . . ."

Klay paused. The two female lawyers were looking at him expectantly. Sehlalo was not in the room. "Help me with something downstairs, will you, Tench?"

Klay led Tenchant across the catwalk and down the stairs to the garage. He took him to the front of the garage out of sight and earshot of Hungry's team.

"Tell me," Klay said quietly.

"It's crazy, right? I mean, we're here for Botha, and somehow it looks like he's connected to their Ncube investigation. But it could help all of us, right? What's the matter?"

"Keep going."

"They used the same address, a beauty parlor owned by one of the Ncube nieces. That address ties to several of Botha's companies and a number held by Ncube's family. Important thing is, they made a mistake. It proves there's a link between them."

"Doesn't 'prove,' suggests." Klay looked up toward Hungry's office. "You told the team you found a link?"

"Maybe I shouldn't have. Chinese wall. But I can help them. Is something wrong?"

"What was their response?"

"They wanted to see it."

"Who did?"

"Sehlalo."

"Did you show it to him?"

"I did."

"What did he say?"

"He didn't say anything. He left."

Klay's jaw muscle flexed. "All right. See what else you can find, but keep it to yourself. Don't share any more." He turned toward the stairs. "I have to talk to Hungry."

"She's not here."

Klay hesitated. "Where is she?"

"I don't know. She didn't say."

"All right." Klay turned for the door. "Get back to it."

"Where are you going?"

"I'll be back as soon as I can."

Outside on the street, he texted Hungry: "Where are you?"

"Silverton HQ. Depos," she responded.

"Need to talk."

"Call in 30?"

"In person."

"The Klipspringer. 3:30?"

He sent a thumbs-up emoji. And later, the room number.

They stood in the middle of a hotel room identical to the one where they'd made love days earlier. A faucet dripped in the bathroom. Sunlight burned through the muslin drapes, casting a yellow stain on the carpet. She'd come straight from the national prosecutor's office. "What is it, Tom?"

Klay sat in a side chair and motioned for Hungry to sit on the bed. The hotel had been convenient to the restaurant that night and sufficiently down-market that she was unlikely to be recognized in the lobby. He hadn't noticed the tacky furniture then and couldn't recall whether the orange bedspread he was looking at now was the same design as in their former room.

Hungry looked at him with a puzzled expression and remained standing.

"I need to know how you arrested Botha," he said.

"How? We pulled him over on N1, outside his game farm in Polokwane."

Klay's phone rang. It was Tenchant. He turned off the ringer and put the phone in his pocket.

"But how did you know to be there, Hungry?"

"We got a tip. We have a corruption hotline. The team monitors it. We get dozens of them every week."

"Dozens? And you respond to all of them?"

"No. Not all."

"So, why did you act on this one?"

"Is this an interrogation?"

"Humor me, please."

"Officer Sehlalo phoned me and told me the tip

looked legitimate," she said warily. "There'd been a break-in at the police station in Polokwane. The safe was opened. According to the tip, an officer on Botha's payroll had done it and Botha would be transporting the stolen rhino horns personally. We got a date and time. It checked out. Rhino poaching is outside my jurisdiction, but Botha has a hand in everything in this country. He knows the president personally. I knew we'd never flip him, but I thought, why not shake his tree, see what falls out. I authorized Julius to proceed. He organized a few of the Hawks and intercepted the car. The tip was accurate. They recovered the horn."

"So, it was Sehlalo?"

"With my authorization. Julius Sehlalo is part of my team, my trusted team."

"I went to see Botha this morning. He said he was in prison for me. Because of me, is what he said."

"I don't know what that means." Her confusion was turning to anger. "I do know that you must not trust Ras Botha. Everything he says is a lie within a lie. He's a master manipulator. You know that."

"He knew things he shouldn't know."

"What things?"

That I am a CIA agent. The thought ricocheted inside his head.

"Is there a chance he got arrested on purpose.

To get inside, somehow? To . . . I don't know . . . to occupy your resources?"

Hungry sat down at the foot of the bed. "What are you saying?"

"He's in prison because of me . . . What if he meant, to give **The Sovereign** a reason to send me? To give you a reason to let me in?"

"That doesn't make sense."

She was right. It didn't make sense. Botha seemed to know he was a CIA asset. But if Botha was in with the CIA, why had Eady and Barrow sent him?

"Let's go back. Does Sehlalo have history with the Americans? With the intelligence community?"

"Not possible," she scoffed.

"What?"

"Sehlalo would never betray me."

"Does he?"

"With your intelligence community? You mean the CIA?" She stood up from the bed. "Do you know what you're suggesting? Are you completely ignorant of our history? Mandela spent twenty-seven years in prison because of your CIA. The CIA helped hunt and kill our comrades in Angola, Botswana, Zambia, Mozambique. And later, when Apartheid fell and the rest of the world said its humble apologies, your CIA and your State Department kept Madiba on your terrorist watch list! Our democratically elected president, an international terrorist, until he was ninety years old!

"Any connection, any appearance of a connection, between my team and the CIA would be fatal. I'd be branded Third Force. We could all wind up in prison. Or dead. This is no game, Tom. No," she said, turning to the window, "Sehlalo would not help the CIA. It would jeopardize everything we're doing, everything I've devoted my life to."

Klay's muted cell phone began buzzing. Something in his gut was buzzing more.

"You have a cache of files."

She did not respond.

"Botha knows it, Hungry. He said to ask you where you got them."

When she didn't respond, he continued, "Was it Sehlalo who brought them to you?"

"Sehlalo did not betray me."

Klay's eyes narrowed. "But there is something?" His voice was determinedly steady. "I can see it. You're not telling me something."

"It's not important. Not relevant," she corrected.

"What?"

Hungry faced him. "It's personal."

"It's all personal."

"I'm engaged, Tom. I'm going to be married."

Something in his chest tightened. He laughed bitterly. First Erin, now Hungry. "Well, I look forward to meeting him."

Her eyes clouded in disbelief. She shook her head. "You already have."

Sehlalo. He sighed. He'd missed that, too. "Well, I'm happy for you," he said.

"It's not public. The staff know. But you see, he would never betray me."

"Not intentionally."

She shook her head. "Not at all."

"CIA can arrange things, Hungry. Arrange them so you don't even know you're working for them."

Her eyes narrowed. "You know this from personal experience?"

He shook his head. "I've seen it. I've seen them succeed with people I know."

She sensed his deception—he could see that—but he had accused Sehlalo of betraying her, and the absurdity of that distracted her.

She stood. "He's a kind man, Tom. A good man. And an excellent detective."

"Good enough to know about us?"

Her eyes narrowed to knife edges. "Good enough to know we all come with baggage. Smart enough not to open mine without asking."

"And if he asks?"

"'Tom Klay and I were close once, just never close enough.'"

Klay nodded. That seemed about right. He reflected on Sehlalo. The hostility he'd perceived scanned differently now. "He seems like a solid guy," he said.

"You have a lot in common actually. It might surprise you to know he also had misgivings about Botha's arrest. He said it was too easy the way we picked him up." She shook her head. "Botha mentioned files? What did he say?"

"He said it at the end. He started out bragging about smuggling diamonds and sable antelope. When I asked him about Kenya, he told me some story about Terry Krieger. Then he said you'd gotten your hands on a cache of files. He said the files were dangerous. He told me to ask you where you got them." Klay paused, but she did not respond. Instead, Hungry's inscrutable expression had hardened. "He said you were on the wrong branch of the tree," Klay continued.

"What story?"

"What do you mean?" Klay asked.

"What story did he tell you about Terry Krieger?"

WHAT HAVE YOU DONE?

Pretoria, South Africa

Tell me exactly what he said about Krieger," Hungry demanded.

Klay sat on the edge of the hotel bed and looked up at her. "He said Terry Krieger took his daughter hunting in Zimbabwe. A place called the Kimber."

"It's a hunting property," Hungry said. "We think Botha transferred it to Krieger in advance of one of his trials."

"That makes sense. Botha said he sold it, but he talked about the property like it was still his. He said Krieger was angry because his daughter wouldn't shoot the lion, she wanted to dart it instead. Krieger hit her, shot the lion himself, and sent her home. The next day Krieger missed a shot on a buffalo, then shot a boy to distract its charge."

"Murdered him?"

"That's what Botha said."

"And you didn't think to tell me this? Just another dead African child . . ." She rubbed her temples. "Julius said it couldn't be coincidence, your coming here."

"I don't understand."

She pulled a chair toward the bed, her voice was nearly a whisper. "I will share details with you because I think Julius was right. But this is not for your magazine and this is not because I trust you. We—Julius and I—must bring Ncube to justice. It's the only way to stop this country's cycle. Do you understand me?"

"Yes," he said flatly.

"No one, Tom, can know."

"You can trust me, Hungry." His words were just sounds in the air.

She responded with the sigh of a prosecutor who was long past hoping for the truth. She took a deep breath and began. "Okay. A year ago we received a tip on our corruption hotline. Go to a certain spaza shop. We went and we found a row of thumb drives taped beneath a shelf. The drives contained over a terabyte of documents. At first we assumed it was simply evidence of corrupt business deals. It turned out to be much larger. Each of the individual deals was a leg, a segment of a leg. There were multiple legs. We don't know how many. They all connect to a single body."

"Who?"

She waited. "No one, Tom, can know."

"I won't tell anyone, Hungry."

"It's an investment fund of some kind run by Terry Krieger. The partners are intelligence agencies from around the world. There's MI6, Mossad, the Australians, our people. The CIA is an investor, Tom."

Klay stood and started to pace, grinding a palm into his forehead. "CIA and Krieger."

She continued, "Ncube is one of their . . . I don't even know what to call it . . . one of their facilitators."

Klay faced Hungry. "How do you know this?"

"We broke the code on one of the projects. A tin mine in Congo. There was an insurrection, Krieger's people took it over. We identified the South African intelligence officer involved. That was our Rosetta stone. We've been slowly deciphering their operations ever since."

"Kisie," Klay interrupted.

"Kisie. Yes, that was the name of the mining town. How did you know?"

Had the Agency used him? Had Eady **used him?**

"I need to meet the intelligence officer you identified," he said.

"Not possible."

"You questioned him directly?"

"We did," she said uneasily.

"Hungry, I need to see him. What's his name?"

"His name was Mo Rademeyer. State Security Agency. And he's dead."

"Tied to this?"

"It presented like a home robbery, but he'd been tortured, beyond the usual."

Klay processed the geometry of what she was telling him.

Hungry continued, "Your CIA and Terry Krieger are colluding with Ncube to prey on my country. Ncube holds the door open for them."

Klay crossed to the window. He edged the curtain away from the wall and looked outside. Across the street was a Wimpy Burger and a KFC. Below the street was lined with cars; pedestrians going places like insects, leading normal lives. "When was it?"

"When was what?"

"When did they kill Rademeyer?"

"It was November. They put his death at November 12."

His meeting with Eady and Barrow at the Confession Club had taken place a week later.

"I need to get you out of here, Hungry."

She gave a short laugh.

"What's funny?"

She pressed her thumbs to her temples. "It's not funny, it's just . . . When I told Julius **The**

Sovereign was offering us two journalists to help with our investigation, he said, 'That's it! That's the CIA's plan!'"

Klay's mind reeled. If Eady was part of this, he surely would have anticipated Klay would find out what Hungry knew about Krieger. But if the Agency, Krieger, and Ncube were in bed together, why send him to help her? In his mind, Klay heard the voice of his father's defense attorney, Saul Kane, the famous Philadelphia mafia attorney who dispensed advice from behind a desk in his moldy cubbyhole office on South Broad Street. "When a client tells me his story, I ask myself, **What is the opposite of this?** And even though I am that one-in-a-million lawyer blessed with clients who never lie to him—so that I know they are all innocent, and the government is always a gang of jackbooted thugs—when I receive my answer, I say to myself, **Now, Saul, what is the opposite of this opposite?** And I ask myself this question again and again, Jack, until I see the fucking truth."

Klay applied the old lawyer's technique to the facts as he knew them. His assignment had been to help Hungry prosecute Ras Botha and to get her files on Ncube.

"I'm not here to help you," Klay said.

"I understand that, Tom."

"Get up." He seized her arm. "We have to go."

"Wait." She pulled her arm away from him. A

text had arrived on her phone. She read it, and Klay watched the blood drain from her face. She looked up at him. "Tenchant is hacking into our computers."

He felt a cold spike shoot up the back of his neck.

There was a knock at the door.

Hungry looked down at her phone a second time, then at Klay. "What have you done?"

THERE'S ALWAYS A WHO

Pretoria, South Africa

The hotel room door burst open. Three black men wearing tactical gear rushed Klay, driving him backwards onto the bed.

They spun him around, pushed him facedown, and flex-cuffed him. Then they jerked him to his feet. A skinny white photographer began snapping photographs. **Click. Click.** The photographer shouted from behind his lens, "Are you Tom Klay?" **Click. Click.** "Are you Tom Klay, the CIA agent?"

Hungry drew herself up and declared, "I am Advocate Hungry Khoza, special prosecutor empowered by the Office of the Public Protector—"

One of the men seized her by the arm, turned her around, and began to cuff her.

"You have no authority here," Hungry barked.

"Restraints won't be necessary." A fourth commando entered dressed in tactical clothes but without a vest or mask. He stood in front of Hungry and spoke with a slight impediment. "Our special prosecutor will surely obey the laws of the state." He began straightening Hungry's collar. She slapped his hands away.

He took a step back to address her. "By the power of the president, Advocate Hungry Khoza, I arrest you on the charge of treason."

The photographer was still shooting.

Hungry and Klay were led down a set of stairs and out the hotel's rear emergency exit, where four black Chevrolet Suburbans waited. They put Hungry in the back seat of the first vehicle. Klay was sandwiched between two men in the back seat of the third. The vehicles sped off.

No one spoke. Klay used the time to run more opposites in his mind:

He had been sent to help Hungry Khoza's corruption investigation.

He had been sent to hurt Hungry's corruption investigation.

He would never intentionally harm her.

What was the opposite of that?

Unwittingly.

How?

Out him as a CIA agent.

If Hungry was shown to be in bed with the

CIA, her case against Ncube would go away. She would be ruined. He would be ruined. Krieger, Botha, and the Agency would be safe.

Hungry Khoza had been in bed with the CIA . . .

CLICK. CLICK. CLICK.

In his mind, he ran more data:

Eady and Barrow had sent him.

The Agency was partnering with Krieger in some kind of investment fund.

Botha was in with the CIA. But Botha's behavior didn't add up. He claimed to have arranged medical care for Klay in Kenya. He had warned Klay about Krieger. Botha had helped him.

And Tenchant. What the fuck was Tenchant doing?

The SUVs stopped in front of Hungry's building. He watched as Hungry was taken out of the first vehicle. Then his door opened and he was pulled out. They cut his zip-cuffs and led him and Hungry through the garage and up the metal stairs to the Wild Dogs' office. Over the stench of grease and motor oil was another smell: gunpowder.

The big steel door was wide open. Klay put his hand on Hungry's shoulder. "Let me go first."

She jerked away and led them forward. Klay saw movement beyond the doorway. There were too many people inside the office and not enough urgency. Urgency meant life.

Two men holding automatic weapons stepped out of her way. Hungry crossed the threshold into the office and paused. Klay looked over her shoulder. The blood was everywhere. It spattered the walls. It ran like thick paint down the whiteboard. Miss Edna was at her desk, her chin on her chest, the back of her head on the wall. Minnie lay crumpled on the floor in front of her. Across the room, Sehlalo lay beneath the whiteboard. Hungry rushed to him.

Klay knelt beside Hungry and put his arm around her shoulders. She seemed not to know he was there.

"Hungry," he said.

She responded as if he had electrocuted her. "GET—AWAY—FROM—ME," she hissed.

Across the room Tenchant's blue jacket hung on the back of his chair. Klay crossed the room and picked it up. Tenchant's wallet was in the pocket. The dozen or so armed commandos ignored him as they went about their work. He glanced inside Hungry's office. Her desk lay on its side, legs out stiff, like a dead cow. Its drawers and papers lay strewn across the room. The bookshelves had been stripped. Two men and a woman were still at it. They stuffed armfuls of files into black garbage bags, and yanked cables from the devices.

A bloody smear ran down the hallway toward the bathroom. Two men in tactical gear were talking outside the bathroom door. The blood trail ran between their boots and disappeared inside. As Klay started down the hall, the men stepped toward him and shook their heads, their weapons nosing up.

"Stay in the main room, please," a voice said from behind him. Klay turned. This man was medium height, lean, with a bush-creased face and sandy hair. He was dressed in the same black tactical gear, including a pistol on his web belt. "Touch anything you like, Mr. Klay. Be my guest." He pointed to a pair of computers and said, "Hurry up with those!"

"Yes, General."

Klay returned to Hungry. She was still on her hands and knees beside Sehlalo's body, holding the dead man's hand, weeping. Blood covered Sehlalo's face and chest. Hungry was red with it now. It covered her hands and her blouse. It was in her pearls. Klay gently laid Tenchant's blue windbreaker over Sehlalo's boots. "Hungry," he whispered, lifting the jacket to show her what he wanted to do. She gave him some room. He pulled the jacket like a blanket over Sehlalo's lower body and felt an ankle holster.

"Gen-er-al!" a voice called.

It was a familiar voice, and yet not familiar. Everyone stopped and looked toward the bathroom. Tenchant emerged from the hallway shirtless, a hand on his belly, the other carrying a pistol. Strips of T-shirt were tied around his abdomen to staunch his bleeding. Blood dripped from the bottom of his pant leg over his boot.

"General Visser. Take your men out!" Tenchant ordered.

"But—"

Tenchant waved the pistol. "Out, General! All of you!"

Visser hesitated, then nodded to his people. Garbage bags dropped and hard drives got one last kick toward a pile in the room's center.

"Close the door behind you," Tenchant said.

The general glanced at Klay. "We still have work to do here."

"Close the door, General," Tenchant said.

The mercenary pulled the steel door closed behind him with his eyes on Klay. Tenchant hobbled across the room and pressed the lock button. Klay heard the low hiss of the door's steel bolts slide into place.

Tenchant turned and wiped his face with the back of his weapon hand. "You should really hear yourself sometimes." He impersonated Klay: "'Don't worry, Tench. I never leave a man behind.'" He snorted. "And that 'who' obsession. You said it to me my first day, you know. You said it on three stories we worked together, and then you said it again on the plane over here like it was the first time." Tenchant spat onto the floor and mocked Klay again: " 'There's always a who.'

"Well"—Tenchant spread his arms wide— "HERE I AM!"

Tattoos raged over Tenchant's upper body. A large sun on each pectoral. A double lightning bolt on his right shoulder, a Celtic cross on his left. His makeshift bandage did not hold. The bullet hole in his abdomen burped blood.

"You kill me. Just the fucking arrogance you bring to it, you know? And the whispering . . ." He mocked Klay's low growl: " 'Back in a minute, Tench.' Making me lean in to hear every goddamn word. Well, now's your moment. You want me to tell her? Or you want to fucking mumble it?"

Hungry, holding Sehlalo's hand, looked at Tenchant.

"He's CIA, honey," Tenchant said. "Always has been."

Hungry shut her eyes and took a steeling breath.

"This is your mess, Klay. I tried to avoid it. I called you on your phone. Over and over. Tried to get you back here. I had them distracted looking for fucking addresses. You could have kept them going." Tenchant pulled a desk chair to the middle of the room and sat down. "But you couldn't be bothered. Miss Edna got hungry, wanted to go out. I asked her to wait, reminded her of her daughter's wedding. But no. The fat bitch had to get her cupcake on. Asked what I was doing."

Hungry glared at him. "She knew you were hacking us."

"That right?" Tenchant seemed to consider that, then nodded at Sehlalo's body. "I should've gone for the greatest risk first, but Julius was right-handed, and he was holding a coffee cup." He grimaced. "He was faster than I expected." He coughed and turned to Klay. "You weren't supposed to get anywhere, but then, well . . ." He pointed his weapon at Hungry. "You got inside the very special prosecutor."

"Let her go," Klay said.

"Unnecessary. All of this," Tenchant continued. He pointed to a red and black thumb drive lying on the floor. "I got a virus into their computer system anyway. Everything's destroyed." He coughed again. "They'll paper this up. 'We regret to inform you . . . Assailant or assailants unknown . . .' You take on corruption in this country, it could be anybody at all."

Tenchant stood up, raised his weapon, and pointed it at Hungry. "He killed you, not me."

Klay drew Sehlalo's ankle pistol, surprising Tenchant. Their two shots sounded almost as one.

The revolver bucked in Klay's hand, but he did not vary his aim. On the fourth shot, Tenchant went down. Klay crossed the room and kicked the gun away. He turned and saw that Hungry had been shot. "Hungry!"

Hungry ignored her wound. She picked up Sehlalo's mobile phone and dialed. "You are going to prison," she spat.

THE NEW ORANGE

**Warden's Office,
Kgosi Mampuru II Management Area
Pretoria, South Africa**

R as Botha leaned forward and tapped a blue visitor's card on the conference table.

"I hear you had some trouble," he said.

Klay did not respond. He wore an orange prisoner's uniform. The knuckles on his right hand showed angry red bottle caps where skin used to be. He was being housed in a communal cell with fourteen other prisoners, not all of them welcoming.

Botha was dressed in a tailored charcoal suit, open-collared white shirt, and alligator boots that matched his briefcase. He set his briefcase on the table, removed an orange, and rolled it across the table. "You'll want that now."

Botha was right. An orange did look different from this side of the table. Still, Klay didn't touch it. Hungry was gone. He had no idea where. Officers loyal to her had surrounded the building and ordered the general and his men to surrender. The general's men were private contractors, paid to fight but not to die. Hungry's people loaded them and the photographer into white vans and disappeared. The team's medic had hardly bandaged Hungry's shoulder when she was on her feet again, issuing orders to secure the crime scene and gather up her team's documents and computers. Once the work was in hand, she walked to a waiting car. She paused at the door and turned to Klay. "How many innocent people have died because of your lies?" She had not waited for an answer.

They brought him into the prison through an underground tunnel left over from the Apartheid era. Klay had not been arrested or charged. He was simply caged.

Botha withdrew a second orange from his briefcase. He raised the fruit to his mouth and bit its skin. He worked his lower lip in and out, nodding as he peeled the fruit. "Wild Dogs dead. Advocate Hungry Khoza ruined. Ncube investigation terminated. My case dismissed . . ."

"Ras," Klay said, "what can you tell me about Hungry?"

"Oh, she's royally sorted. A masterful fucking you gave that one. She's a CIA operative helping the Americans oust our legitimate president. Bring back white rule. Don't you read the papers? Well, you couldn't, could you?"

"Which is all bullshit," Klay countered. "I did some interviews with her for **The Sovereign** working on a story . . ."

"You did." Botha shook his head and laughed. "Yes, you did." He laughed some more as he laid newspapers on the table. "Ncube called in your ambassador for a full dressing-down. Fucking international incident you've caused."

It was all a game for Botha.

"What do you want?" Klay asked.

Botha pointed at the newspapers. "Take a look."

It had been ten days. Klay skimmed the articles, all front page. Hungry had issued a press release before disappearing: "Intruders as yet unidentified raided the field office of the Wild Dogs Anti-Corruption Task Force, Office of the Special Prosecutor, Office of the Public Protector, killing Advocates Edna Sebati and Minenhle Mthembu and Chief Investigator Mr. Julius Sehlalo, formerly of the Hawks. A visiting American journalist, David Tenchant of

The Sovereign magazine, was also killed during the raid. The Wild Dogs Task Force was formed under a mandate by . . ."

"Then there's these . . ." Botha withdrew more newspapers and web page printouts. These were pro-government tabloids with racy headlines: "I, Spy!" . . . "Hungry's Last Supper!" . . . "A Very Spe-CIA-l Prosecutor."

An op-ed in one of them began, "Advocate Hungry Khoza, a pawn of White Monopoly Capital, has been doing the bidding of her CIA masters, attempting to undermine the office of the presidency and incite unlawful regime change . . ."

None of the stories mentioned Tom Klay. Someone had fed the tabloids their CIA angle. He went through the papers again to be sure. "She did you a favor," Botha confirmed. "Lord knows why, but she kept your name out."

Klay looked more closely at the printouts of the online stories, focusing on publication dates and times. A Perseus Group tabloid in Johannesburg had been first out with the story. PGM coverage then spread around the world, mutually triggering news and social media algorithms, feeding the beast.

Klay was confident he had pieced together most of the puzzle. He had been the CIA's Trojan horse, sent to carry Tenchant into Hungry's office to destroy her files, not copy them. The Agency, Krieger, and Ncube had all won.

The puzzle piece that didn't fit was sitting across the table from him. Ras Botha seemed to know everything. But he didn't seem to want anything. And Klay needed Botha to want something from him because Klay very much needed something from Botha. Botha was his only way out.

Desire is opportunity. It creates leverage. It was a basic rule of tradecraft. But Botha didn't seem in need of anything at all now. A man without desire was invisible. Botha was a ghost.

There are no truly invisible men, Klay reminded himself. Every person wants something. He inventoried what he knew. Botha was here, so that meant: ego. He'd brought a stack of media reports: authority. And an orange: power. Botha hated anyone with leverage over him. And that translated into a single word. Botha's abiding desire was for respect. Hunger for validation fueled his outbursts at trial, his refusal to wear a prison uniform, all of the special accommodations he demanded here. It was in every one of his stories. His tales of conquests over women, grand money-making schemes, and powerful friends all added up to a lifelong search for respect.

Klay looked at the orange in front of him.

Terry Krieger had stolen the Kimber from Botha. To take a Boer's land was just short of taking his life. It was humiliation.

Klay picked up the orange and bit into its skin. "Last time we did this," he said, slowly peeling the fruit, "you told me, 'I'm in here because of you.' What did you mean by that?"

Botha didn't respond. He chewed his own orange and watched Klay's fingers. Klay kept peeling, slowly, as if he didn't care. As if he didn't have any desire of his own. When he had the fruit peeled, he looked across the table for Botha's answer. Botha raised his eyebrows and indicated Klay's orange with his eyes.

Klay put an orange wedge into his mouth and began to chew.

Botha cleared his throat. "Now do you hear me, counselor?"

"I'm listening," Klay said.

"You're listening. I need you to hear me. Do you hear me?"

Klay swallowed the slice. He looked directly into Botha's eyes. "You haven't said anything."

Botha smiled. "You are Agency property. Sum and total, that's all you are and all they want. You"—he stabbed a finger hard into Klay's chest—"don't exist for them."

Play along, Klay told himself. **Go with the flow until you see it.** "That's right," Klay said. "What they want is my shadow."

"Your shadow?"

Klay watched Botha roll the word around in his mind.

"Okay," Botha said. "Yeah, that's good. Your shadow is what they want. They'll cut your throat to keep your shadow alive. And you don't mind because you're looking the other way, happy to be rid of what's behind you. You don't want to be you. That's what makes you useful. Makes you a good asset. Do you hear what I'm telling you?"

"I hear you," Klay said in a tone suggesting he was still waiting for Botha to say something meaningful.

Botha nodded. "When they told me the plan, I said yes just to fucking meet you again. I said yes just to lock eyes with the fucking guy that could be so fucking good and still fall for it."

"Well," Klay said, "I hope you're duly disappointed."

"Oh. I would have to say, overall, yes, counselor, I am heavily fucking disappointed." Botha sat back and folded his arms across his chest. "You're a writer, but you couldn't see the plot. You're their agent, but you couldn't figure out your mission. And you still don't realize who you're working for. So, now do you know yet what cage you're in?"

"Who am I working for?"

Botha raised a finger and made a few circles

with it pointed at the ceiling. "The fucking lord and master of us all."

Klay could feel Botha's rage. But there was something else. Botha didn't just hate Terry Krieger. He feared him. Hate and fear, those fraternal twins, showed themselves bloodthirsty in Botha's face. A man consumed by hate and fear lost his invisibility. For the first time, Klay could see Botha.

"Krieger put you up to all this, right?" Klay said.

Botha's eyes darkened. Then, suddenly, he smiled. He wagged a finger at Klay. "You—" He grinned. "You might learn something useful yet." He leaned forward and spoke slowly and quietly. "Remember I told you how Krieger killed that boy on the buffalo hunt. And that boy never knew he was fair game? What if that boy had known? Isaac was strong, quick. What if he had even fucking suspected? The old man Njovu carried a good knife. What if he had known what Terry had in mind for his son? Things might have gone differently, don't you think?"

Botha sat back to let his lesson sink in, enjoying himself. This wasn't merely a game for Botha. This was a big game hunt. Botha, the professional, tracking spoor, planning a kill. He was baiting Klay and exhausting him at the same time. To what end? Good tracking follows a trail. Great tracking leads it. **Get in front of him,** Klay told himself.

Klay moved his orange peels aside, drew three letters on the table with his finger. **C. I. A.** Pointed at Botha.

Botha smirked. "You Yanks are all the same. You think because it's your eyes seeing it, it must be what it is."

"What should I have seen, Botha?"

"I don't know. You went to Kenya. What did you see?"

"My friend killed."

"What else?"

"A politician killed."

"And?"

"No elephant. Faulty technology. Perseus technology . . ."

"Then you go to the Philippines. Why?"

"What are you talking about?"

"You think those stories were random? He weaponized you. That's what Tots does. You're the pigeon in that diamond mine. The one who flew through the window for me. Little packet tied to your foot. They built the coop for you." Botha looked around the warden's office. "Fed you. Gave you water. Trained you up, eight kilometers a week, see how you'd fly."

A guard knocked on the door, then opened it. "Five minutes, Ras." The guard was enormous with a shaved head and huge arms.

"Thanks, Thabo," Botha said. "We're just about finished, if that's all right."

"That's all right." Thabo closed the door.

Botha was on a roll now, so Klay didn't interrupt. "I'm out now, and I'm going to stay that way. Ach." Botha nodded at a portrait of Ncube hanging over the warden's desk. "I was never a prisoner in here. I'm my own man wherever I am. You, you're a prisoner wherever you go. Anyone ever tell you that? I saw it the moment you walked in here. Right proper dagga boy, looking for a fight, charge anything that moves. Reminded me of Minotaur. You remember him?"

"The myth?"

"No, my buffalo. The one Krieger missed." Botha eyed him. "You hearing me now? You were their prisoner before you ever walked through that gate."

Klay held his tongue. There was plenty of truth in those words.

Botha moved his chair closer. "Tell me what you think is going on," he said quietly.

"I saw the intel. They were your poachers in Kenya."

"Ja. And Advocate Khoza saw intel I broke into that police station for rhino horn. Intel is what it needs to be. Somebody opened the police safe, stole that horn? But it wasn't me. They made me an offer I couldn't refuse. Said it would bring you over. You're obsessed with me, or some fucking shit . . ."

"Who said?"

Botha didn't respond.

Klay tapped the spot on the table where he'd written the three letters. "You know they sent me . . ."

"Ach," Botha scoffed.

"Krieger? You're telling me this has all been Krieger. Terry Krieger's running CIA?"

"Did I say running? You need it in black and white to see what's in front of you? Not a lot of zebras in this world for a reason. Leverage, Klay. Leverage is the tail that wags the dog. I'll ask you again, counselor. Cui bono?"

Klay responded in a low whisper. "They destroy the files, hang me out as Agency, it kills Hungry's investigation. Ncube benefits."

"And?"

"And I end up in here, falsely accused."

"Come on, counselor. You can do better than that. And—"

"All right," Klay said, his anger rising. "And they get rid of the Dogs, who found a link between intelligence services and Krieger. An investment fund. The South African was—"

"Mo Rademeyer," Botha said. "Good oke. Greedy. Said goodbye to him personally."

Klay sat back in his chair. "You did?"

Botha shrugged. "You think you're not," Botha said, "but you're in the life deep as me. Maybe deeper. You were the gun. I told you. You don't see that?"

"I was the gun? You're talking about my stories?"

Botha laughed. "No one cares about your fucking stories, counselor."

The door opened and Thabo stuck his head in. "Time, Ras."

"Thank you, Thabo. I'll wrap up. Just one minute, please."

Thabo nodded.

"Think bigger, Klay. A fucking magazine? An investment fund? That's nothing. It's nothing to me, and I'm almost nothing to him. Krieger's mind works on a global level. You're in a box, counselor. You want things lined up nice and neat, but the world doesn't work that way." He tapped Klay's forehead. "You're in Africa now."

Botha organized his papers and returned them to his briefcase. "Truth is I don't know the big picture. If I did, I'd have my Kimber back. But I guarantee he's got one. It's you that has to figure it out, not me." Botha knocked his knuckles on the table and smiled. "You got the hunter in you. I do know that. After all, you almost got me, right?"

Botha gathered up their orange peels and wiped the table with a napkin. He dropped the remnants into a wastebasket and clapped his hands clean. "I got you switched to my old cell. Left you a few items. Maybe next time we meet, you can tell me which one you're going to be."

"Which one?"

"The hunter, the buffalo, or the boy." Botha grinned.

UNARMED IN THE COMPANY OF KILLERS

Kgosi Mampuru II Management Area
Pretoria, South Africa

Thabo escorted Klay down a long pale hall to Botha's former cell, a battleship gray, steel-doored isolation unit in the prison's C-Max unit. "Used to hang us on the other side there," Thabo said, nodding toward the cell block's opposite end. He handed Klay a cloth laundry sack. "From Ras."

Botha's cell smelled of Pine-Sol. Against one wall was a single bed bolted to the floor. On it was a folded wool blanket, a set of sheets, and a clean pillow. Against the opposite wall was a metal desk with a big screen television on top of it. A cable ran from the TV through a small hole in the concrete wall. The toilet was in the back, blocked from view by a metal dresser.

On the walls hung several **Playboy** centerfolds and a poster of Sylvester Stallone as Rambo. There were blank spaces and bits of old tape on the walls where someone had recently removed small photographs. On top of the desk was an unopened bottle of Courvoisier XO and a glass.

Klay sat down on the bed and fished through Botha's gift bag. Some toiletries, a laptop, and a note. Klay set the laptop beside him on the bed and read the note. "Research, counselor. Nobody bothers you less I say. Do what you do. Enjoy the conyac. —Ras." The note included the warden's Wi-Fi password.

Klay set the sack on the floor and lay back on the bed. He put his arm over his eyes to block the fluorescent bulb. After a moment the scenes began. Sehlalo's ankle pistol in his hand, the disbelief on Tenchant's face. Then Hungry, blood-smeared, kneeling beside her fiancé's body, folding the blue windbreaker into a pillow and placing it gently under Sehlalo's head. He watched her wipe the blood from his face, straighten his collar, and adjust his arms and legs. She crawled to Miss Minnie and did the same for her, and then to Miss Edna doing what she could to give the dead their dignity.

He'd watched people tend to corpses thousands

of times. They straightened eyeglasses, fixed neck-
ties, picked away bits of makeup, adjusted stray
hair. They leaned into caskets and kissed the
dead on the forehead, the cheeks, the lips. They
spoke to them.

Klay had seen so many dead he couldn't remember his first, but he didn't understand it. A
corpse was not a person. It was a thing—an aban-
doned thing, no more worthy of sentiment than
was a dead person's shoes or toothbrush. His view
formed on the morning of his mother's funeral.
"This is life, Tom," his father had explained,
standing in the doorway to their funeral home's
main chapel before approaching her. "And this
is death." Jack Klay switched off the light and
darkness filled the room. "Death is always present, but death is afraid of the light." His father
switched the light back on. "Your mother was a
light." He squeezed Klay's hand. "You are a light,
Tom. But when a light is switched off, the world
is back to its natural state. Do you understand?"

Klay said he did. He took from the lesson a
message his father had not intended: if the fun-
damental state of the world is darkness, it is foolish to grieve. He did not want to be foolish. His
mother wouldn't like that. And so to honor her he
swore he would not cry at her funeral. He would
not mourn her, or anyone. It wasn't easy to do.
He trembled beside her closed casket, knotting
his toes in his shoes and squeezing his stomach

muscles. He bit his tongue so hard it bled. From then on he practiced. He said goodbye to his first dog, Shelby, with some tears, but to the next, Brutus, and to two cats without any at all. He was dry-eyed as he pulled socks up over the dead feet of Julie, his motorcycle-riding neighbor, whom he'd had a crush on. He was emotionless holding his grandmother's fluffy-haired head with one hand while he repositioned her plastic head block with the other. He was steady as he embalmed Little Victor from the neighborhood.

Without realizing it, his definition of darkness expanded over the years so that it wasn't just grief over a lost life he silenced. He found ways to switch off his feelings for all sorts of things that might end: friendships, loves, dreams. Over time, his idea of what constituted an end expanded, too. He learned to protect himself not just from the prospect of grieving, but from any loss, any pain. He began pulling the plug on possibilities earlier and earlier, shutting himself off from everything he might care deeply about before it had a chance to hurt him by dying in front of him—the way his mother had.

Now, lying in a prison cell, exhausted and alone, an unbearable wave of pain broke over him, and he asked himself for the first time what the opposite of his light-switch philosophy might be. He pressed his fists against his eyes. He could not stop their faces. His mother walking past him, his father on the drive to prison, the boy and his bicycle lying under his car. He saw Bernard jingling up a mountain in front of him, Lekorere lifting his beer bottle in salute, Hungry kneeling in Sehlalo's blood.

He stood up. He exhaled. So much death. All these years he had dismissed those who mourned a corpse in a box, while he had been mourning something far less rational, and far more destructive. While the world around him grieved death, he had grieved life.

He hadn't turned his back on death; he was living it, mourning every moment, chasing criminals to distract himself, grieving a light that could never be switched on again. "Mom," he whispered. He knew that if he lay down on the bed now and closed his eyes, her red coat would appear. Her polished black shoes would walk by. He would call to her as he struggled with his shoelace, but she would not turn. In all these years, dreaming over and over again of that terrible day, she had never once paused to listen to him. She walked out of the living room, through the kitchen, and down the ramp to her death.

He lay back down on the bed. He closed his eyes.

He allowed himself to remember.

—

He was nine years old, standing beside his father on the Atlantic City boardwalk, watching a dollar-green Cadillac convertible roll toward them. His father wore a light gray suit and dark tie. He and Sean wore their navy-blue Easter suits. The car had its top down. The governor of New Jersey, Brendan Byrne, sat on the car's shiny trunk, his shoes on the tan leather back seat, waving. People cheered.

"Hey, Jack, whaddaya think?" a man chewing a cigar asked Klay's father. It had been like that all morning. Ever since they arrived, men had been greeting his father, peppering him with questions about what he thought, whether he was in. Klay was used to rough men like these. They came by the funeral home, knocked on the side door, then shuffled foot to foot, peering through the glass, never stepping inside unless invited, asking, "What horse looks good, Jack?" "Which jock you like?"—working their way around to the same question they always asked. "Jack, would you think I can borrow the box tickets, you're not using them?"

Today they worked their way around to different questions. Was Resorts Casino going to get its license? If it didn't have a 24-7 license, what good was investing? Was he in anyway?

"Are you, Jack?" they asked. "Are you in?"

His father answered each of them the same: "We're all in anyway, aren't we, boys?"

The green car pulled to a stop and Governor Byrne stepped out. Above, the sun was already hot. Seagulls flapped and cawed. He walked to a long table in front of Boardwalk Hall and took his seat. The table had blue and white bunting draped along the front, and a podium at one end with a microphone. Local politicians gave their speeches first. Bored, Tom watched a large man in a dark suit with a shaved head and dark sunglasses skim sweat off his head using a credit card. He was part of a group of Italian-looking men standing beside the boardwalk railing watching the politicians speak.

Finally, the governor got up. Byrne was handsome, with a strong jaw and blond hair that reminded Klay of Tarzan on television. He said tax revenues from Atlantic City's gaming industry would go to help care for senior citizens and the disabled. He didn't use the word "casino." He said "gaming." He said the gaming industry would stay on the island, but jobs would go to people all over the state. When he was done talking, he picked up a pen and signed the Casino Control Act, opening Atlantic City to gaming. Then he raised his right fist high above his head and shook it. "I've said it before and I will repeat it again," he shouted. "To organized crime: Keep your filthy hands off Atlantic City. Keep the hell away!"

A brass band struck up "Happy Days Are Here Again." The date was June 2, 1977.

. . .

The lights were off in most of the building when Nicky Scalise's black Cadillac pulled up in front of Klay Funeral Home a few weeks later. Klay had his shoes off and had been shuffling over the carpeting, building up static energy through his socks, touching his fingertip to lamps and door-knobs and casket lids, seeing which gave off the best shock. He was testing the front door latch when Scalise's car arrived out front. He paused and watched. A man got out of the front seat and stood beside the car with his hands folded in front of him. Then the driver got out—it was the big man with the shaved head from the boardwalk. He circled the car and opened the back door.

Scalise stepped out onto the sidewalk. He looked in both directions as if checking for traf-fic; then he adjusted his cuffs and started up the funeral home steps.

"Who is it, Tom?" his father called from be-hind him.

Everybody in the neighborhood knew Little Nicky.

Klay heard his father's footsteps increase—no doubt he had seen Scalise's car out front. "I'll get it, son," his father said, just behind him now.

But Klay didn't wait. He opened the door and let the boss of the Philadelphia–Atlantic City crime family into his family's home. Klay's first thought was that he had never seen such a tiny adult. Scalise removed his hat. He had silver hair combed straight back, the most perfectly cut hair Klay had ever seen. He wore a shiny silver suit with pointy lapels that fit him so perfectly it looked like the skin of an eel. He wore a white shirt, silver-gray tie, and dark sunglasses.

"Nice boy," Scalise said, rumpling Klay's hair.

"Good morning, Nick," his father said, placing a hand gently on Klay's shoulder. Scalise crossed their crimson carpet and disappeared into Jack Klay's office.

"Go see what your mother needs," his father said. Then he turned and walked into his office and closed the door.

Klay wanted to watch through the door's keyhole the way he often did, but Scalise's men stood beside it. So he opened a box of prayer cards and began inserting them in the slits in the oak holder. He rearranged flower baskets in the chapel, pulled flower sprays off one rack and stuck them onto another. He wiped the casket down with a chamois cloth. An hour passed. He repositioned more flower sprays. He spilled a box of prayer cards and knelt down to pick them up. He tacked photographs of people who weren't related to the body in the chapel onto the memory board.

Finally, his father's door opened and Scalise emerged.

"I'm sorry, Nick," his father said.

Scalise didn't respond. He adjusted his French cuffs. He nodded curtly to his driver, who went outside to start the car. The other man crossed the lobby and took a position beside the front door with his hand on the latch. When Scalise reached the door, the man opened it. But Scalise paused. He turned and looked directly at Klay. Tom had never encountered eyes like Scalise's. They were small and the deepest black he had ever seen. "This your boy?"

"That's my son," Jack Klay answered.

Scalise put on his hat and left.

It was Christmastime now, still 1977. The kitchen smelled like sugar cookies. His mother asked if he and Sean wanted to help her pick out a tree. Klay ran into the front room to get his coat and mittens from the closet under the stairs. Sean ran upstairs to get their mother's purse. Klay's shoe had come untied. "We do not have untied shoes, uncombed hair, or shirttails out" was one of his father's rules. Klay sat on a bench in front of the living room's faux fireplace to tie his shoe. He was bent over, fumbling with his laces, when his mother walked past. She wore a red wool coat and black shoes.

"Wait for me," he said, his outsized fingers fumbling the laces.

She kept walking.

He called to her again.

Finally he got his shoe tied. He was racing Sean down the morgue ramp to the driveway when his mother turned the key in the ignition. The explosion tore the doors off the garage. Klay and his brother were thrown into the street.

Nicky Scalise sent white Asiatic lilies to the funeral. "My condolences to you and your remaining family," the card read.

Klay lay on the bed in Botha's damp prison cell. He wept until he had nothing left. Then he got to his feet. He was calm. He could see beyond this room, beyond the cage he'd put himself in. He had been the boy on Krieger's buffalo hunt. Naïve to the danger standing next to him. Unarmed in the company of killers.

Eliminating him was the CIA's next logical move. Botha believed it. Why else move him to solitary, with Thabo posted outside his cell? Klay didn't look at Botha's laptop. He didn't need to do research. He knew what was coming.

He poured a glass of Botha's cognac and waited. He did not have to wait long.

A DIFFERENT SET OF TEETH

Zambian Airspace

K lay woke bound in dual shoulder restraints. Barrow sat in an oversized leather recliner across a table from him. They were in the air. Behind Barrow the private jet's interior looked like a well-appointed home theater. The plane appeared to be empty.

"Mistakes were made," Barrow said, dabbing his cheek. "Possibly we should have involved you from the beginning. Hard to know. These things can go so many ways."

Klay had a pounding headache, a sore neck, and pain in the middle of his back. He didn't remember anything. The swelling under Barrow's left eye might explain his restraints.

"We're not renditioning you here." Barrow

chuckled, running his eyes over the jet's zebra-wood paneling. "Wanted to get that out of the way straight off. Ketamine does pack a punch, though."

"Fuck yourself, Barrow. If that's even your name."

"It is."

"Good. I'll want that for my story."

"Oh, I don't think there'll be a story here." Barrow reached beside his seat and set a briefcase on the table. It was an old barrister-style leather bag that opened from the top. Barrow removed a thick accordion folder. He found the file he wanted, opened it, and laid a large color photograph on the table in front of Klay.

It was Bernard's body on an army cot. A white plastic sheet had been pulled back to make the photograph. Barrow tapped the photo with his pen. "This gentleman, not wanting all those Perseus bells and whistles on his elephants, had to go."

He removed another photograph. It was Simon Lekorere, the politician, dressed as he'd been in the passenger seat of Bernard's Land Rover. His throat was sliced wide open. "Like a vacuum cleaner hose," Barrow observed. "Collateral."

Another photograph. A fat man hung by a rope, eyes bulging. It was the purple Croc on the floor beneath the body's bare foot that brought it around for Klay. The Filipino priest. Martelino.

"Suicide. Or the look of it. Maybe he hung himself. Maybe he got hung. Your story made it a question with an answer."

"The priest's dead?"

"Very," Barrow said. He tapped the photo. "Krieger was pleased with this one, yessir. His troublesome priest. Some lovely stuff you've done."

Klay gritted his teeth with fatigue and frustration. "What's the point of this?"

"Then there's Mr. Gatt. Found him washed up on Cebu, Bobby Maxwell–style. We're not sure how he fits in yet. Did you know him?"

Klay looked. An obese man's body was pale and swollen to sea-creature proportions. "I have no idea who that is. What are you telling me?"

Barrow continued, talking as much to himself as to Klay. "Krieger dismissed your Mr. Eady at first. Called him a lackey. But Eady kept at it, didn't he?" Barrow tapped each of the photographs. "Desperate to find his way in. Drove him crazy. Tried a couple of PR stories. 'Angola's New Hope.' 'Congo's Christian Warriors' . . ." He dropped a copy of **The Sovereign** onto the table. "That was the first one, far as we can tell. Like a serial killer, he was cautious at first. Seeing if he had the stomach for it." Barrow chuckled. "Turns out he did."

"What the fuck are you talking about?" Klay would have stood if he weren't trussed like an animal.

"Vance Eady couldn't know what your stories were worth, no market price for propaganda, so he kept trying different angles. Fiddled the books a little and convinced the board to sell your magazine at a good price. Still"—Barrow tapped the photographs—"nothing a billionaire valued. Nothing worth the ante."

Klay fought against exhaustion. It had been days since he'd slept. "You're saying Vance used my stories to help Krieger and the Agency? You are the Agency."

"Oh, we have our part to play in this, Tom. And I'll get to that. But this here"—he indicated the photographs—"is something else. CIA? No, sir. A rogue group of treasonous bastards, that's what I'd call them. Some of them ours—yes. But only some.

"Vance Eady didn't use you to help Krieger, Tom. He used you to buy in. Terry Krieger runs a fund. Not really a fund, my people tell me, but that's what he calls it. Or **funds** I guess is better."

"The investors are intelligence agencies," Klay said. "I know about it."

Barrow's eyes narrowed. "The buy-in for the South African was twenty million dollars. He's dead now. She tell you about him, too? Mo Rademeyer?"

Klay nodded slowly.

"Vance Eady wanted into something bigger. Price, we think, is seventy-five million dollars.

He didn't have that, of course. Not even close. But he had you."

Klay's mind raced as Barrow picked up the photos from the table and laid them down again one at a time. "Your friend," he said, laying down Bernard's picture, "the Kenyan, got in the way of Perseus's tribal-surveillance project. Your priest here, the peace negotiator, got in the way of Krieger's plans to buy a deepwater port. Ms. Khoza's value you understand. Eady was making Krieger's problems go away, earning his way in piece by piece."

Barrow cleared his throat. "Let me introduce myself to you properly, Tom." He laid a thin leather wallet down in front of Klay. "I'm not working with Vance Eady. I'm hunting him."

Klay didn't recognize the credentials as CIA. Only a single blackbird on a blue-and-yellow background.

"IG?" Klay asked.

Barrow tapped an incisor with his fingernail. "Different set of teeth. I read a story one time how it's all about teeth. Evolution, I mean. Who we are. What we want. Cows grind, lions tear. Humans do both. Your Hungry Khoza got her teeth into something big. Something that could hurt Krieger. Tear the meat right off his leg. We still don't know who leaked those files to her. Maybe it was local. Maybe it was his competition. A Russian named Yurchenko fits that bill.

"We do know the cost. If it got out Terry Krieger was playing varsity for more than one team, well, that's the kind of thing not even a presidential pardon can help with. Avoiding life in prison, or the death penalty—that would be worth $75 million to him. Yessir. Hungry Khoza's intel put Vance Eady into a whole new class altogether."

"I was your bait," Klay said.

"You want a drink?"

Barrow pressed a button on the arm of his chair. A door opened in the back of the plane. A large man appeared. Klay recognized him as one of the men who'd subdued Thabo to enter his prison cell. "Sir?"

"Troy, bring Tom and me a couple of bour-bons. Booker's, isn't it? And some picky things, nuts or something. And let's cut him loose."

Troy unlocked Klay's restraints. Barrow didn't speak again until they had been served their drinks and snacks, and Troy had returned to the back of the plane. Then he raised his glass. "To the Confession Club," he said acidly.

When Klay didn't touch his glass, Barrow set his own on the table, too. "Beginnings," Barrow said. "Best place to start in my opinion. This whole thing begins with an accident. One of our people gets dragged by her husband to one of those Washington, DC cocktail parties nobody likes. Her husband's a tax accountant, so it's worse than usual. She's had her fill of double declining balances or whatever those people talk about. She's at the bar, getting herself another gin and tonic, when she overhears this British fella saying how he runs a sniper operation overseas. Says he picks the targets, his man over there in Africa pulls the trigger for him. Takes out bad men all over the world, he says. Goes on and on about it. Well, she doesn't realize it's just some magazine editor talking metaphorically. She files a report like she's supposed to. We put some people on it, track down your Mr. Porfle. Find out he works at **The Sovereign.** Figure out his assassin is you." Barrow ate a handful of nuts.

"I'm not an assassin," Klay said, taking a drink of bourbon.

Barrow's mouth was full. He nodded. "At Langley," he continued, "everybody's in their silo. You come up as Vance Eady's asset. So does Porfle."

To the look of surprise on Klay's face, Barrow said, "No, no, no. It's common. It's the culture. First thing our people do overseas is register every foreigner they meet as an asset. You'd be shocked how many dry cleaners and housekeepers pose a class two threat to this nation's security. Most never know they were listed. Eady's got half the magazine down as his assets. Problem is nobody remembers Eady. Remembers? Hell, he's been filing reports for so long, the guy who's supposed to look at them is dead.

"So, our people take a look. They review Eady's file and realize we don't know what this Tom Klay is up to. They see a possible overlap with your work and the interests of one Terry Krieger, so they send the tickler up to me, as required. Because that's what I do, Tom. I hunt the rotten apples. I sniff them, test the soft spots, and when it's appropriate, I . . . well, you get it.

"I take a look at Eady's reports and my little man goes off. You ever see that one? Edward G. Robinson? The insurance investigator with a little man inside tells him when something's not kosher?"

Klay did not respond. He looked at the age spots on the top of Barrow's balding head, the wrinkles along the buttons of his yellow dress shirt straining to hold his belly.

"It's a helluva picture. Well, I look at what he's got going, and mine goes off like a ten-year-old boy on the Coney Island Cyclone. Wooot!"

Klay leaned forward. "I don't give a shit about you and your little man, Barrow," he sneered. "Why should I believe a fucking thing you say?"

Barrow squinted at him for a long moment. "Okay," he said, and dusted salt from his hands. "I'm going to tell you about it because I need your help, and I believe the best way to make a man trustworthy is to trust him. That's the only reason I'm telling you any of this by the way"— his jovial tone turned cold—"instead of letting you rot in Gabriel Ncube's prison." Barrow took a sip of his bourbon. "Krieger's focus is China. China's Ultimate Silk Road Project. Biggest public works project the world has ever known. It began—"

"I know. Everybody knows about it."

"Of course you do. Krieger follows the Chinese around like a cattle bird, providing security for President Ho's investments, making his own moves. He's got a thousand men running security for Chinese Development Bank oil interests in Angola. He's the spear for China's Djibouti base. He got them the Darwin port. Now he's got them Mindanao. He's locking up the coast from the Persian Gulf to the South China Sea. If that leads to conflict someplace, he sells one side, or both, the weapons—"

"I was in the Congo," Klay interrupted. "I know how he operates."

Barrow paused, assessing him again.

"It's a modern world, Tom. You ever hear that? I always think what the hell else could it be—every day's more modern than the one before it—but that's me. You got High Tech. High Finance. Maybe now we got High Intelligence. I don't know. I don't have to know. My job, most of the time, is follow the money. Same as you." Barrow adjusted in his seat.

"Krieger didn't come out of nowhere with this fund idea of his. We're in a race, Tom. Our spies have to keep up with their spies. But how do you do that? Our in-house engineers aren't exactly Silicon Valley's finest. And we can't buy off the shelf. We need what hasn't been invented yet. Our people put together a venture capital firm called Maven-Q. The company's genuine—our people do trade shows, hand out Maven-Q ball caps and ink pens," Barrow said with a chuckle. "It lets us invest in promising ideas, steer product development, lock up end products."

"Let me guess," Klay speculated. "The CIA with its own investment fund. You wouldn't leave management of a venture capital firm to intelligence officers. You hired outside?"

Barrow nodded.

"Wall Street?"

Barrow waited.

"You hired Wall Street bankers, but you couldn't pay Wall Street–sized bonuses with tax-payer dollars. You told them they had the oppor-tunity to serve and protect, they said screw you, so you . . ." A bitter smile formed on Klay's lips. "You told them they can eat what they kill, and they took you up on it . . ."

"Well, they've made some very good investments,

so they tell me. But they did make one that put our ass in the jackpot."

"They invested in Perseus Group."

Barrow raised his glass in acknowledgment.

Klay sat back in his leather seat. The CIA had invested in Perseus Group. "So now Krieger has your money and your secrets," he said, and laughed. "And now it's your money funding those port acquisitions. Providing China's security. Killing Congolese. Anything he does, you're tied to."

"Langley didn't see that one coming," Barrow said. "Too excited about the gadgets, I expect. We got out, of course. His fund program started right after. With nobody looking, a few of our people peeled off and went rogue. Sequence isn't important really. Hell, number one search term our people type into Google these days is 'Perseus.' How many skew their work to audition for Terry Krieger I don't know."

Barrow sat back. "So that's how it started. Those funds are made up of rogue intelligence officers from all over the world, working together, for Terry Krieger. Conspiracy. Bribery. Fraud. Murder. It's a long list that ends in treason. I am no goody two-shoes. But treason I do not abide. Which brings us back to Vance Eady." Barrow swallowed the rest of his drink and pressed the call button. "Leave us the bottle, Troy." He topped off Klay's drink.

Klay looked at Barrow, not really seeing him. Instead he pictured Eady in his office that last day. Around them Eady's artifacts packed up, outside movers hammering shipping crates together. Eady talking about his cancer before explaining the sale to Krieger. "This was not my decision. Krieger pitched the board in Davos. I was brought in after. For appearances, I expect . . ." Klay felt his anger turning to rage, his stomach in knots.

"So, Tom—"

Klay spoke through a clenched jaw, "Tenchant."

Barrow nodded. He opened the briefcase again, found the file he wanted, and withdrew a photograph. "Hitter. Kicked out of the Marines." In the photo, Tenchant was loading bags into a Land Rover. There were camera bags at his feet, one bag especially long. The photo was date stamped. In the background was a Kenyan car rental agency.

Barrow laid out more documents and photos of Tenchant. "Started as a babysitter on you, we think."

"You could've stopped him. You let my friends die."

"Not 'let.' We didn't let anything. And let me make this clear. There is no 'we' here, Tom. My God will judge me for my decisions, but anyone I took this up the chain to might have been compromised. Half the people above me are compromised, for Chrissake. I had no idea how far up it went—"

"Now you do?"

When Barrow didn't reply, Klay upended his glass and set it down hard. Barrow reached out to pour him another, but Klay waved it away. He wanted to wave away the voice in his head, the one saying, **You could have stopped him, Tom . . . You were the gun . . .**

"Hungry was always going to be sacrificed," Klay said.

"We would not have let her proceed, that's true. We care about predictability, tolerable risks. That part of investing we do understand. Ncube has proven himself to be a reliably corrupt ally, but hanging you out was Eady's plan from the beginning. Keep that fact firmly in your mind, Tom. Destroying your lady friend was Vance Eady's idea. But the plan wasn't moving fast enough. Krieger was impatient, offered to send one of his operators, a woman named Mapes. She and Tenchant crawled out of the same dark hole a long time ago. Kinetics is their specialty." Barrow shook his head. "So the plan got accelerated."

"What about Botha? He's yours?"

"That man's a skeleton key. He who has the cash gets to turn him. Eady turned him for this project. We went along. Your white whale, Eady called him."

"Does he have cancer?" Klay asked.

"Eady? Oh, I expect Vance Eady's got himself a terminal disease, all right," Barrow said. "Cancer's not what they call it. No."

Barrow kept talking, but Klay wasn't listening. He was going back, retracing. That night at the Confession Club, Barrow's aggressiveness made sense now. Barrow had been hostile to force Eady to state explicitly what he had in mind. Klay had been in Barrow's shoes plenty of times. You found a good branch, laid out plenty of rope, and waited for your target to hang himself. He wondered if Barrow had recorded the conversation that night. He had no doubt Barrow was recording their conversation now.

"You said you wanted my help," Klay said. "You're going to prosecute Eady?"

Barrow gathered his photographs into their files and returned the files to his briefcase. He closed the lid, laid his forearms over the top, interlocked his fingers, and looked at Klay. "No, Tom. I don't expect so, not the way you mean." He separated his hands and tapped a fingernail against an incisor. "Different set of teeth."

MARCHING ORDERS

Chadian Airspace

The plane shivered. The pilot made an announcement. Klay and Barrow fastened their belts. Barrow explained that a look-alike, carrying Klay's passport, was currently flying on Delta Air Lines flight 9470 from Johannesburg to Washington, DC. The flight had a regular stop at Amsterdam's Schiphol Airport. "We're headed there now," Barrow said. "You'll pick up your passport and continue on home. We papered it with the embassy. You were never officially arrested—Ms. Khoza helped you there. You're not a fugitive. You're a victim. Eady has antennae of his own. He may try to meet you at the airport. He'll suspect you've caught on to him, but he can't be sure. He'll want to be sure.

Our people will approach you at Dulles Airport, just for show. Refuse to talk with them. Make a scene if you're up to it." Barrow touched the skin under his swollen eye. "Nothing permanent."

"And then?"

"Be yourself. That move Ms. Khoza pulled with her press release was clever. He doesn't know you were there. It's not foolproof, and Eady's no fool, but it opened us some space."

"Space for what?"

"Get some rest, Tom. We'll discuss it."

Troy brought Klay a blanket and a pillow. He put his seat back and closed his eyes. He fought it but the movie in his head began to play: Sehlalo's ankle pistol . . . surprise on Tenchant's face . . . Hungry adjusting the bodies. The scenes speeding up, spiraling. Bernard's smile . . . shots fired . . . brakes squealing . . . her red wool coat . . . "Wait for me" . . .

Klay sat up.

Barrow looked up from his paperwork. After a moment, he removed his reading glasses, set them on top of his papers, and rubbed the bridge of his nose. "You know what keeps me up at night?" He poured himself another drink. "It was that day in September. Whole city had a smell to it. Smell of what we used to call the ash can." He tapped his pen on the table. His voice softened. "It was the people in the streets, you know? Not just that morning, with the dust on their shoes, but for weeks. Complete strangers saying hello to one another. 'Are you okay? May I help you with that?'" He chuckled. "Russians called me at home. 'You okay, comrade? Anything I can do for you?'"

"You were there?"

"I had a lunch date that day. Took the Amtrak up. It's a habit, I show up early. Not early enough . . ." He coughed and cleared his throat. "It was my daughter, Julia. She loved her work, yessir," Barrow said. His voice trailed off.

"She was there?"

"She was," Barrow said.

"I'm sorry, Will," Klay said.

"We looked at all sides of that date. Krieger, he'd opened up a small logistics company, registered in Cyprus. Called it Executive Prospects. Moved highly placed individuals out of harm's way. A valuable service in a world gone mad. Invisible exfils. No fingerprints."

"You mean for the Saudis who got out. Right afterwards."

"Oh, the Saudis, sure. That prince with the embassy, the cousins. I'm talking about timing. Krieger registered that exfil company a month before the Towers."

Klay stared at Barrow. "I never heard any 9/11 reference to Krieger . . ."

"No, I expect you didn't. It's not in those twenty-eight pages, either. Had to go to the FBI to get that information. Agent who gave it to me was working for Raptor Systems when I got a hold of him." Barrow shook his head.

As the plane flew north toward Europe, Klay slipped back into his own thoughts. **How many innocent people have died because of your lies . . . ?**

"What happens to Krieger?" Klay asked grimly.

Barrow cleared his throat. "We'll block his export applications, bar him from government work. Work with our allies to make his life difficult, but unofficially, he's got what you might call spousal privilege. He's outside of scope, son. I'm sorry."

Klay felt his stomach turn. "Outside of scope" was what he'd said to Bernard. Part of his "I'm no safari ant" speech. He'd been wrong to say that, wrong to stand by, wrong to not speak out about Congo and so many things he'd seen, even if his voice was unlikely to be heard. He'd been wrong for so long, confining himself to the page, the deadline, the script.

Hungry said he was afraid to take on the unwinnable case, and he had laughed. He was a mortician's son, he said. They were all unwinnable cases. Life was an unwinnable case. But now he realized the unwinnable was the only thing worth fighting for.

His father had stood up to Nicky Scalise—and the cost had been immeasurable. But the cost to stand by—to not enter the fight, regardless of the odds—was to let darkness win. Taking a risk to help someone—knowing you might lose—was not folly; it was the test of a man. Without sacrifice, all the world was darkness. His father's voice: **You are a light, Tom.**

"Your focus needs to be Vance Eady," Barrow continued. "He's a flight risk and he's a suicide risk. We're counting on you to keep him alive for us. He won't make any decisions until he finds out what you know. So we need you to string him along a bit. Not long."

"And then?" Klay asked.

Barrow shrugged.

Klay looked at Barrow. "I want to talk to my father."

Barrow sighed deeply. He pressed the call button.

Klay reclined his seat and closed his eyes. An hour later Barrow woke him and handed him a phone. Barrow walked to the back of the plane, a symbolic gesture of privacy. The call would certainly be monitored and recorded. Klay and his father spoke for ten minutes. When he was through, Klay set the phone down on the table and waited for Barrow to return to his seat.

"I want him out of prison."

"Can't do it," Barrow said.

"You lost your daughter. I lost my mother. He lost his wife. What would you do to have your daughter back? To protect her from that day? My father did what it took to protect his children."

The two men evaluated each other. A father and a son. Mist and rock.

"I'll see what I can do," Barrow said. "After you deliver."

"Fair enough," Klay said. He would keep Eady alive until Barrow's men arrived.

As the plane made its descent into Schiphol, Barrow went over it all again. "Eady can't feel threatened. But don't be a pushover. You're angry. Get angry. Channel your anger in a way that makes sense to him."

"I got it," Klay said.

"You'll have the Tenchant funeral and then—"

"I got it," Klay said.

MISCHIEF REEF

Dangerous Ground
South China Sea

Terry Krieger stood in the stern of the **Raptor,** a mile off Mischief Reef in the South China Sea, an area aptly known as Dangerous Ground. The area is poorly charted. Accurate information on ocean currents is not available for Dangerous Ground. Charted depths are unreliable, soundings give no warning, radar is of little value. Low islands, sheer drops, and sunken reefs abound in these blue-green waters. The US military's chief geospatial intelligence agency, which offers guidance to Navy vessels, minces no words when it comes to the area: "Vessels in Dangerous Ground must rely heavily on seaman's eye navigation and should not normally enter the area other than in daylight. Avoidance of Dangerous Ground is the mariner's only assurance of safety."

A brisk morning breeze blew Krieger's hair. He wore a blue Perseus Group windbreaker and khakis. Beside him, a wall of five flat-screen computer monitors had been set up, served by a single brushed-aluminum keyboard on a white table, all of it secured against the area's sudden winds and unpredictable currents.

Standing before Krieger was Vice Admiral Meng Jingchen of the People's Liberation Army Navy, commander of China's South Fleet, accompanied by his two most trusted men. The three officers wore their service dress whites.

When he described the capability he intended to offer China's military, President Ho had replied simply, "Convince Meng."

If he failed to get Meng to think outside the box this morning, Krieger knew he would suffer more than just the loss of a business deal. He'd be gored. Yurchenko would see to it.

"A small gift," Krieger said. Using both hands, he presented Meng with a book. Mapes, fluent in Mandarin, acted as his interpreter. Meng nodded curtly and accepted the gift. The book was **The Sovereign Field Guide to Hawks of North America.**

Meng smiled. "Raptor!" he said, and nodded to indicate the yacht, which brought light laughter from his team. Meng admired the book's cover and turned the first few pages, lingering over the author's signature and Krieger's inscription: "Tempus fugit, memento mori. —Terry Krieger." He turned at random and lingered over a photograph of a bird power-diving. Meng did not look at the bird's description. **"Falco peregrinus,"** he said, and told his men it was the world's fastest raptor. Mapes translated for Krieger.

"Yes," Krieger said. "Not everyone approaches the world's challenges in the same way. After this morning, I hope that you and your country will join me in looking at the world from a raptor's perspective.

"Admiral Meng, before our demonstration, I'd like to recount a story," Krieger said. "It is a story you are no doubt familiar with, but it will take us to a place from which we might all become raptors. In 1996, the US Navy announced it would develop a new, technologically superior battleship designed to ensure American naval dominance into the twenty-first century. It called the program Smart Ship. Instead of reconceiving the idea of a warship, however, the Navy hired Griffon Industries to backfit an old one. Griffon retrofitted the **Yorktown** with a new bridge, automated her navigation and propulsion systems, fused her SAMs and torpedoes to operate in sync with Aegis. To make it all work, Griffon laid four miles of cable and fiber optics through the ship, then they installed twenty-seven desktop PCs and ran the ship's entire system on Microsoft Windows. Let me repeat that: the American Navy ran the most technologically sophisticated warship in history on the same business software used by my children's school.

"A week after her relaunch, **Yorktown** was off the coast of Nicaragua in pursuit of a Colombian drug trafficker when the entire ship lost power. Every system down, **Yorkie** dead in the water, humiliated, towed to port. Unfortunately for the Navy, a reporter from the news program **60 Minutes** was on board that day, filming a story about America's drug war. The most advanced warship in history went dark on national television. Millions of Americans saw the American Navy fail. I'm sure you saw it, too."

Meng nodded, though Mapes had only begun to translate. Krieger waited for her to finish.

"What caused the failure?" Krieger asked rhetorically. He held up his thumb and forefinger in the shape of an okay sign. "Zero," he said. "Officially, the Navy said the ship went dark as part of a covert maneuver. The truth was a systems tech accidentally typed a zero into a database field calling for a denominator. You cannot divide a number by zero, but instead of issuing a warning, the ship's entire operating system crashed. And America's Smart Ship program sank with it."

He looked at Meng. "The greatest threat any

military can face is doubt. It took ten years for the Navy to risk automating its ships again. Smart Ship Two, they called their next attempt. Perseus Group bid on it. We proposed a fully automated, virtually unmanned naval capability using smaller, more agile platforms—a computer that happens to float and shoot. We were not successful. The Pentagon and our Congress think Big War, and our idea made things small. Instead of reconceiving battle, they green-lighted another retrofit."

Again, Meng nodded. He knew all this, as well.

Krieger let Mapes finish her translation; then he looked at Meng and smiled. "China is not afflicted with doubt, Admiral. Your military has the full support of your leaders, whether it's your new Type 055 Renhai destroyer, your Type 002 carrier, or your own fully automated civilian smart ship. When it comes to naval technology, China leads the world. More important, China understands the art of war. As Sun Tzu once said, 'The supreme art of war is to subdue the enemy without fighting.' Americans don't understand that."

Krieger gestured to the stern. The Chinese officers turned and exclaimed, clearly surprised to see an American warship coming into view. The ship's profile indicated she was a Ticonderoga-class cruiser. The number 67 painted on her hull signaled her identity, the USS **Shiloh,** a $1.5 billion warship, carrying 370 sailors.

"**Shiloh** is armed with Aegis," Krieger said. "It's the most advanced defense system in the US Navy, able to track ballistic missiles in flight, coordinate the ship's vertical launch system, and shoot down threats without human intervention." Krieger shook his head dismissively. "Aegis is fifty years old, gentlemen."

The Chinese were not listening. They were focused on the incoming warship. **Shiloh** was not supposed to be anywhere near Mischief Reef. She was part of a joint exercise taking place several hours north.

Krieger had their full attention now.

"Modern warfare will not be fought on the battlefield. It will not be fought in the sky, or on the high seas. It will be fought online, by keystroke and algorithm. America was built on ambush and surprise, but we have forgotten that. We fear another zero in our denominator."

Krieger stepped forward and tapped one of the computer screens. "As you know, the Seventh Fleet, including the **Shiloh,** and Japan's Self-Defense Forces are currently engaged in joint exercises. Here you see what every geospatial indicator on earth sees: **Shiloh,** seventy nautical miles north of our position, holding the picket during a refueling and missile-transfer exercise, which is what commanders across the Seventh

Fleet see." Krieger's monitors, mirroring those on warships throughout **Shiloh**'s carrier group, showed red, green, and black triangles representing the area's crowded commercial sea traffic, with yellow ships indicating the joint naval exercise underway. One by one Mapes tapped the triangles and the naval vessels' identities popped up. Every capital ship was in its place, including the operation's designated perimeter guardian, the **Shiloh,** located beyond visual range of the exercise.

"And here is what the world sees at our present location," Krieger said.

Mapes zoomed in on **Raptor**'s location. Nearby islands fell away until eventually only light blue filled the screens, signifying open water. The warship bearing down on them did not exist. Like **Raptor,** it was a ghost. "Every monitoring system in the world indicates the same profile. We have been cloaked, too."

While the United States, Russia, and China scrambled to improve their ability to cloak their own armed forces, Krieger had done their spoofing efforts one better. He had developed a way to cloak one's enemies. No longer could military leaders be 100 percent certain that the forces they were commanding electronically were actually where their computers said they were. The US Navy thought its **Shiloh** was seventy nautical miles north. But here she was.

Compared to his new enemy-spoofing technology, hacking into a computerized warship, taking control of her systems—from comms to propulsion—was easy.

Krieger turned to Meng. "You may wish to check with Zhanjiang, Admiral. They'll find **Shiloh** in its scheduled position. And they'll find no vessels indicated at ours."

Mapes offered Meng an encrypted phone.

But Meng did not move to take it. Instead, with his hands behind his back, he studied the incoming American warship. After a minute, he issued a short grunt and his second officer stepped forward and accepted the phone from Mapes. The officer dialed the phone, spoke for a few moments, and waited. Another minute passed. The officer spoke briefly to Meng and then returned the phone to Mapes.

"Confirmed?" Krieger asked.

Meng nodded.

"We are in disputed waters, gentlemen," Krieger said. "The Philippines and China claim Dangerous Ground. The Philippines is a US ally. One cannot afford a conflict here. One can afford peace. I would like . . . Perseus Group would like to offer China a new weapon, based on the latest technology. A demonstration of this capacity is my gift to China."

A numeric code appeared on the center monitor. "Admiral Meng"—Krieger gestured to the keyboard—"the future is yours to deliver. You need only press the enter key."

Meng tilted his head slightly, his expression curious.

"You cannot destroy a ship that does not exist," Krieger encouraged. "You will be dividing by zero."

Krieger waited.

Meng offered no indication of what he was thinking. His latest orders, Krieger knew, were to expand China's occupation of reefs and islands within Dangerous Ground. The United States challenged China's claim to the waters, diving her bombers at China's new Spratly Island airbases, slicing the waters with its ships, and interfering with China's secret efforts to map an internal sea-lane navigable by its nuclear-powered ballistic submarines. If China's boomers were able to sail Dangerous Ground, then a third of the world's population would come within reach of China's ballistic missiles.

Krieger spoke again. "The ship's own navigational error put it here, Admiral. That error will compound throughout the ship's systems in a manner adverse to survival. The fault will lie entirely with the US Navy. Complete mortality. Untraceable. The latest in a string of accidents in these waters . . ." Krieger added a phrase he had been practicing. **"Yi chang meiyou xiaoyan de zhanzheng,"** he said. War without smoke.

Still Meng did not react. He stood staring out at open water. Krieger believed he knew what Meng was thinking. So many unexplained American naval accidents recently. Collisions, systems failures, even groundings. Blame for the accidents had been widely distributed. First, to the other party—drunk Jordanian tanker captain, a broken Vietnamese drive shaft. Then, to those on the bridge of America's warships— poor seamanship in the channel, failure to man all stations, dereliction of duty to train operators. Analyses of the ships' electronic bridge and navigation systems and log data found nothing wrong with the computer systems.

Meng would be asking himself whether the rumors could be true: that America's South China Sea problems had not been accidents.

Meng turned to Krieger. "You are betraying your country," he said in perfect English.

"I have served my country honorably, Admiral," Krieger replied. "This is business."

"They were your client," Meng said, glancing down at the keyboard.

And they might be again, Krieger thought.

"Contracts—like civilizations—end, Admiral. I deal in the future. The future, as I'm sure you'll agree, is with China."

Meng stepped away from the keyboard. He held Krieger's eyes. "Then as a businessman you will understand, China requires that **you** demonstrate the capability of your product."

Krieger had hoped Meng would be unable to resist the opportunity to wield the power he offered, but he was fully prepared for the alternative. Hard decisions were what Kriegers made. He stepped to the keyboard and pressed enter.

A flock of small, dark birds hovered above the **Shiloh.** The birds were quick and maneuvered in perfect harmony. Meng watched them for several moments, then whispered something quietly under his breath. "That species does not fly so far out to sea."

THE UNDERTAKER'S SON

Washington, DC

Klay walked to the Gray Pigeon. He'd had the dream again about his mother in her red coat. For the first time since he was a boy, she had paused, then turned and looked down at him struggling with his untied shoelace. "What is it, Tommy?" she asked. "What's wrong?"

He pulled on the bar's door, but to his surprise the Pigeon's front door was locked. A cocktail napkin was taped to the door's glass. "Closed," it said. It was mid-afternoon. He peered inside. The lights were off. There were half-empty glasses and beer bottles on the bar. In all the years he had been coming to the Pigeon, Billy had never closed the bar during business hours. Not during the city's worst blizzards or when a water pipe upstairs had burst. Maybe he was sick. Klay had spent more time with Billy than just about anyone he knew, and he didn't have a phone number for him. Didn't have a phone number for the bar, either. When he wanted a drink, he walked over.

He looked up Pennsylvania Avenue toward the Capitol Building. He didn't want to drink at home today. Somehow it felt disrespectful to Billy to drink anywhere else on the House side, so he crossed Pennsylvania Avenue and walked north to Massachusetts Avenue.

Everything was sunnier on the Senate side. The restaurants were more sophisticated. The bodegas were called groceries, and had aisles wide enough for two people. The bagel place made their bagels in a brick oven, rather than his usual, a serve-yourself in Saran wrap with lumped cream cheese already inside. Why did he live the way he did? It was only a few more blocks to walk to these places. He should come up here more often, he told himself, change his habits. He'd do it tomorrow, he decided, order himself a cappuccino and a poppy seed bagel warm out of the oven.

He chose a bar in the middle of the block with a brick patio out front that was as big as the entire Pigeon. In the summers, the patio filled with loud congressional staffers holding chardonnay and vodka tonics in plastic cups. "One of them goddamn fern bars," Billy called it. Sebastian's was bright inside with an exposed brick wall and little glass flower vases on the tables. It was early enough that only one table was occupied, five young men in college sweatshirts and designer jeans drinking craft beer and watching the game. Klay took a seat at the bar. The bartender, older than Klay had expected for this place, set a napkin in front of him and placed a glass of iced water on top of it. "What can I get you?"

"Booker's. Neat," Klay said.

The bartender shook his head. "Sorry. No Booker's. Kids all drink this." He took down a bottle of Bulleit bourbon.

"I'll have a beer," Klay said. He checked the tap handles. "Guinness."

It was in motion now. He had his role to play in Barrow's plan and then he would be free.

The bartender poured the stout. It arrived in front of Klay with a little shamrock design in the foam. Klay took a sip and looked up at the flatscreen television maybe four times the size of the one at the Pigeon. All of the television's colors were what they were supposed to be, too.

"Would you like some pita chips?" the bartender asked, setting a basket in front of him, along with a dish of hummus.

Klay chuckled.

"What's funny?"

He reached for a chip. "I'm usually over at the Gray Pigeon. Billy's not much for snacks."

The bartender's face fell. "It's a crying shame," he said.

Klay got a sick feeling. "What is?"

"You don't know?" The older man picked up the remote and began flipping channels. "It's all over the news."

"Hey!" The Hill rats looked up from their nachos. "The game!" they said. "Turn it back!"

The bartender ignored them. A PGM news anchor with that somber, post-tragedy newscaster expression was interviewing someone via video link. The camera cut to the interviewee, and Klay sat up. Tanned face. Perfect teeth. Ollie North haircut. A banner beneath the man's image read "Terrence Krieger, Perseus Group CEO."

"We grieve for their families," Krieger said. "We grieve for the Navy. This situation is all the more painful because this type of accident—one of six major accidents in the past two years—could have been avoided . . ."

A chyron scrolling beneath Krieger's image screamed, "BREAKING NEWS. The US Navy reports a major accident has occurred aboard the USS **Shiloh** during US–Japan joint exercises in the South China Sea. Dozens of bodies have been recovered. No survivors have yet been found. Search and rescue continues . . ."

"Avoided how?" the reporter asked.

"Proper technology. We don't yet know the details, but we do know that this ship was near retirement age and terribly off course. Sadly, its Aegis radar system has been around since Richard Nixon, and its navigation software was not designed for this platform. At Perseus Group we've developed AI-based systems to eliminate these kinds of disasters. We've offered to assist the Navy to evaluate its entire fleet—free of charge. We want to make sure this type of accident never happens again."

Stock footage of the USS **Shiloh** filled the screen.

The news anchor returned. "Unexplained systems failures . . . Explosions . . . Possibly an entire crew lost. When we come back, we'll have the man responsible for the Navy's Seventh Fleet, Vice Admiral Everett Tighe . . ."

Klay stared at the screen, processing what he was seeing: Krieger, again. The universe conspiring to show him something. Billy's grandson was on the **Shiloh.**

Another terrible Naval accident.

What was the opposite of that? Klay asked himself.

Not an accident.

Krieger offering to help the Navy.

What was the opposite of that?

Klay closed his eyes. He could hear Botha's voice: **Who benefits, counselor?**

Answer: Krieger, if he could convince the Navy to hire Perseus Group. But hadn't Krieger been blackballed by the US government?

What if a US Navy contract wasn't Krieger's objective?

The next biggest defense contract opportunity in the world was with China. Taking the Ultimate Silk Road Project into consideration, the opportunities for security contracts and attendant services were the greatest in the world. Barrow himself had said Krieger followed China around like a cattle bird. Barrow had it wrong, Klay realized: The target in Kenya was not Bernard. The target was more likely Simon Lekorere, the politician who stood in the way of China's Ultimate Silk Road Project. Bernard's death was collateral. No, he checked himself. Bernard was not collateral. He'd been killed to keep Klay chasing Botha. Both murders were planned.

"Forget Krieger," Barrow had urged, patting Klay's shoulder. "Chuck Yeager was a helluva pilot. But he never went to the moon. Didn't have to. Moon was for other folks."

"What other folks?" Klay had asked. "In this particular case."

Barrow hadn't tapped his incisor at that. Instead, he'd shrugged. When it came to Terry

Krieger, Barrow was toothless. So was the rest of the world.

It wasn't that different from how Little Nicky took over Atlantic City, only on a much larger and more lethal scale. Anyone paying attention could see what turning the keys over to Terry Krieger meant. But instead of objecting, they gambled. People took what benefitted them and ignored the rest. Conservationists gratefully accepted Krieger's wildlife-tracking technology. Farmers deployed his agricultural drones. Governments used his security services. People tuned in to his easy-to-digest, hate-mongering Perseus Group News. Even the CIA had invested in Perseus Group stock. The list went on. Behind Perseus Group's new and popular technologies was a second truth: many of those same technologies were being used for terrible ends. Everyone knew it, but no one did anything about it. They got what they wanted and left policing Krieger to someone else. But there was no one else. Barrow had confirmed that.

Someone had to stand up to him.

"Something wrong?" the bartender asked.

Klay looked up. He'd been talking to himself. "No," he said. "Just something a friend of mine said once. About history repeating itself . . ."

"It tends to do that," the bartender said, but Klay didn't hear him.

He didn't hear the bartender calling to tell him he'd left too much money, either. He was moving too quickly. Outside, on the sidewalk, Klay took out his cell phone and dialed South Africa.

"Botha," he said. "It's time to go hunting."

HERE LIES TOM KLAY

Greenwood Cemetery
Alexandria, Virginia

He had killed before. That was his thought. A boy riding a bicycle. It was raining now, too, a soft rain, nearly a mist. Klay stood out of view on a rise far above the grave site, near the grave digger's utility shed, watching Tenchant's mourners arrive. He reminded himself that what he was seeing was their reality, not his. Tenchant was the victim of a terrible crime. Klay was in mourning **for** Tenchant, not because of him.

"My husband," Maggie had cried into the phone. "You promised," she wept. "You promised me."

"Wife has no idea," Barrow had said with a

firmness suggesting he had gone to some length to be sure.

"I'm so sorry, Maggie," Klay said, and recited a version of what he knew she'd already been told. **They went after the prosecutor's task force, and Tenchant was there . . . It happened in seconds . . . He felt no pain . . .**

The hearse arrived. The funeral home's staff opened umbrellas. Klay did not recognize the pallbearers. Three looked to be ex-military. The pallbearers lifted a blue steel casket, and the minister led them across the wet grass to a grave under a canvas tent. He wondered how many plots Maggie had purchased. Neither of them was from the area, he knew. He hoped life would carry Maggie and her unborn child too far away to ever come back to Tenchant's side. Tenchant's mother looked frail and older than Klay would have guessed. He found himself trying to imagine what had happened in that home to create Tenchant. What had happened in Krieger's home, or in Eady's? He knew what had happened in his.

Fox and Snaps arrived in Fox's Mazda. They waited for Erin and Grant before approaching the grave site. Erin's heels stuck in the soft earth as she walked, and she took her fiancé's arm for balance. Klay's eyes lingered on the couple. Porfle showed up in an old brown MGB roadster he was restoring. A tear in the soft top had been patched with silver duct tape. He opened a pocket umbrella and joined the staff.

Sharon stepped out of a white Range Rover, popped an umbrella, and waited for her husband. She nodded hello as she passed Porfle and the journalists. She paid her respects to Maggie. Porfle broke off from the journalists and walked toward her. A gust of wind caught his umbrella, and he paused to fix it. Then he appeared unsure which way to go. He looked expectantly from Sharon and her people back to Snaps, Fox, and the others. In the end he stood alone.

"She'll be taken care of," a gravelly voice said. Klay stiffened. Eady took Klay's elbow in his gloved fingers. "It was an Agency assignment, technically," Eady said, looking down the hill at the mourners. "She and the baby will be taken care of. I will see to it."

The boy's family will be taken care of. I will see to it.

"Good," Klay said. It was all he could manage.

Eady stepped into Klay's view. He wore an Irish driving cap and a gray trench coat. "I thought I might see you sooner," Eady said, studying Klay.

"I needed some time," Klay said.

"It will be difficult," Barrow had advised. "You'll need to maintain your self-control. Give him no indication that you know. You'll have talked to me. He'll want to confirm that. Be honest. Make him curious."

"Barrow reached out to you, I presume," Eady said.

"He did."

When Klay didn't say more, Eady said, "We do what we do to protect them, Tom. The people here. This nation of ours. Sometimes we fail. Tenchant respected you. He was grateful to have had a chance to work with you."

Klay knew if he didn't access genuine grief he would lose Eady. He forced himself to remember his mother's casket lying above its grave. He recalled his grandfather standing beside him and his brother, Sean. His father standing alone. It was the only time he would ever see his father cry. Sadness sparked on the flint, then caught. Klay wiped a tear from his eye. "You spoke to him?"

Klay wanted to take Eady's throat in his hands.

"I did. Just before the attack, I expect," Eady replied. "He was happy, excited. He said you found something . . . ?"

"I did. Did he tell you?"

"I didn't want him to use the unsecure line. I told him to have you call me back . . ."

Eady waited, but Klay did not respond. "He told me he was doing good work, Tom. That's what each of us hopes for in the end, isn't it? To say, 'I did a good job with the time God gave me.'"

Klay watched the undertaker hand each of

Tenchant's mourners a carnation. One by one they stepped forward and laid a flower on Tenchant's casket.

"Come see me. My apartment," Eady said. "We'll talk."

Klay shook his head no.

"We need to talk, Tom."

"Don't be eager, but don't play too hard to get," Barrow had counseled.

"I don't want to see anyone, Vance."

"Come out to the farm then. Ruth is visiting her sister. We'll catch a trout for supper. Just the two of us. I have something, Tom. Something you need to see."

"Did you know?" Klay said.

"Did I know?"

Don't tell him you suspect anything. Too risky.

"Barrow didn't send me to help Hungry. He sent me to discredit her."

Eady lowered his umbrella. His eyes narrowed. Raindrops hurried along his face and dripped off his chin. "Why on earth would he do that?"

Klay wiped the rain from his own face. "Barrow's got something going with Terry Krieger."

Eady was fully alert now. "Barrow does?"

Klay nodded. "He's got to be stopped."

A DEATH IN CAMELOT

Fauquier County, Virginia

Klay drove his Land Cruiser west toward Eady's Virginia horse farm. The Toyota was more than thirty years old with two hundred thousand miles on it, but it was in good condition. He took the Warrenton exit and headed south on 29, then west again, horse farms of Virginia's wealthy galloping up beside him. He wound his way through the narrowing country roads, wondering as he always did if he'd missed his turn, when a white three-board fence appeared, the Eadys' front pasture.

Klay's most recent visit had been Fourth of July. Eady and his guests had shot skeet from the back hill. Vance, not surprisingly, an excellent shot.

The property had been purchased by Eady's

banker father, a dollar-a-year man under McNamara. "His brothers and sister haven't set foot here since the funeral," Eady's wife Ruth confided once. "Haven't looked at a bill, either, though they're happy enough to question our expenses. Hyenas waiting for Vance to stumble . . ."

Klay wondered if it could be that simple. He guessed Eady earned about a million dollars a year as head of **The Sovereign.** Then there was his Agency pay.

Klay followed the paved driveway nearly a half mile up toward the main house. The house had been an inn originally. It had nine fireplaces, four upstairs and a big walk-in that filled the dining room. There was a flagstone patio in the back. Most of the horse stables had been converted to a kennel, where Eady kept his prizewinning Jack Russell terriers. Two seldom-used guest cottages lay south of the stables. The spring-fed pond was stocked with rainbows, blue catfish, and triploid grass carp to keep it clean.

Klay pulled into the drive's final horseshoe and parked behind Eady's Grand Cherokee. Anyone who knew Eady well enough to visit knew he kept a key under the mat outside the summer kitchen door. No one who visited twice ever bent to look for it. The Eadys never locked the house.

Klay stepped from his vehicle, and a dog shot toward him from beneath a row of boxwoods. A screen door slammed. "Goddamn it!" Eady yelled as he strode briskly across the driveway, flanked by a pack of Jack Russells. "Off!" he yelled.

The jumping dog was big for a Jack Russell. Klay didn't know whether to pet it or catch it. He was trying to do both when Eady kicked at it, nearly losing his loafer.

"Off!" Eady repeated. "Sorry, Tom. Hankins down the hill lets his goddamn heeler roam free. Got on Integrity's Desire. I drowned 'em all but this one got away. Off!"

Klay looked down at the energetic mutt. It had the head of a Jack Russell, but its tall body was thicker and spotted the color of newspaper. There was a black bull's-eye above its right hind leg.

"Anyway, thanks for coming, Tom," Eady said in his phlegmy bass, offering his hand.

Klay's mind flashed to Barrow's words. **Bring him into the light,** he had said. **We'll take care of the rest.** Meaning: find a way to make Eady vulnerable.

Klay turned and reached for something inside his vehicle.

"Did you bring an overnight bag?"

Klay looked up to see Eady moving toward the back of his Land Cruiser, talking, trying to see inside.

"Just this." Klay showed Eady his backpack.

"Good." Eady turned. "Good. Okay. Come on in, Tom."

Klay followed Eady and his tide of Jack Russells

through a door into the summer kitchen. Eady continued through the room and stepped into the main house, causing the dogs to surge ahead of him. "Good dogs," he called, and shut the door.

Klay and Eady stood alone in the summer kitchen with its thick whitewashed stone walls, deep-set windows, and cool Mexican-tile floor. It was appropriate that it would happen here, Klay thought. This had always been his favorite room in the house. It smelled of woodsmoke, fresh fish on newspaper, and cloves. Klay's father used to say that smell was the most powerful of man's senses. The smell of this room was what Klay conjured when he thought of home. Not lilies or embalming fluid.

This was the room where Eady and Ruth shared morning coffee sitting at the round maple table. A bottle of Lagavulin and two glasses were on the table now. One of the glasses, with liquor already in it, was in front of the spindle-back chair Eady favored. Klay took the chair opposite. Eady's fishing hat lay in the seat of a third chair on top of the day's **Washington Post,** folded to the crosswords.

Eady filled two glasses of water from the sink, served Klay, and sat down. His hair didn't look as if he'd recently worn a hat.

"Could use this," he growled, pouring Klay a whiskey. He raised his glass, hesitated when Klay didn't join him, then drained his scotch in a swallow. He set his glass down on the table in front of the third chair, but did not release it. Klay looked at Eady's hand. It was too close to the table edge, too close to the hat in the third chair. "That the way you want to play this, Vance?"

Eady tilted the glass to look into it, tapped it hard on the table, and refilled it. He folded his hands in front of him and turned to look out the small window.

It was a bright, clear day. Klay knew the view without taking his eyes off of Eady. Below the window was a flower garden with a bird bath held up by a concrete cherub whose arm had broken off. Farther on, down the hill, was Eady's trout pond.

"Do you remember how you started, Tom?"

"You are a murderer," Klay said.

Eady unfolded his hands. "Not at the magazine," he continued. "How you and I started. Your training . . ."

Klay wanted to smash Eady's head into the table, lean on his skull until his temples caved and his blue eyes leaked. But that was outside of scope, he told himself. "We were down there," Klay said flatly, nodding out the window. "You looked at my fingers and said if I learned to tie a Parachute Adams and could catch a rainbow on a double-haul cast in a good wind, I'd know everything I needed to know about espionage. Wouldn't need the Farm."

"And you never did. Need it, I mean," Eady said, adding, as he had those many years ago, "Make the fish see what you want them to see . . ."

"Well, you did that," Klay said.

"We're all the fish. Tom."

"I'm counting on that," Klay replied. He was done humoring this remorseless bastard.

Eady nodded, poured himself another, and looked across the kitchen at a framed photograph of himself standing beside Nelson Mandela. Eady had covered Mandela's release from Robben Island for **The Sovereign.** In the photo Mandela, gray haired, dressed in a gold and brown silk Madiba shirt smiled fondly while Eady, still on assignment, cameras slung over both shoulders, beamed admiration.

"Both of my brothers are Wall Street bankers, did I ever tell you that, Tom?" Eady said, still looking at the photograph. "Eight figures a year. My sister, a heart surgeon. You know what they've got?"

Klay didn't trust himself to respond. Rage was coursing through his body.

Eady tapped his glass, nodding at something on his mind, and looked at Klay. "Satisfaction," he said, drawing out the word. "They've been rewarded for their dedication. Their children respect them . . ." Eady held an imaginary camera and moved the tip of his index finger. "I took photographs. Snapshots of extinction on four legs." He laughed. "On two legs," he said with a bitter glance toward Mandela. "I thought I could make a difference. Were they grateful? Did they change? I was a fool. A naïve fool."

He drank. "There's always a who, you like to say. Who am I? That's what you want to know. Well, I'm a man who stopped pretending things would get better, that the cream always rises, that we'll see more enlightened times. I stepped off that two-bit amusement ride and invested in the amusement park instead."

"You fucking smug . . ." Klay fought to control himself. He checked his watch. Almost time.

Eady ignored him. He continued his monologue, drinking and looking toward the window. "At the Agency, we did exactly what Terry Krieger is doing. Or tried to. And who benefited? No one! We fucked it up, over and over. Say what you will, but Terry Krieger has vision. War is octagonal now. A multidimensional puzzle. Krieger versus Krieger versus Krieger. What value do I have in a world like that? What legacy do I leave?" Eady smiled. "But then I found one. I gave the puzzle master a piece he didn't have."

"You sit here on your gentleman's farm ordering the murder of innocent people to pad your fucking bank account? To feel meaningful? You recruited me with that song and dance about taking on Hitler, doing good in this twisted world. You are one of them, no better than the leg breakers I grew up with. Worse. You deserve what's coming to you."

Eady leaned forward in his chair and peered out the window. "You came alone?"

"Nobody's in my truck, Vance."

"But I haven't much time?"

Klay stared at him.

Eady got to his feet, then bent over slowly and picked up his fishing hat. Beneath it a Browning Hi-Power pistol lay coiled like a rattlesnake.

Eady looked down at the pistol.

He put the hat on and crossed to the sink, leaving the pistol on the chair. He picked up a bottle of orange juice from beside the sink and returned it to the refrigerator. He put a loaf of bread back in the bread box. "You could have your Pulitzer for this, Tom, if you play it right. It's not too late. This story could have a different ending. Nobody would need to know. I'd support you, and Barrow would find a way to make it disappear. PGM will make you a hero. We can celebrate Hungry . . . her sacrifice. You're a damn good journalist," he said, with a question in his face.

Klay picked up his backpack. "It's over."

Eady sighed. The old man walked into an alcove beside the refrigerator, sat down on a bench, and began removing his loafers and socks. He reached for his waterproof boots. His hands were trembling.

"You didn't kill him," Eady said, getting to his feet.

"I know that. You did."

"Not the Kenyan," Eady said. "The boy."

"The boy?"

"The woman in Jakarta was one of ours. She drugged you. We found a body at the morgue, tossed it under your car."

Klay felt life rush from his body like a tide. His heart dropped, his stomach fell, his legs turned as flaccid as seaweed. He saw the broken body of a dead boy lying on a damp street. The loss was real but it had not been Klay's fault. In place of darkness, Klay felt a sublime emptiness. He had not killed that child.

Klay looked into Eady's eyes as he considered what Eady had done and why. The old man had staged the boy's homicide to destabilize Klay, opening him to his CIA offer, ensuring that either way Klay would keep it quiet, leveraging Klay's guilt over his mother's murder to manipulate and control him for **years.**

Klay struck Eady then, connecting just below the older man's cheekbone. Eady went down, taking a net and fishing rods to the floor with him. He could have killed Eady with one punch, but he didn't have to.

"You become what you kill," Bernard had warned him once. "So choose wisely."

Klay lifted Mandela's photo off its nail and threw it across the room.

Outside, he started his Toyota. In his rearview mirror he watched Eady emerge from his house wearing a fisherman's vest and make his way unsteadily down the grassy slope, a fly rod in one hand, trailed by a pack of dogs.

Klay adjusted his rearview. On the opposite slope two men descended toward the pond.

He put the Land Cruiser in drive. After a few yards he stomped on the brake. The mutt with the bull's-eye on its leg was sitting at the edge of the driveway, watching him with an expression that reminded him of a little chicken-stealing Kenyan dog he'd seen looking down at him from a rooftop.

Klay opened his door and gave a short whistle. The dog didn't jump in. It flew.

WE BURY THEM ONE AT A TIME

Kimber Conservancy, Zimbabwe

Krieger's G650 made another low pass to scare off a few stubborn waterbuck before circling wide and touching down on the Kimber's airstrip. Pete Zoeller waited beside a freshly washed dark green Land Rover, his big sleeveless arms crossed over his thick chest.

"Howzit, Pete?" Krieger said as he descended his jet's final step.

"We got the boys on him, Mr. Krieger," Zoeller said, taking a duffel bag from Krieger, knowing well enough not to ask for his briefcase. Knowing enough to erase Krieger's previous attempt at Minotaur from his memory, too.

"Mr. Krieger is it?" Krieger said, and quick-scanned the perimeter.

Zoeller, the deaf bastard, had not heard him. Krieger took a deep breath, sending his mind to the .45 he wore on his belt. He was glad to be in and out in two days, yet concerned that such a narrow window made him an easy target. Botha was out there somewhere, and a sniper-quality shot. Krieger was drawn to the challenge presented by Botha on the loose, refusing to bring his bodyguards with him. Or Mapes. She would meet him back in Jo'burg. The Kimber was the Kimber. He came here to be alone.

"Did you want to freshen—"

"No, Pete. And she's zeroed. Let's go. I'm wheels up by midnight." His instincts suddenly told him to alter his schedule, narrow the threat window even further.

"Right," Zoeller said, accepting the change. "Well, we're set for you. 'Bout an hour out to him."

"All right."

Krieger climbed into the Land Rover's passenger seat. Zoeller took the wheel. He glanced at the pair of teenage trackers sitting in the back of the Land Rover. New boys. That was good.

He had been watching a Pats game in his den when Zoeller's email arrived. The big buffalo,

Minotaur, had killed some villagers, got his name in the damn newspaper. The community was in an uproar. The Saudis were asking about him, too, wanting to schedule a hunt. "Somebody's going to take him, Tots," Zoeller had written.

Krieger studied the animal he'd missed. Rock-hard bosses gnarled like oyster shells, ears worn like aged moth wings, chest as broad as a truck. The old bull lived alone now. Moving at his own pace. Many considered the Cape buffalo the most dangerous game in Africa. Black Death, they called it, Africa's widow-maker. Miss your shot and, well, that had happened once already. Krieger had sent Zoeller a single-word response: "Mine."

Under his safari shirt, Krieger wore the new Vulcan bulletproof undershirt, manufactured by a Perseus Group subsidiary in Mexico using chitin harvested from mantis shrimp. It was a terrific product, a little stiff but lightweight and effective against just about any handgun out there. When the first shipment arrived, a few ex-operators got a kick out of donning Vulcan shirts and shooting each other in the chest. It was great for morale—and the YouTube videos didn't hurt sales—but then a couple of his guys from Dallas got the idea to put the bulletproof shirts on passed-out homeless men. They woke them up and shot them center mass. The videos were the funniest thing he'd ever seen. Had to fire them all, of course.

Undershirts didn't help against a headshot. Krieger pulled his Filson hat down over his eyes and lay back in his seat. Not sweating what he couldn't control was one of his rules.

An hour later, Zoeller tapped his shoulder. "The boys have him over the next rise," he said, slowing to a stop. Krieger examined the setting. Wide-open tall grass, no trees. Minotaur over the next hill. Or maybe something else.

Zoeller seemed to be his usual self. Old Pete had been on the Kimber since Krieger was a boy. Krieger thinking he had to learn to trust somebody someday, then laughing inwardly at himself. Sure, and yoga—he'd take up yoga, too.

"Sticks?"

"No sticks," Krieger said.

He knew the whole thing bothered Pete. Driving up on a target violated Pete's rules. You gave fair chase. But Krieger didn't have time for that. He'd brought a double rifle this time, the H&H in 600. A true cannon. No time for nostalgia. He wanted his trophy. He deserved his trophy. The Chinese were completely on board with his cloaking program. He had sold China the power to impose doubt on its enemies.

From now on, no one would know what was an accident and what was an act of war—it was disruption on a new and lucrative scale. Minotaur scale.

The new boys were eyeballing him. They'd heard what he'd done, of course. No secrets on the Kimber. Which meant they knew what he was capable of. **Stay in your lane, boys,** Krieger thought, **and nobody gets hurt.**

At the top of the rise, Krieger paused. Grass turned from brown to green as the land below fell away into a deep vale with knots of acacia trees along a river's banks. Krieger lifted his binoculars and glassed the land. The grass was thick and tall until it reached the river, where it lay matted by animals that had braved the crocodiles to drink. Krieger could see the crocs lolling on rocks, their bellies full. Some zebra looked in his direction. A few buffalo grazed peacefully. No sign of Minotaur.

"Wallowing other side of those trees, I'll bet," Zoeller said.

It would be a long, slow walk down to the buffalo through grass as tall as he was. Krieger rechecked the sight lines. Nothing higher than him at the moment. Whatever it was, the action would come in the trees below.

"Light's burning, Pete," Krieger said. "I don't want any surprises."

Zoeller signaled. The taller boy plunged into the grass in the direction of the trees. He did it without hesitating. Krieger liked that.

While Krieger searched the landscape for Minotaur, Botha emerged silently from under a tarp in the back of the Land Rover. He came up behind Krieger and put a pistol in his ribs. "Hunt's over, Tots," he said, lifting the big rifle from Krieger's hands.

Krieger's right hand flew to the pistol on his hip. Pete Zoeller caught it there, the older man's iron grip swallowing weapon and hand as one. Zoeller removed the pistol from Krieger's hand as easily as if Krieger were a child.

Krieger laughed. "Okay. Bravo. Well done." He looked Botha up and down. "None better. Back of the truck, right?"

"Where the servants are," Botha said.

"Well, bring me the papers."

Botha whistled. The Land Rover came up, driven by the tracker who had disappeared into the long grass. Botha reached into the back of the vehicle and withdrew a set of contracts for the sale of the Kimber. "Lawyer in Polokwane drew them up for me." He handed Krieger a pen.

Krieger signed his name.

Botha turned a few pages. "And here. And there. And then another round. Attaboy, Tots."

Krieger scribbled without reading. His lawyers were going to tear these documents to pieces.

No contract in Zimbabwe would stand up to his money. Botha knew that, too, surely.

"That it?" Krieger asked.

"That's it, Tots," Botha said.

The teenager slipped from the driver seat and joined the other tracker in the back of the Land Rover. Zoeller climbed behind the wheel.

"Going to shoot me now? Hunting accident?"

"No," Botha said. He fired two shots from Krieger's rifle, each shot deafening, with a recoil powerful enough to put an unsuspecting man on his back. But Botha handled the rifle like it was a pellet gun. "Fuckin' Pommies," he said, admiring the engraved rifle. "Am I right, Tots?"

Botha took the rifle by the barrel and flung it high and into the grass, then climbed into the passenger seat, leaving Krieger standing beside the road. Zoeller tossed Krieger's pistol into the grass and started the truck.

"You know who wins from this?" Krieger said. "Yurchenko. You think he won't be worse than me?"

"Ya. I told the man that," Botha said. "You know what he said?"

"What?"

"He said, 'We bury them one at a time.' Crazy motherfucker."

Botha gestured over his shoulder to the trackers. "That's Isaac's brothers in the back. One's John on the left. Other's Isaiah. Say hallo, boys."

Krieger barely looked in the boys' direction, and the boys showed no sign of hearing Botha. They stared at Krieger with hate-filled eyes. Botha pointed. "That's the father, Njovu, coming up the hill now. You might remember him."

This time Krieger did look. An old man was walking slowly up the track toward them, carrying a rifle.

"An elephant never forgets," Botha said.

Krieger tilted his head.

"Did you forget your Chichewa, Tots? 'Njovu' means elephant."

Krieger watched the older man.

"I'm sure he remembers you," Botha said.

Zoeller put the Land Rover in gear and drove Botha and the sons away.

Krieger remained focused on Njovu. "Njovu!" he called. "Njovu! We have an opportunity now. Just you and me. You have a family. I can make you very—"

Njovu took a knee. He chambered a round, pushed the bolt forward, and took aim at Terry Krieger.

Krieger began to run.

The first shot took Krieger behind the left knee and he went down. He cried out, but after a moment he gathered himself, got up, and limped hurriedly for the tall grass. Njovu opened the bolt, ejected the cartridge, and reloaded.

The second shot took Krieger's right knee and he understood. He lay at the edge of the grass looking up as Njovu approached. The father of the boy Krieger had killed knelt down to him, pulled up Krieger's shirt and bulletproof undershirt so that Krieger's arms were extended over his head, withdrew a fixed-blade knife, and began to gut him like a zebra.

HOME

Catskill Mountains, New York

A golden vibration followed by an explosion, violent and white. Klay wet his hands in the cool water, reached down and removed the fly from the trout's lip. He watched the fish swim off. It was enough for the day. He waded toward shore, sliding his feet carefully over loose river stones. As he approached the river's edge, he gave a short whistle. A rustle began deep in a grove of rhododendron and then a missile sailed off the embankment, touched a fallen tree, and kept coming.

Klay had named the dog Rocket. Rocket was not the purebred Chesapeake Bay retriever he had always dreamed of, but he was definitely the incorrigible mutt he loved.

Barrow had come through. Jack Klay had been released. Klay offered to bring his father up to the Catskills, but the old man had refused. "You got your own life up there now, champ," he said. "That clean mountain air will make me sick." It was his way, they both knew. His father had decided to move to Florida, a community called the Villages. "Some FBI guys down there I might want to talk old times with," he said.

Trout fishing in the Catskill Mountains was to die for, the brochures all agreed. He'd found a quiet stretch of river, a remote piece accessible only by walking through an old cemetery and then climbing carefully down a cliff of fallen pines and sturdy white oaks. At the bottom was a quiet pool below a riffling fall. The climb back up was the hard part. He wouldn't be able to enjoy this spot forever, but for now it was more than worth the trouble.

He'd bought a cabin. It was a half an hour away. Everything was a half hour away in the Catskills. Out of milk? Half an hour. Mail a package? Half an hour. GPS reading 6.1 miles? That was still a half an hour. He liked it that way. The victory of time over distance.

He lowered the Land Cruiser's tailgate, broke his rod down, and laid it in the bed. He took off his waders, folded them, and set them in a milk crate. Rocket jumped on the tailgate and made his way to the front of the vehicle, where he took his place in the passenger seat, waiting. It was his vehicle now, Klay just lucky to be the dog's chauffeur.

Klay drove to Van Guilder's Mercantile for fuel. As usual, Norman Van Guilder was sitting in a rocking chair on the front porch as Klay pulled up to a pump, the old man dressed in the same flannel shirt, torn carpenter pants, and work boots he'd been born in. Not playing chess this afternoon, though often he was, completing the picture. The old man nodded hello.

Norman's usual chess partner, Russell, the town fire chief, owned a farm a half hour away, a nice property on either side of a rural county road where he raised beef cattle, hogs, and chickens. A few years back, traffic on the road got heavy enough that the township decided to improve Russell's road for him. They repaved the whole thing "smooth as a black snake," Russell said. The only change for Russell was that the leaf lookers from the City drove faster through his property now. The county put up some yellow signs for the tourists about slowing down, but it didn't do any good. It got to be dangerous, so Russell made up a sign that got straight to the point. He painted it himself and staked it into the rocky ground just before the turn onto his property. The sign read, "Stop Killing My Chickens!"

When he noticed people were slowing down to

photograph his sign, Russell built a lean-to just beyond the sign with a table under it, and placed a small refrigerator and a freezer on it. For power he ran an orange extension cord across his yard, up the steps of his front porch, and through a cracked window into his house. A sign told you how much the steaks, sausages, chicken parts, and pork chops inside the freezer cost, though it was hit or miss what you might find on your particular visit. Russell vacuum-sealed the meat and wrote the date the animal was butchered on the plastic wrap with a Sharpie. Another sign asked you to raise the red metal flag welded to the refrigerator to let him know when he was out of eggs. The supply of both eggs and chickens generally depended on the foxes.

The eggs were expensive as eggs went, but Klay liked to say hello to a person every once in a while, so he stopped by Russell's place two or three times a month, whether he needed eggs or not. He went the long way to get his gas at Van Guilder's for the same reason. There was another reason he stopped by Russell's lately. Russell's daughter was a doctor in the City, but on her visits home Grace was a farmer's daughter in mucking boots and overalls. They talked easily. When Grace was working for her father, Klay found it could take half the morning just to pick up a dozen eggs. She had a wonderful smile and she didn't ask him about his past. He felt like he didn't have a past in her company. On her most recent visit, she had handed him a piece of paper with his eggs. It was her phone number. This weekend they were planning to go on their first date.

He brought the pump to ten dollars even and went inside Van Guilder's to pay. He put his money on the counter and weighted it down with a smooth gray river stone resting beside the cash register for that purpose, same as usual. Van Guilder's Mercantile sold milk, assorted candy bars, motor oil, and fishing and hunting supplies, including three pairs of Wolverine brand work boots in unlikely sizes. A red fox with one paw raised as if to say hello was mounted to a birch branch in the store's front window, its fur moth-eaten and bleached to a pale yellow. A cardboard "Be Back Soon" clock hung inside the door for when Van Guilder was away. Someone had drawn antlers on the six with a ballpoint pen. Klay hadn't been to Van Guilder's during deer season yet, but he was looking forward to the venison stew everybody talked about.

He touched the silent clock on his way out. Capturing time on paper had been his life for so long. Suddenly he recalled the clocks scratching away in the Confession Club. It was remarkable the things that rose unbidden from his mind. The past was not ever dead. It lived with him, bodies and all. If not for Eady, he might still be with Hungry. If not for Eady, he might still be a journalist. Who could tell the impact of that one blood-covered stone tossed into the pond of his life. He did know one thing. The ripples were quieter now that he'd done something about it.

He paused to greet Van Guilder, same as usual.

"See your story got the cover again," the old man said, nodding toward a news rack. The rack held copies of **American Angler, Truck Trader, Guns & Ammo,** and a few local papers, along with the **New York Times.**

When the news finally broke that Klay was a CIA asset, Porfle had sent him an email telling him he was fired. "Dear Mr. Klay," it began. When the story subsequently went viral, Sharon had emailed him: "Tom! Come back! We want to give you your own column. 'The Sovereign's Agent.' It will be your BRAND! I'll send you a mock-up. What do you think?"

He declined.

The Agency's plan had been to reengage with Krieger, to wrap him up in noncompetes and NDAs, overwhelm him with carrots and pretend they could control him. But Krieger had them by their secrets, and as long as that was the case, Klay knew where their hearts and minds would be.

Botha had texted after it was done. His message was short: "Never knew he was fair game." Klay didn't write back. Porfle had been right about snipers and editors. An investigative journalist fires his shot from a long way off, sitting alone at a desk, and waits for word of a result. Klay bent down and picked up a copy of the **Times** from Van Guilder's rack.

He had been more than happy to send Raynor McPhee what he had, including recordings he'd made of Eady's final confession: "I stepped off that two-bit amusement ride and invested in the amusement park instead . . ."

Raynor's first story had run on the front page above the fold. The article, taking up two more pages inside, had vindicated Hungry, and already she and her anti-corruption effort had been reinstated, her task force granted even more power. Ncube was on his way out. Today's article was the second in a three-part series. It was also front page.

"MURDER PORTFOLIO: Rogue Intelligence Funds Kill for Profit."

He scanned the first few grafs. It was all there: The Fund, Eady's "suicide," Klay's double life, Krieger's hunting accident. After the hyenas got to him, there had been little left of the billionaire, the article said.

Klay got back in his Land Cruiser and started the engine.

"They say he might win a Pulitzer," Van Guilder called out to him.

But Klay was gone.

ACKNOWLEDGMENTS

A young Togolese journalist seated in the auditorium's front row raised his hand and asked, "How long have you worked for the CIA?" I was in Lome, finishing up a lecture on wildlife crime and journalism, part of a series I would give across West Africa sponsored by the U.S. State Department. I had by that time interacted with intelligence officers overseas, more than I knew probably, and I'd run some creative international investigations of my own, but I had never worked for the CIA. His question got me thinking.

This is a work of fiction. The characters, scenes, and plot are invented. Truth may be stranger than fiction, but fiction can be more illuminating. What is not invented are the rapidly escalating threats around the world to journalists and other truth seekers; the dangers of privatized defense and intelligence services, of divisive entertainment masquerading as journalism, and of the rising surveillance state.

I would like to acknowledge the many rangers, conservationists, journalists, scientists, diplomats, soldiers, and more who work tirelessly in the field to conserve and protect life around us. I owe a special debt of gratitude to **National Geographic,** which for years was my home as an investigative journalist.

I am grateful to my publisher, Mark Tavani, at Putnam and my agent, Jennifer Joel, at ICM for their support and expertise.

My uncle, FBI Special Agent Kevin Flannery, retired, took me under his wing years ago and taught me investigation.

Most of all, my wife, Jennifer, saw this book from one "What is the opposite of that?" moment to the next, editing countless drafts with both her lawyer's pen and her artist's brush, making this novel better than it ever would have been without her. The same can be said of me.

ABOUT THE AUTHOR

BRYAN CHRISTY is the former head of Special Investigations at **National Geographic** and the 2014 National Geographic Society "Rolex Explorer of the Year." His criminal investigations have been the subject of two award-winning **National Geographic** documentaries and his crime writing has been anthologized in **The Best American Science and Nature Writing.** He is the author of the nonfiction book **The Lizard King.** His education includes Penn State, Cornell's FALCON Program, University of Michigan Law School, Tokyo University Law School, and time at the Iowa Writers' Workshop.